Phule's Company

CAPTAIN WILLARD PHULE: the galaxy's youngest mega-millionaire – and the only commander whose military career *began* with his court-martial.

BRANDY: the Amazonian first sergeant terrified superiors and subordinates alike – until Phule took charge of Omega Company.

TUSK-ANINI: the giant alien had the face of a warthog – and the heart of a dove.

SUPER GNAT: the smallest Legionnaire – but don't call her that to her face!

BEEKER: the only civilian in Omega Company. He was more than a soldier, he was . . . *the butler*.

They were the best darn fighting force in the whole Space Legion.
Or maybe not . . .

The Myth Books by Robert Asprin

Another Fine Myth
Myth Conceptions
Hit or Myth
Myth-ing Persons
Little Myth Marker

PHULE'S COMPANY

Robert Asprin

CENTURY
A LEGEND BOOK
LONDON SYDNEY AUCKLAND JOHANNESBURG

First published in Great Britain in 1991 by Legend, an imprint of
Random Century Group
20 Vauxhall Bridge Rd,
London SW1V 2SA

Century Hutchinson South Africa (Pty) Ltd
PO Box 337, Bergvlei 2012
South Africa

Random Century Australia Pty Ltd
20 Alfred St, Milsons Point, Sydney, NSW 2061
Australia

Random Century New Zealand Ltd
PO Box 40–086, Glenfield, Auckland 10
New Zealand

The catalogue data record for this book is available from the British Library

ISBN: 0 7126 5001 6

Phototypeset by Intype, London
Printed in Great Britain by Mackays of Chatham Plc, Chatham, Kent

INTRODUCTION

Journal File #001

It has been said that every great man deserves a biographer. I have therefore taken it upon myself to keep a private record of my employer's activities during his career in the Space Legion. If there are those who would, perhaps, contest his qualifications as a great man, I would answer that he is the closest thing to a great man that it has been my privilege to associate with on close enough terms to keep such a journal. I would further point out that, in certain circles, Genghis Kahn and Geronimo are considered to be great men.

To introduce myself, I am a gentleman's gentleman, or what would be referred to in military circles as a batman. (For the less literate-minded, I would ask that you refrain from associating that label with any comic book character you might be familiar with. I have always felt that capes were an unnecessary fashion statement and have endeavored to discourage my employers from resorting to such tacky, attention-seeking ploys.) I am called Beeker, and neither require nor seek additional titles of address.

Although I was with my employer since the time of his enlistment and before, I feel that the truly noteworthy portion of his career began at his court-martial. To be specific, at his first court-martial.

The waiting room had the kind of decor one would expect of the greenroom of a down-at-the-heels acting troupe. Two ancient sofas of indeterminate color were sagging against opposite walls, surrounded by an assortment of folding and wooden chairs that would have been cheap if new, and the magazines strewn on the only table would have made an archaeologist sit up and take notice.

Two men shared the space, more at home with each other than with their surroundings. One was a chunky individual of medium height, decked out in impeccable but conservative civilian clothes, or civvies, as they were known in these quarters. His ruddy face had the bland expression of one used to waiting as he dominated one sofa, idly staring at the pocket microcomputer in his lap and steadfastly ignoring his companion.

The other occupant was anything but calm in appearance or manner. Whiplash lean, he seemed to radiate barely suppressed energy as he paced the room's confines. If tigers stood vigil in maternity waiting rooms while awaiting delivery of their young, there would be little difference between their display of anxiety and that shown by the young man's nervous prowling. Perhaps panthers would be a better comparison, as his uniform was the midnight black of the Space Legion – a color chosen not for its aesthetic or camouflage value as much as the fact the dye could hide the origins of any military surplus uniform bought in lots by the budget-strapped Legion. Not that he was wearing a standard-issue uniform, mind you. His collar pips marked him as a lieutenant, and like most officers he had his uniforms tailor-made, taking full advantage of the Legion's lack of uniformity among their uniforms. The quality of the fabric and workmanship in his garment was several notches above normal, though he had deliberately chosen one of a more somber cut for this occasion.

'For cryin' out loud, how long does it take them?'

The question burst almost unbidden from the lieutenant's lips as he began his fiftieth circuit of the room.

The man on the sofa didn't even glance up.

'It's really not my place to say, sir.'

It was the first response to any of his muttering, and the lieutenant seized on the words as a focus for his irritation.

'Don't give me that "subservient butler" guff, Beeker! Since when have you ever not had an opinion on something or been hesitant to share it with me . . . asked or not?'

Beeker's gaze shifted from his reading to the lieutenant.

'Well, actually you've been a bit more close-minded than usual since you joined the Space Legion, sir . . . or rather since you made up your mind to join. In this specific case, however, I was under the impression that what you voiced was a rhetorical question.'

'It was . . . but answer it, anyway. Come on, Beeker. Talk to me.'

With careful deliberation, the butler set his reader aside.

'Certainly, sir. Could you repeat the question?'

'What do you think's taking them so long?' the lieutenant said, resuming his prowling, but more slowly now that he was verbalizing his thoughts. 'I mean, I did plead guilty.'

'Forgive me for belaboring the obvious,' Beeker said, 'but if the question of guilt has been settled, then what remains is the sentencing. It would seem the court is having some difficulty in deciding precisely what punishment is correct for your offense.'

'Well, what's so hard about that? I made a mistake. Fine. I'm sure other Legionnaires have made mistakes before.'

'True,' the butler said. 'However, I'm not sure how many others have duplicated the exact nature and magnitude of your indiscretion. I'm certain that if anyone else had strafed the ceremonial signing of a peace treaty, I would have noted it in the media releases . . . sir.'

The lieutenant grimaced at the memory.

'I didn't know what was going on at the time. Our communications gear was on the fritz, so we never got the cease-fire order. Besides, we'd been ordered to maintain com silence.'

Beeker nodded patiently. He had heard all this before, but understood the lieutenant's need to go over it again.

'As I understand it, you were ordered to stand silent picket duty . . . to note and report any ship movement off-planet. Period. There was no authorization for an individual ship to make a strafing run.'

'I wasn't ordered not to! Battle usually goes to the side that seizes initiative when opportunity presents itself.'

Beeker raised his eyebrows expressively.

'Battle? I thought there was no resistance.'

'That's why I made my move. Our instruments showed that they had dropped their defense net, so I thought if I moved quick we could scare them with a little demonstration of firepower and bring this whole revolt to an early close.'

'It was already over,' Beeker pointed out dryly. 'That's why they dropped their defense net.'

'But I didn't know that! I just saw the net go down and –'

'And talked the hot-shot pilot on duty into going in on a strafing run. All in the time it took the ship's captain to go to the john.'

'It was a simple case of bad communications,' the lieutenant grumbled, avoiding his comrade's eyes. 'How mad can they be? We deliberately aimed at property and not people, so no one got hurt.'

Beeker stared innocently at the ceiling.

'I'm told the property damage was in excess of ten million credits . . . '

'Hey. I told them I'd . . . '

'... and that you shot their flag to shreds while it was flying over the ceremony ... '

'Well, it was ... '

'... and of course, shooting up the ambassador's private space yacht was unwise at best. That's *our* ambassador ... '

'They didn't have their ID beacon on!'

'Possibly because there was a cease-fire on.'

'But ... Oh, damn it all, anyway!'

The lieutenant ceased his struggles and his pacing and sank wearily into the couch opposite Beeker.

'What do you think they'll do to me, Beek?'

'At the risk of sounding disloyal, sir,' the butler said, picking up his reader again, 'I frankly don't envy them that decision.'

As the court-martial involved a junior officer, Legion rules only required three officers to try the case. An air of discomfort seemed to hang over the deliberations, however, mostly due to the senior officer present.

It was said that everyone in the Legion had three names: the one he was born with, the one he chose when he joined the Legion, and the one he deserved. Though the records showed the second, most were known by the third, the nickname they acquired through their personality and actions while enlisted, though few officers formally acknowledged what the lower ranks called them.

Colonel Battleax was one of those rare cases where her chosen name and nickname were in accord. She was a drab, horse-faced woman with piercing eyes that left respect, caution, and no small amount of fear in their wake, and the prim no-nonsense cut of her uniform added an implied note of disapproval for those Legionnaires who favored a more flamboyant style in their wardrobes. There was a stern air about her that could only be called intimidating and did little to set people at their ease when in contact with her, much less the focus of her attention. The overall effect was that one was being taken to task by one's ageing mother, except that in this case the party sitting in judgment could not only heap guilt on one's head but also scuttle a career with a raised eyebrow and a terse notation on one's personal file.

This alone would have caused discomfort in the other two officers of the court . . . but there was more. The colonel had arrived unannounced from Legion Headquarters specifically to preside over the court-martial, and while she did her best to pass it off as a routine visit, simple logistics dictated that she would have had to be dispatched within hours of receipt of the notification to have arrived as soon as she did. The implications of this were clear: Headquarters had a special interest in this case and wanted to be sure of its outcome. The problem was that neither of the other two officers had a clue as to what was expected. While their best guess was that the lieutenant was to be made an example of, they chose by unspoken agreement to proceed cautiously, playing good guy/bad guy while waiting for some clue from the court president. After an hour of this, however, the colonel had yet to give any indication as to which way she was leaning, contenting herself to listening intently as the other two 'argued.'

'Do you want to review the court recordings again?'

'What for? They haven't changed!' Major Joshua snarled. Olive-complexioned and naturally hyper and intense, he had easily assumed the bad-guy role. At this point, however, he was tiring of the game and eager to bring things to a head. 'I don't know why we're still debating this! The man's guilty as sin – hell, he even admits it! If we don't come down hard on him, it'll look like we're condoning what he did.'

'Look, Josh – I mean, Major – there were extenuating circumstances involved.'

The rotund Captain Humpty had no difficulty playing the good-guy devil's advocate. It was his habit to champion the underdog, though this case was trying even his generous tolerances. Still, he rose gamely to the challenge.

'We keep saying we want our junior officers to show initiative and leadership. If we slap them down every time they try something that doesn't work, then pretty soon no one will have the courage to do anything that isn't under orders and by the book.'

The major snorted in disbelief. 'Incentive! Bloodthirsty opportunism is more like it – at least, that's what the media called it, if I remember correctly.'

'Are we letting the media set our discipline these days?'

'Well, no,' Joshua admitted. 'But we can't completely ignore our public image, either. The Legion is already considered to be the bottom of the heap. It's disasters like this that have everyone thinking we're a haven for criminals and losers.'

'If they want Boy Scouts, there's always the Regular Army, not to mention the starfleet,' said the Captain dryly. 'The Legion has never been a home for angels, including, I'll wager, all of us in this room. We're supposed to be judging this man's questionable action, not trying to salvage the Legion's reputation.'

'All right. Let's look at his action. I still don't see any redeeming factors in what he did.'

'He inspired one of those Dudley-Do-Right pilots you're so envious of to make an unauthorized strafing run. I know commanders who haven't been able to get that kind of cross-service support even when the pilots were under orders to cooperate. Do you think it's wise to squelch that kind of leadership potential?'

'That depends on if you're differentiating between "leadership" and an ability to incite disobedience. What your young lieutenant *really* needs is a couple years in the stockade to calm him down. Then maybe he'll think twice before he goes charging off half-cocked.'

'I don't think we want to do that.'

Both men broke off their argument and turned their attention to the colonel, who had finally entered into the discussion.

'While you have made several valid points, Major, and your proposed sentence would be in line with those points, there are certain . . . factors to be considered here which you are not aware of.'

She paused, as if weighing each word for correctness, while the other officers waited patiently.

'I am extremely reluctant to bring this up – in fact, I rather hoped it wouldn't be necessary. As you know, each Legionnaire starts with a clean slate when he or she joins up. We aren't supposed to be biased by, or even be aware of, their personal history prior to their enlistment. To maintain that illusion, I'll have to ask that not only what I tell you be kept in strictest confidence, but also the fact that you were told anything at all.'

She waited until both men had nodded their agreement before continuing, and even then seemed reluctant to speak directly.

'It goes without saying that the lieutenant comes from money. If he didn't, he wouldn't be an officer.'

The others waited patiently for information that was news. It was known that the Legion raised money by selling commissions . . . or rather by charging hefty fees to anyone who wanted to test for one.

'I did notice that he has his own butler,' the captain said, trying to be amiable. 'A bit pretentious, perhaps, but nothing the rest of us couldn't afford if we were so inclined.'

The colonel ignored him.

'The truth is . . . have either of you considered the significance of the lieutenant's choice of a name?'

'Scaramouche?' Major Joshua said with a frown. 'Aside from the obvious reference to the character from the novel, I hadn't given it much thought.'

'I assumed it was because he fancied himself to be a swordsman,' the captain put it, not to be outdone by his colleague.

'Before the novel. Perhaps I should say that the *real* origin of the name and title is a stock character from Italian comedy – a buffoon or a fool.'

The men scowled and exchanged covert glances.

'I don't get it,' the major admitted at last. 'What has that got to do with –'

'Try spelling "fool" with a "*ph*" . . . as in *p-h-u-l-e*.'

'I still don't –'

The colonel sighed and held up a restraining hand.

'Take a moment and study your sidearm, Major,' she said.

Puzzled, the officer drew his pistol and glanced at it, turning it over in his hand. As he did, a sharp intake of breath drew his attention and he realized that the captain had successfully put together whatever it was that the colonel was driving at.

'You mean . . . ?'

'That's right, Captain.' The court president nodded grimly. 'Your Lieutenant Scaramouche is none other than the only son and heir apparent to the current owner and president of Phule-Proof Munitions.'

Stunned, the major gaped at the pistol in his hand which bore the Phule-Proof logo. If the colonel was correct, then the lieutenant he had been about to throw the book at was one of the youngest megamillionaires in the galaxy.

'But then why would he join . . . ?'

The words froze in the major's throat as he barely caught himself on the brink of the worst social gaff a Legionnaire can commit. Suddenly uncomfortable, he turned the pistol over in his hands again to avoid the icy stares of the other officers. While it was a definite breach of regulations for the colonel to reveal the lieutenant's personal background, the one question no one was ever allowed to ask of or about any Legionnaire was 'Why did he or she join?'

After an awkward few moments had passed, the colonel resumed the discussion.

'Now, what we need to consider before reaching our verdict is not only that Phule-Proof Munitions is the largest arms manufacturer and distributor in the galaxy, not to mention the current supplier of arms and munitions for the Space Legion, but also that it is the largest single employer of Legionnaires who quit or retire. I think we have to ask ourselves whether the lieutenant's offense was so great that it's worth jeopardizing the relationship between the Legion and its main supplier, not to mention our individual careers.'

'Excuse me, Colonel, but didn't I read somewhere that the lieutenant and his father were on the outs?'

Colonel Battleax fixed the captain with her coldest stare. 'Possibly. Still, family is family, and I'm not sure I'd want to bet on how the father would react if we threw his only son into the stockade for a few years. Then, too, assuming the lieutenant eventually inherits the company, I wouldn't relish going to him for a job when I retired . . . not if I was one of the ones who sentenced him to jail.'

'It would be a lot easier if he just resigned,' Major Joshua muttered darkly as he mulled over this new development.

'True,' the colonel said, unruffled. 'But he didn't . . . and you know Legion regulations as well as I do. We can level any kind of punishment we want on a Legionnaire, but we can't drum them out of the service. He can resign, but we can't force him to quit.'

'Maybe if the sentence was rough enough, he'd resign rather than accept it,' Captain Humpty suggested hopefully.

'Perhaps, but I wouldn't count on it. I, for one, don't like to bluff if I'm not willing to live with the consequences if it's called.'

'Well, we've got to do something to him,' the major said. 'After all the coverage he's gotten from the media, we'd look silly if we didn't make an example of him.'

'Perhaps.' The colonel smiled tightly.

Major Joshua scowled. 'What do you mean by that . . . sir?'

'I mean it wouldn't be the first time a Legionnaire has been renamed to keep the media hounds off his track.'

'You aren't seriously suggesting that we let him off scot-free, are you?' the captain broke in. 'After what he's done? I don't favor ignoring –'

'I wasn't suggesting we let the lieutenant escape unscathed,' Colonel Battleax interrupted hastily. 'I merely think that in this particular situation, it might be wisest if we considered some alternatives to confinement in the stockade for punishment. Perhaps we could find a new assignment for our misfit . . . a tour sufficiently unpleasant that it would leave no doubt in his or anyone else's mind as to the opinion this court has of his little Wild West show.'

The officers lapsed into silence then, as they searched their minds of a posting that would fill their needs.

'If he were a captain,' the major said to himself, breaking the silence, 'we could ship him off to the Omega crew.'

'What was that, Major?' The colonel's voice was suddenly sharp.

Joshua blinked as if waking from a dream, jolted into remembering that the court president was from Headquarters.

'I . . . Nothing, sir. Just thinking out loud.'

'Did I hear you say something about an Omega Company?'

'Sir?'

'Do you know anything about this, Captain?'

'About what, sir?' Captain Humpty said, mentally cursing the major's loose tongue.

The colonel swept both men with an icy glare before speaking again.

'Gentlemen, let me remind you that I've been in the Legion twice as long as either of you. I'm neither blind nor stupid, and I'll thank you not to treat me as if I were.'

The other two court members squirmed uncomfortably, like schoolboys in a principal's office, as she continued.

'The Space Legion is smaller and less glamorous than the Regular Army, more like security guards than an actual fighting force. We don't enjoy the advantage they have of fielding units made up entirely of soldiers from one planet, hence our policy of accepting all applicants, no questions asked.

'Now, I know this policy has always caused problems for field officers such as yourselves. Despite our loose discipline and regulations, there are always those who don't fit neatly into military life – misfits or losers, depending on how polite you want to be when describing them. I'm also aware that, in direct disregard for standing orders regarding the treatment of Legionnaires, from time to time there develops an Omega Company – a dumping ground for problem cases that field officers are too busy or lazy to deal with. They are usually broken up as soon as they are discovered by Headquarters, but they continue to pop up, and when they do, the word gets passed quietly through the Legion until someone inadvertently leaks the information to Headquarters, and then the game starts all over again.'

Her forefinger began to tap impatiently on the table.

'I'm aware of all this, gentlemen, and now I'm asking you bluntly: Is there an Omega Company currently operating in the Legion?'

Confronted by the direct question, the other officers had little choice but to respond, and respond truthfully. Honesty was a primary requirement within the Legion (it didn't matter much what you told outsiders, but you weren't supposed to lie to your own), and while field officers were masters of half-truths and omissions, this particular approach left little maneuvering room . . . which was why the colonel used it.

'Ummm . . . ' Major Humpty farbled, searching for words to sugarcoat the confession. 'There is a company that seems to be drawing more than its share of . . . Legionnaires who are having difficulty adjusting to life within –'

'Losers and problem cases,' the colonel cut in. 'Let's call a spade a spade, Major. Where is it?'

'Haskin's Planet, sir.'

'Haskin's Planet?' The Battleax scowled. 'I don't believe I'm familiar with that one.'

'It's named after the biologist who explored the swamp there prior to settlement,' Captain Joshua supplied helpfully.

'Oh yes. The contract with the swamp miners. So that's the current dumping ground, eh?'

Humpty nodded curtly, relieved that the senior officer seemed to be taking the news so calmly.

'The CO . . . the commanding officer there has been consistently . . . lax in screening his transfers . . . '

'And in everything else, as I recall,' the colonel added grimly. 'Lax . . . I like that. There may be a future for you in media relations, Major. Please continue.'

'Actually the situation may correct itself without Headquarters intervening,' the captain said, hoping to evade the stigma of having betrayed their fellow officers to Headquarters. 'Scuttlebutt has it that the CO's tour is over soon, and no one expects him to reenlist. A new CO will probably put a stop to things out of self-preservation.'

'Maybe . . . maybe not.'

'If you're worried about reallocating the . . . problem cases,' the major put in hastily. 'I'm sure normal attrition will –'

'I was thinking about our problem of sentencing Lieutenant Scaramouche,' the colonel interrupted dryly. 'If you'll recall, that is the subject of our discussion.'

'Yes . . . of course,' Humpty was relieved but surprised at the apparent change in subject.

'What I was about to say,' Battleax continued, 'was that in light of this new information, I think Major Humpty's earlier suggestion has a certain degree of merit to it.'

It took the other officers a moment to follow her train of thought. When they did, they were understandably taken aback.

'What? You mean transfer him to the Omegas?' Captain Joshua said.

'Why not? As I just pointed out, Omega Companies are a fact of life in the Legion. While Headquarters generally disbands them as being too easy a solution for our problems, at times they have their purposes . . . and it seems to me this is one of those times.'

She leaned forward, her eyes bright.

'Think about it, gentlemen. An unpleasant, no-win assignment may be just what's needed to convince our young lieutenant to resign. If not, he's conveniently out of the way and in no position to cause us further embarrassment. The beauty of it is that no one, including his father and the lieutenant himself, can accuse us of not giving him a chance at redemption.'

'But the only officer's post available there is – or will be – the CO slot,' the major protested, 'and that position calls for at least a captain. That's what I was saying when –'

'So promote him.'

'Promote him?' the captain said, painfully aware they were talking about a rank equal to his own. 'We're going to reward him for fouling up? That doesn't seem right.'

'Captain, would you consider it a reward to be placed

in command of an Omega Company . . . even if there was a promotion attached?'

Joshua made no effort to hide his grimace.

'I see your point,' he conceded, 'but will the lieutenant realize he's being punished? I mean, he's new to the Legion. He may not even know what an Omega Company is.'

'If not, he'll learn,' the colonel said grimly. 'Well, gentlemen? Are we in agreement?'

With this decision, made out of desperation, a new chapter was begun in the Space Legion's already spotty history. Without knowing it, the court officers had just provided a head, not to mention a soul and spirit, to the group that was to become known as the Omega Mob, or, as the media liked to call them, Phule's Company.

1

Journal File #004*

Some have commented that the executive mind tends to expand work to fill, or overfill, available time. While I will not attempt to comment on the overall accuracy of this statement, it was certainly the case during our preparations prior to departure for my employer's new assignment.

For my employer, this meant countless shopping expeditions, both in person and by computer. As you will note in these chronicles, unlike many of his financial level, he was never reluctant to part with his money. In fact, when confronted by a choice of two items, he seemed to invariably solve the dilemma by simply purchasing both – a habit I found less than endearing as I was the one required to store and track these acquisitions.

Of course, his pursuit of equipment and wardrobe meant that other important chores tended to be neglected . . . such as conducting research on the situation which we had been thrust into. As is so often the case, I felt compelled to step into this void rather than allow my employer to begin this new endeavor without proper preparation.

The Port-A-Brain computer system was designed to be the ultimate in pocket computers. Its main strength was that it enabled the user to tap into nearly any data base or library in the settled worlds, or place an order

*Throughout this journal, there will be file gaps where I have deleted or withheld files which are either pointlessly caught up in the petty details of the time or contain evidence which might be utilized in court should certain activities of this period ever come to public attention.

with most businesses above a one-store retail level, or communicate directly with or leave messages for anyone or any business which utilized any form of computerized telecommunications, all without so much as plugging into a wall outlet or tapping into a phone line. What's more, the unit, complete with folding screen, was no larger than a paperback book. In short, it was a triumph of high-tech microcircuitry . . . but there was a small problem. Each unit cost as much as a small corporation, placing it well out of the financial reach of the individual and all but the most extravagant conglomerate executive officers; and even those who could afford one usually contented themselves to use the cheaper modes of data access, particularly since their job positions were lofty enough to allow them to delegate such menial tasks as research and communications to lower echelon staffers. As such, there were fewer than a dozen Port-A-Brain units in actual use in the entire galaxy. Willard Phule had two: one for himself and one for his butler. He reasoned the expense was worth avoiding the inconvenience of waiting in line for a pay terminal.

Camped in one of the spaceport's numerous snack bars, he had been putting his personal unit to good use for the last several hours, tirelessly tapping in message after message in his clawlike two-fingered style. Finally he signed off with a flourish and replaced the computer in his pocket.

'Well, that's all I can think of for now, Beek,' he declared, stretching mightily. 'The rest can hold until we've had a chance to look over our new home.'

'Nice of you to curb your enthusiasm, sir,' the butler said dryly. 'It may enable us to be on time for our transport.'

'Don't worry about it.' Phule started to finish his cardboard cup of coffee, then set it aside with a grimace when he realized any trace of heat in the liquid had long since fled. Some things remained untouched by technological advances. 'It's not like we're taking a commercial flight. This ship has been hired specifically to transport us to Haskin's Planet. I doubt it'll leave without us if we're a few minutes late.'

'I wish I shared your confidence, sir. More likely the pilot will cancel the flight completely and make do with half payment for a no-show.'

Phule cocked his head quizzically at his companion. 'You're certainly a Gloomy Gus today, Beeker. In fact, you've been more than a bit dour ever since the court-martial. Anything in particular bothering you?'

The butler shrugged. 'Let's just say I don't have the greatest faith in the generosity of the Legion, sir.'

'For example?'

'Well, for one thing, there's this chartered flight. Considering the tight-fisted nature of the Legion, I find it a bit out of character for them to allow the added expense of a private ship rather than using normal commercial transport.'

'That's easy.' Phule laughed. 'The commercial lines only fly to Haskin's Planet once every three months.'

'Exactly.' Beeker nodded grimly. 'Has it occurred to you that this new assignment is more than a bit away from the mainstream of activity?'

'Beeker, are you trying to say you suspect that my promotion and subsequent assignment are something less than a reward?'

There was an edge on his employer's voice that made the butler hesitate before answering. While normally pleasant enough to deal with, Phule also had a temper that ran to icy exactness rather than blind rage, and Beeker had no wish to become the focus of it. Still, there had always been an unspoken agreement of total honesty between them, so he summoned his courage and plunged onward.

'Let's just say I find the timing of both to be . . . questionable, considering the fact that you were being court-martialed at the time. If nothing else, their insistence that you change your Legion name would seem to indicate there's more to the matter than meets the eye.'

'I'm afraid I'll have to disagree,' Phule said coldly, then flashed one of his sudden grins. 'I don't think there's any question at all. The whole thing stinks on ice. Whatever I'm headed into, it's a cinch I'm not supposed to enjoy it.'

Beeker experienced a quick wave of relief.

'Forgive me, sir. I should have realized you couldn't be totally unaware of the situation. It's just that you seem abnormally cheerful for someone who knows he's being, as they say, set up.'

'Why shouldn't I be?' Phule shrugged. 'Think about it, Beek. Whatever's waiting for us on Haskin's has got to be better than rotting in a stockade for a couple years. Besides, I've always wanted to command a company. That's why I went for officer status in the first place.'

'I'm not sure it's safe to assume this assignment is preferable to a stockade,' the butler cautioned carefully.

'Oh?' The reply was accompanied by a raised eyebrow. 'Is there something in the company's personnel records I won't like?'

'I am virtually certain of it, sir.' Beeker smiled tightly. 'I've taken the liberty of loading them into your personal computer files so you can review them without having to deal with hard copy. I know you've never mastered traveling light.'

He gave a slight jerk of his head toward the porters standing by their luggage.

'Whoops! That's right. We've got a flight to catch.'

Phule surged to his feet and gestured to the waiting baggage handlers.

'Follow me, men. Time and spaceflights wait for no one. C'mon, Beeker. Let's roll.'

'Captain Jester?'

It took Phule a moment to recognize his new name and rank.

'That's right,' he acknowledged hastily. 'Are we about ready to depart?'

'Yes, sir. As soon as you . . . What's that!?'

The pilot had spotted the caravan of porters wheeling three cart loads of baggage with them.

'Hmm? Oh, that's just my personal luggage. If you'll show them where to stow it, they'll take care of the loading.'

'Hey, wait a second! All weight for a flight has to be cleared in advance. You can't just waltz up here at the last minute with a load like that and expect me to let you on board with it!'

Inwardly Phule sighed. He had been afraid something like this would happen. Though under contract to the Legion, on board ship the pilot had ultimate authority. Like many minor bureaucrats, this gave him an exaggerated opinion of his power. Fortunately Phule had been raised on bureaucratic infighting.

'Look . . . Captain, is it? Yes. If you'll check your manifest, you'll notice that the cargo that's been loaded so far is lighter than the weight you were contracted to transport – substantially lighter. My baggage is the balance of that weight. While it's more than is normally allotted to military personnel, I've paid for the extra poundage out of my own pocket, and am therefore understandably reluctant to leave it behind.'

The pilot had indeed noticed that the loaded cargo was light, but had figured it for an oversight, mentally licking his lips over the extra profit from saved fuel. Now he saw that extra profit slipping away.

'Wellll . . . if you're sure all that stuff is still within the paid-for poundage. Just don't expect me to load it for you.'

'Certainly not,' Phule soothed. 'Now if you'll direct the porters, they'll take care of everything.'

Beeker hefted the two suitcases that contained their necessities for the trip and started up the gangplank.

'I'll go ahead and start unpacking, sir,' he called back over his shoulder.

'Now, who's that!?' the pilot snarled.

'That's Beeker. He's my butler and traveling companion.'

'You mean he's coming with us? No way! The Legion hired me to transport one – count it, one – person and you're it!'

'Not surprising, as Mr. Beeker is not enlisted in the Legion. He's attached to me personally.'

'Fine. That means he's not going.'

Phule studied his fingernails.

'Actually, if you care to check the weights, you'll find that the extra poundage I purchased includes allowance for Beeker.'

'Oh yeah? Well, there's a big difference between baggage and transporting a person.'

The Legionnaire was studying the ship.

'That's a Cosmos 1427, isn't it, Captain? I believe it sleeps six comfortably. Realizing this is a charter flight and there are no other passengers, I'm sure we can find room for Beeker somewhere.'

'That's not the point,' the pilot insisted. 'It takes paperwork and clearances to transport a person to another planet. I got no orders for this Beeker guy.'

'As a matter of fact,' Phule said, reaching into his jacket pocket, 'I have the necessary paper right here.'

'You do?'

'Certainly. I couldn't expect you to break regulations on my say-so, could I?'

He dropped something onto the pilot's clipboard.

'Hey! This isn't . . . '

'Study it carefully, Captain. I'm sure you'll see that everything's in order.'

The pilot stared in silence, which wasn't surprising.

In fact, Phule found it was the usual reaction of laymen when suddenly confronted with a thousand-credit note.

'I . . . guess this will cover the necessary clearances,' the pilot said slowly, unable to take his eyes from the money.

'Good.' Phule nodded. 'Now, if you'll just show the porters where to stow my luggage, we can be under way.'

Journal File #007

In reviewing my entries so far, I notice that the comments regarding my employer's preparations for his new assignment seem less than complimentary. Please realize that we are two separate people with different modes of setting priorities. While we more than occasionally disagree, my noting of those differences is not intended as criticism, but rather an effort for completeness. The fact that I am the one keeping this record gives me a certain advantage in stating my opinions and preferences, and while I shall endeavor to keep my observations as impartial as possible, there is an understandable slanting where my own role in the proceedings is concerned. I trust you will take that into account in your readings.

In actuality, my employer is far more extensive in his research than I – once he gets around to it. My earlier concern was whether he would get around to it in time for it to be useful upon assuming command, and acting on that concern had prepared myself to be able to give him at least a basic briefing should time run out. As it turned out, the flight allowed more than ample time for him to complete his preparations.

Speaking of time, you may have noticed that I am merely keeping this journal in sequential sequence, occasionally noting the lapse of time between entries. Dates and times tend to become meaningless to travelers . . . particularly when one travels between planets or solar systems. For specific reference points to your local timeline, simply check in your local library for media coverage of the various events I record.

Glancing up from his lap computer, Phule noticed that Beeker had apparently fallen asleep in the cabin chair. In many ways, this wasn't surprising. There was a sense of timelessness to space travel . . . days and nights being defined by when you turned the lights on or off. For Phule, this was ideal, as it allowed him to set his own work schedule, pausing only occasionally for a meal or a nap. Beeker, however, was less flexible in his need for regular sleep patterns, so it was not unusual that the two men often found themselves on different cycles. Normally this was no problem. At the moment, however, Phule found that he wanted to talk.

After struggling with his conscience for several moments, he decided on a compromise.

'Beeker?' he said as softly as he could.

If the butler was really asleep, the words would go unnoticed. To Phule's relief, however, Beeker's eyes flew open in immediate response.

'Yes, sir?'

'Did I wake you?'

'No, sir. Just resting my eyes for a moment. May I be of assistance?'

That reminded Phule of how tired his own eyes were. Leaning back, he massaged his temples gently with his fingertips.

'Talk to me, Beek. I've been staring at these files so long they're starting to run together in my head. Take it from the top and give me your thoughts.'

The butler frowned as he mentally organized his own reactions to the assignment. It was far from the first time that his employer had asked for his opinion on key matters, though there was never any doubt as to who had the final responsibility for any action or decisions. Still, Beeker was gratified to know that Phule respected his counsel enough to ask for it from time to time.

'The settlement on Haskin's Planet is self-sufficient and numbers about one hundred thousand,' he began slowly. 'That in itself has little to do with our assignment, other than the potential of providing us with a bit of culture on our off-duty hours.

'On the surface, the assignment seems simple enough,' he continued. 'Though the mineral content of the swamps on Haskin's Planet is too low to warrant full commercial exploitation, there is a handful of individuals who eke out a living by mining those swamps. There are no major dangers in the native flora and fauna, mind you, but a swamp is a swamp and hazardous enough that it's impossible to keep watch and concentrate on mining at the same time, so the miners banded together and hired a company of Legionnaires to give them protection while they work.'

Beeker pursed his lips and paused before launching into the next portion of his summary.

'To make the job even easier, pressure from various environmental groups requires that the miners only work the swamp one day a week . . . and that within strict limitations. As an aside, though it's never stated in so many words, I suspect the assignment is actually of a duo nature: guarding the miners and policing them to be sure they remain within the environmental guidelines. Whatever the case may be, the Legionnaires are actually only required to stand duty once a week . . . which I consider to be the first sign of serious trouble. While it may sound like easy duty, I suspect that having that much free time on their hands is not a good thing for the Legionnaires posted there.'

'Which brings us to the subject of the Legionnaires,' Phule said grimly.

The butler nodded. 'Quite so. It has never been a secret that with its open-door policy, the Legion is made up, to a large extent, of criminals who chose the service as a preferable alternative to incarceration. After examining the personnel files of your new command, however, one is forced to assume that this outpost has more than the expected percentage of . . . um . . . '

'Hard cases?'

'No. It goes beyond that,' Beeker corrected. 'Even without reading between the lines, it becomes obvious that the company can be divided into two major groups. One, as you note, is comprised of those rougher elements who do not take easily to military life, regardless of what they signed on enlistment. The second group is at the other extreme. If anything, they are pacifistic by nature or choice – a trait which also makes them difficult or impossible to absorb into a normal military structure. I think, however, it is necessary to note that apparently all of your new command falls into one or the other of those groups. In short, it's my considered opinion that you've been assigned to a force comprised entirely of . . . well, losers and misfits, for lack of better titles.'

'Myself included. Eh, Beeker?' Phule smiled wryly.

'It would appear that you are viewed as such in certain quarters,' the butler said with studied indifference.

Phule stretched his limbs.

'I agree with your analysis, Beek, except for one thing.'

'Sir?'

'When you refer to them as falling into one of two groups . . . I'm not seeing any of the cohesion necessary for a group, either in the categories you mentioned or in the company itself. It's a cluster of individuals with no real sense of "group" or of "belonging".'

'I stand corrected. "Group" was simply a convenient label.'

Phule was leaning forward now, his eyes bright despite his obvious fatigue.

'Convenient labels are a trap, Beek. One I can't afford to fall into. As near as I can tell, convenient labels are what got the bulk of the personnel transferred into this company as . . . what did you call them?'

'Loser and misfits, sir.'

'That's right, losers and misfits. I've got to mold them into a group, a cohesive unit, and to do that I've got to see them as individuals first. People, Beeker! It always comes down to people. Whether we're talking business or the military, people are the key!'

'Of course, you realize, sir, that not everyone in your command falls under the category of "people",' the butler commented pointedly.

'You mean the nonhumans? That's right, I've got three of them. What are they? Let's see . . . '

'Two Sinthians and a Voltron. That is, two Slugs and a Warthog.'

'I'll have none of that, Beeker,' Phule's voice was sharp. 'Species slurs are the worst kind of convenient label, and I won't tolerate it . . . not even from you, not even in jest. Whoever they are, whatever they are, they're Legionnaires under my command and will be treated and referred to with proper courtesy, if not respect. Is that clear?'

The butler had long since learned to distinguish between his employer's occasional irritated temper flares, which were quickly forgotten, and genuine anger. While he had been previously unaware of this particular area of sensitivity, he made a mental note of it.

'Understood, sir. It won't happen again.'

Phule relaxed, confident that the matter was settled.

'I'll admit,' he mused, 'that of the three nonhuman species that we've made alliances with, I'm surprised to find individuals from those two species in my command. I suppose it would have been too much to hope for to get a Gambolt or two.'

Beeker almost said 'The Cats?' but caught himself in time.

'I believe that members of that species inclined to enlist usually sign onto the Regular Army,' he commented instead. 'In fact, I've heard there's an entire company of them.'

'It figures,' Phule grimaced. 'With their combat reflexes and abilities, they can pretty much pick their assignments.'

'Certainly a different breed of . . . a different caliber material than you've been given to work with,' the butler agreed readily. 'Tell me, sir, do you really think you can mold such a . . . diverse collection of individuals into an effective unit?'

'It's been done before. Specifically, the Devil's Brigade . . . the first Special Service force, which eventually became . . . '

'The Special Forces,' Beeker finished. 'Yes, I'm familiar with the unit. If I might point out, however, that was a joint U.S.-Canadian force. At the beginning, the Americans provided a motley assortment of rejects and criminals, as opposed to the Canadians, who donated a crack fighting unit. While you definitely have your allotment of criminals, I fear you're lacking the offsetting crack fighting unit to serve as an example.'

'*Touché*.' Phule laughed easily. 'I should know better than to try to reference military history in front of you, Beeker. Okay. To answer your question, I don't know if it can be done, or more to the point, if it can be done by me. I do know I'm going to give it my best shot.'

'Which is all anyone can ask and definitely more than they deserve.' The butler stretched and yawned. 'For now, however, unless there is something else . . .?'

He let the question hang in the air.

'Go ahead and turn in, Beek,' Phule said, reaching for his lap computer. 'Sorry to keep you up, but I appreciate the talk.'

Beeker paused, eyeing the terminal.

'And yourself, sir? You'll want to be well rested when we arrive at Haskin's Planet.'

'Hmmm? Oh. Sure . . . in a bit. I just want to do a little checking on who's who in that settlement. I'd like to know what I'm up against.'

The butler shook his head as he watched Phule hunch over the computer again. He knew all too well the kind of detail his employer required when researching business rivals – credit checks, educational background, family, police records – and assumed he'd settle for nothing less in this new campaign he was undertaking. There would be hours, if not tens of hours, of painstaking work involved, work begun long after most men would have collapsed from fatigue. Still, he knew it was pointless to try to cajole or jolly Phule from his chosen path once he was on a roll. All Beeker could do was to be there to support this extraordinary person when and if he did wobble.

Still shaking his head, he left for his cabin.

2

Journal File #013

I was not personally present at the assembly where my employer first addressed his new command. Though I had complete knowledge of the Legionnaires' personnel files, and was later to get to know many of them intimately, not being officially in the Legion would have made it inappropriate for me to attend the meeting.

I therefore took it upon my self to eavesdrop on the proceedings by tapping into the compound's two-way paging system. This is merely a high-tech improvement of the time-honored tradition of listening at key holes. While one's employer is entitled to his privacy, it is next to impossible to meet, much less anticipate, his requirements without proper knowledge of his activities and the pressures at work in his life.

(Admittedly I have never discussed this openly with my employer, but while I have often acted on information I was not given directly, he has never commented on or chastised me for my having that knowledge.)

The company recreation hall, though the largest room in the compound, was usually virtually deserted evenings. At one time it had merely been depressing in its lifelessness, but over the last several months the Legionnaires had stopped picking up after themselves, and a little of moldy, half-eaten food added a new air to the environs. More simply put, it stank.

Tonight, however, it was full to capacity. Word had been passed that the new company commander wanted to address the troops, and the possibility that a roll call might be taken was sufficient threat to guarantee everyone's attendance.

There were not enough seats to go around, even including the perching points on the pool table and radiators, and the pecking order among the company could be readily seen by who yielded their spot to whom as the room slowly filled. Though they tried to maintain an air of bored cynicism, the Legionnaires were nonetheless curious about the new commander, and that subject dominated the conversation, particularly among the younger, more clean-cut segment of the group.

'It's sure taken him long enough to call this meeting,' one such was grumbling. 'He's been in residence almost a week and hasn't talked to anyone . . . just keeps sending that butler of his to the mess hall for food or into town on errands.'

'Anyone ever hear of an officer having his own butler?'

'Who cares? They're all spoiled rich kids, anyway. Whatdaya expect in an outfit where ya gotta buy a commission?'

'What do you think he's going to say?'

This last comment proved to be too tempting to pass on for the company's first sergeant, who had been lounging nearby, eavesdropping on the conversation. She was a rough-complexioned woman in her early thirties, and of normal enough proportion that it wasn't until she stood up that one realized how large she was.

'I'll tell you what he's going to say,' she announced with theatric boredom.

'What's that, Brandy?'

Aside from her rank and size, the first sergeant had an easy smoothness and confidence in her movements that earned her deferential treatment and attention whenever she chose to speak.

'It'll be the same as any CO would say taking over a new outfit,' she said. 'First, he'll tell a joke. I think it's written in the Officer's Manual that you have to open with a joke when you're addressing enlisted personnel. Anyway, he'll start with a joke, then tell us that whatever's happened before is in the past, that he's going to make this the best unit in the Legion. Of course, he won't say how, just that he's going to do it . . . which means we get drills and inspections for a few weeks until he gives up on this ragtag bunch and starts trying to pull strings to get transferred out.'

A few of the more seasoned Legionnaires within earshot grunted their agreement or simply grinned in amusement at the top sergeant's analysis. They, too, had heard it all before.

'Basically you've got two choices,' Brandy continued. 'You can wait him out, or you can toady up to him and hope he'll take you with him when he transfers out of this sewer.'

There were several moments of uncomfortable silence before one of the newer Legionnaires voiced the thought that was on all their minds.

'Do you think we could get a better deal in another outfit, Sarge?'

The top sergeant spat noisily on the floor before answering.

'That all depends on what you think a better deal is. Standin' guard in a swamp is no picnic, but it beats getting shot at. As far as the company itself goes . . . '

She shot a glance at the company's two lieutenants fidgeting in opposite corners across the room and lowered her voice.

' . . . all officers are pretty much the same, and none of them are good for much except signing reports and holding the bag. If you're asking what I think of the working end of the company, the grunts, well . . . do you know what an Omega Company is?'

The sudden crash of chairs being knocked about and voices raised in cheers and catcalls drew the attention of everyone in the room, at least momentarily. That was all the time it took for most of the company to realize it was only Super Gnat on another one of her rampages and return to whatever they were doing before.

Super Gnat was the smallest Legionnaire in the company, and had a fiery temper that exploded at any provocation, real or imagined. In particular, she was sensitive to any comment made about her height . . . or lack thereof.

'I wonder what set the Gnat off this time?' Brandy mused, half to herself.

'Who knows?' one of her listeners said. 'The other day she jumped me in the chow line at breakfast. All I did was ask the cook for a short stack of pancakes.'

'That sounds like her.' The top sergeant nodded as the others chuckled appreciatively. 'You know, with as much fighting as the little runt does, you'd think she'd be better at it. Look at that.'

The Legionnaire under attack was laughing openly, keeping Super Gnat at arm's length by the simple tactic of holding his hand on the top of her head as she flailed away blindly with her fists.

Brandy shook her head sadly.

'It looks more like a schoolyard than a Space Legion company. That's what I was starting to say about Omega Companies. Counting up all the oddballs and basket cases we've got in this outfit, it's a cinch that –'

'*Ten-HUT*!'

Lieutenant Armstrong's voice reverberated off the walls, but no one paid it much heed. He was rumored to be a reject from the Regular Army, and had never rid himself of the reflex of calling a room to attention when a superior officer entered. Such traditions were not practiced in the Legion. Courtesy between the ranks was a matter of personal preference rather than required performance, and as such was generally ignored. His eruption did call attention to the fact that the new CO had just entered the rec room, however, and all the Legionnaires craned their necks to see their new commander.

Framed by the door behind him and poised in a parade-rest stance that was at once relaxed and vibrating with restrained energy, the figure that had just entered the room dominated the assemblage with its mere presence. His uniform was a glowing black jumpsuit edged with gold piping and tailored to flatter his slim body. A rapier with a polished brass swept basket hilt that hung at his side by a baldric might have made him look comical if it were not offset by the icy gaze he leveled at the company. So unsettling was the stare and the silence which accompanied it that several Legionnaires nervously rose from their seats and drew themselves up into an approximation of the position of attention. The CO seemed not to notice, any more than he noticed those who remained seated.

'They tell me you're all losers and misfits,' he said flatly without introduction. 'I don't believe it . . . though it's clear most of you think you're losers from the way you conduct yourselves.'

The company exchanged glances, suddenly self-conscious of their soiled uniforms and the garbage in the room. A few eyes were turned toward the first sergeant as if to ask what had happened to the expected joke. She ignored them, making a show of concentrating on the CO's words as he continued.

'I'm aware that you are all lacking in the abilities or character traits that usually define the so-called perfect soldier. I'm also aware that the perfect soldier doesn't exist in reality. I'm not looking for you to be perfect soldiers, just effective soldiers. "Effective" means getting the job done with whatever or whomever you have handy . . . not letting the job or the world run over you while you moan about what you haven't got. You've all spent so much time concentrating on your shortcomings that it's hard for you to see your own strengths. That's where leadership comes in.'

He swept the room with that gaze again.

'My name is Captain Jester, and I'm your new commanding officer. Since I've seen all of your files and know quite a bit about you, I thought I'd return the favor and let you know a bit about me . . . even if it means departing from the Legion tradition of secrecy. My actual name is Willard Phule, and my father owns Phule-Proof Munitions. As you might guess from that, I'm quite rich.'

There was a minor stir at this information, but most kept their attention on the captain.

'Some of you resent the practice the Legion has of raising money by charging a fee for the commissioned-officer examination . . . "selling commissions", as it's often referred to. I won't apologize for the system or for using it to my advantage. Purchasing commissions was common at one time in the British empire, and they did quite well militarily. There is another tradition from that time I intend to implement, however; that the commanding officer supplements the units under his command with his own finances. I'll get to that in a moment, but first I'd like to make one point clear. I didn't inherit my money. While my father provided some seed money at first, it was in the form of a loan long since paid off. I was a multimillionaire before I was out of my teens, and I did it by buying companies and corporations that others thought were losers and turning them into winners. That's what I intend to do with this unit. Developing and making use of raw material is the job of management, and if this company can't become an effective force, it'll be my fault, not yours.

'Now then, as to special gear . . . '

Phule held up one hand and used the other to pull back the sleeve of his uniform, revealing a wide leather band housing a watchlike mechanism.

'You will each be issued one of these. It's a wrist communicator and can be used as either a paging system or a private phone. They will enable you to stay in touch with each other and with Headquarters at all times, and vice versa. As you notice, I'm wearing one as well. I will be available to any of you at any time, day or night. Obviously I have to sleep sometime, as well as take care of other matters of importance. At those times, my number will be monitored by either a clerk or my butler. I can be awakened or interrupted at any time if it's important . . . but be sure it's actually important or we'll have a few words.

'Speaking of my butler, you've probably heard of him if not seen him by now. His name is Beeker, and in addition to being my employee, he's also my friend and confidant. I have a great deal of respect for him, and would appreciate it if you treated him with the courtesy he deserves. I can't and won't order it, but I will ask it. Remember, however, that he is not in the Legion and therefore not in your chain of command. Anything he says should be treated as his opinion only and not an order or official policy statement from me or the Legion. Similarly you will find that he will respect and keep any confidence you care to share with him, so feel free to speak with him or in front of him without fear of it being reported back to me or anyone else in the chain of command. If some of you feel that his job is demeaning or subservient, I'll share with you the fact that after several years of working for me and investing his savings, he is currently independently wealthy in his own right. In short, he's working for me because he wants to, not because he has to.

'That brings me to another point. I don't know what plans any of you have for life after your enlistment is up, or if you're saving any of your wages toward that day. I do know that if you aren't preparing yourself financially, you should. Well, handling money is something I do well, and I hereby place that skill at the disposal of the company . . . just as I hope some of you will be willing to use your strengths and skills, however praiseworthy or dubious, to the benefit of all. I will be opening a portfolio of stocks to enable any of you who wish to participate to invest your savings or whatever portion of your pay you wish to assign to that purpose. While I can't guarantee success, I have never managed a portfolio that lost money. Personally I would suggest setting aside one third of your wages for this purpose, but again the amount is completely up to you, as is your participation at all. If any of you have questions on this, feel free to talk to me during breaks or off-duty hours.'

The captain surveyed the room again.

'While there's a lot more to cover, it can wait. I just wanted you all to get an idea of who I was and what I had in mind for this unit. We all know, however, that talk is cheap, and I'm sure you're all more interested in my actions rather than my words, so I'll keep the speeches to a minimum for the time being.

'I'll be meeting with each of the officers and cadre members in my office after we finish here. Are there any immediate questions before we break up?'

There was a low buzz among the Legionnaires, then a voice floated up clearly from the back.

'We hear that the governor's decided to post a color guard on his office.'

The commanding officer cocked his head.

'This is the first I've heard of it, but I'll check into it first thing tomorrow. Off the top, however, I don't see any problem with it. It could make a nice break from swamp duty.'

'Umm . . . excuse me, sir?' Brandy drawled. 'I don't think you quite understand. Scuttlebutt has it that he's invited Regular Army to perform that duty instead of us. They get to show off their pretty dress uniforms in town while we sit out in the swamp . . . same as always.'

A low growl rumbled through the assemblage. Phule

noted it, as his lips compressed into a thin line of annoyance.

'We'll see about that,' he said grimly. 'All right. Anything else that won't keep until tomorrow?'

He waited a moment, then nodded at the silence.

'Very well, then. The last note is that I want you all to assemble your personal gear and stand by to move out first thing in the morning. We're going to be moving out of these quarters for a while.'

Scattered groans greeted this announcement. It sounded like the new CO was going to make them camp out while taking their measure.

'Why? Are you going to have the place fumigated?'

Phule seemed not to notice the snickers that answered the question which had been shouted anonymously.

'Actually I'm going to have the place remodeled,' he said casually. 'In the meantime, we're going to move into the Plaza Hotel in town.'

Thunderstruck silence followed his words. The Plaza was the ritziest, most expensive hotel on the planet. The few times that Legionnaires had attempted to stop in the cocktail lounge for a drink, they had been driven out by the prices and dress codes.

For the first time since entering the rec room, Phule allowed himself a small smile.

'Like I said, gentlemen . . . and ladies . . . things are going to be different from now on. Officers and cadre . . . outside my office. Now!'

3

Journal File #014

Honoring the tradition of the Space Legion, my employer did not have, nor did he request, any information regarding the lives of those under his command prior to their enlistment. Not being a member of the Legion, however, I felt no obligation to be so restrained, and consequently had compiled substantial dossiers on the individuals that would be affecting my employer's, and therefore my own, life and well-being for the foreseeable future.

For the most part, this was relatively easy to accomplish. A computer check of the police records and news items around the time and place of each Legionnaire's enlistment provided a starting point for most of the searches. There were some, however, that required much more extensive research, and occasionally I was forced to resort to mere extrapolation and guessing. Such was the case of the two lieutenants my employer had inherited with his command.

'Good evening, Lieutenant Armstrong . . . Lieutenant Rembrandt. Please, have a seat.'

Phule had deliberately kept his office as small and spartan as possible. It was his belief that large meetings were useless for anything except announcements. Consequently there were only two visitor chairs in his retreat.

Rembrandt nodded her thanks and reached for one of the seats. She was of medium height – which made her look small beside Lieutenant Armstrong's six foot plus – with dark hair, a round face, and a vaguely rotund body . . . not fat, but broad across the rump and far from slender.

'Thank you, sir. I'd rather stand.'

Armstrong, recruiting-poster correct in his parade-rest stance, barked out his response just as his counterpart's rump was beginning its downward movement toward her chair. At his outburst, however, Rembrandt abandoned her maneuver, electing instead to stand beside Armstrong in a rough, approximation of his posture. From her grimace and his smirk, it was apparent to Phule that this little game of one-upmanship was nothing new between them.

'Very well,' he said. 'I'll try to keep this short.

'I'm probably going to be rougher on you two than on anyone else in the company . . . with the possible exception of myself. Being an officer is more than paying for your exam fee. As I said in the general meeting, this company needs leadership, and if we're going to inspire and lead the Legionnaires, we're going to have to stay one jump ahead of them. You two are going to be my stand-ins when I'm otherwise occupied, but though I'll try to be understanding while you're learning my priorities and style, I will not tolerate laziness. In fact, the only thing I detest more than sloth is thoughtlessness. I want you two to be thinking and analyzing all the time. For example . . . Lieutenant Armstrong.'

'Sir?'

'From your manner and performance reports, you fancy yourself to be a disciplinarian . . . a by-the-book man. Right?'

For a moment, Armstrong's apparent confidence was shaken.

'I . . . that is . . .' he stammered, obviously unsure of what response was expected.

'Well?'

'Yes, sir.'

'All right.' The Captain smiled. 'Then consider

this . . . By the book is it better to order soldiers to shape up or to lead by example?'

'Lead by example, sir.' Armstrong replied briskly, back on familiar ground.

'Then why don't you?'

The lieutenant under fire frowned, his eyes wandering from their straight-ahead stare to look directly at the commander for the first time since the interview began.

'I . . . I don't understand, sir,' he said. 'I try to conduct myself in an exemplary manner. I thought I was . . . I try to be the best Legionnaire in the company.'

'You have that potential,' Phule acknowledged easily, 'but I think you're overlooking one vital element. Most people don't want to be seen as a tight-assed, overbearing prig . . . which is what you tend to show them. If anything, your manner is driving them away from proper military behavior because no one wants to be like you.'

Armstrong opened his mouth to reply, but the commander cut him off with a gesture.

'I don't want to talk about it, Armstrong. I want you to think about it. Then maybe we'll talk about specifics. If you can temper your rigid manner with a little compassion, show that someone can be a bandbox soldier and still be human, then the troops will follow you anywhere because they want to, not because they're ordered to.'

The lieutenant wrenched his gaze back to its original distant stare and nodded once, curtly, as his only acknowledgement of having heard Phule's words.

'As for you, Lieutenant Rembrandt,' the commander said, swiveling his chair to face the second of his subchieftains, 'it appears you don't expect, or want, anyone to look to you for an example.'

The dark-haired lieutenant blinked at him in surprise. She made no effort to duplicate Armstrong's distant stare, but met Phule's eyes directly as he continued.

'From the notes on your record, it would seem you're content to let the sergeants run the company when you're supposedly in command, while you wander off with your sketch pad looking for things to draw.' He paused and shook his head ruefully. 'Now, I'm all in favor of art, Rembrandt, and I don't mind at all your pursuing it as a hobby during your off hours. I may even be able to pull a few strings to help you get a showing when your enlistment is up. However, during duty hours I expect your attention to be focused on the company. The sergeants may be experts in their own right and may think they run the company, but their focus is on the immediate job and not the long term. That's your job, as well as Armstrong's and mine, and if we don't do it, the company will flounder. We can't do that job if we don't know what's going on or aren't familiar with the performance of the Legionnaires as individuals and as a group. Now, the three of us will be meeting on a weekly if not daily basis to discuss the troops and the company, and I'll expect you to take an active and knowledgeable part in those discussions. Do I make myself clear?'

'I . . . I'll try, Captain.'

'Good. As long as people are willing to try, I can work with them. That goes for you, too, Armstrong. The three of us have to be the eyes and the brains of the company, and that means functioning as a team within the team. Which reminds me . . . '

He stabbed a finger into the air between the two lieutenants and made a little stirring motion.

'I don't want to see any more little games between the two of you as to who's the better soldier. As of now, you two are partners . . . and your first order of business is to start building a tolerance for your differences. It's my belief those differences will work in your favor if each of you can learn to rely on the other's strengths rather than envying them. I won't ask for respect, though I'm hoping that will come with time. Just realize that you're holding opposite sides of the same bucket, and you're going to have to learn to move together to keep it from falling or splashing.'

The commander leaned back in his chair and made a little shooing gesture.

'Now, I suggest you get out of here and hole up over coffee or a drink and start figuring out what you have in common . . . '

He allowed a ghost of a smile to flit across his face.

' . . . aside from the belief that your new commander is an unreasonable and unjustly demanding sonofabitch, that is.'

Escrima, the mess sergeant, was a wiry, swarthy little man with wavy black hair, dark wide-spaced eyes, and a nearly perpetual grin that beamed from his wrinkled walnut face. It was the 'nearly' part that made him someone worth watching.

Phule returned his somewhat exaggerated salute and studied him for a few moments before speaking.

'Without meaning to break the rule against prying into backgrounds, Sergeant, am I correct in assuming from your name that you're of Philippine descent?'

The little sergeant bobbed his head in quick acknowledgement, the smile never wavering.

'I've always heard that the Filipinos were some of the best cooks and some of the fiercest fighters on Old Earth.'

That earned the commander a modest shrug, though the smile broadened slightly.

'Then perhaps you can tell me why the food in the mess isn't better.'

Phule had planned the phrasing of that question very carefully. According to his record, Sergeant Escrima had attacked people who criticized his cooking on three separate occasions, hospitalizing two of them. It was therefore important to be sure to say only that the food could be better, not that it was bad.

Even with the added precaution, the cook's dark eyes glittered for a moment. Then the look passed and he gave another of his shrugs.

'Mmmm . . . I am given a menu by the Legion. They say . . . they tell me I should cook what it says. And the meat they give me . . . is, how you say, stiff . . . tough. I tell the supply sergeant, I say to him, "How can I cook with this meat? Look at it! Here, you show me!" but he just shrug and say, "That's all the Legion budget can afford. Do the best you can." So I do the best I can with the meat he gives me . . . and the Legion menu . . . but . . . '

The sergeant let his oration die off with a more exaggerated shrug and a meaningful jerk of his head at Phule.

'I see. Well, forget about the budget . . . and the menu. I want the company to eat well, and we don't pay them enough for them to eat out all the time. While I'm commander and you're the cook, I want this to be the best-fed company in the Legion.'

Escrima bobbed his head in quick accord.

'Good,' he said curtly. 'It's about time.'

'Then I'll consider the matter handled.' The commander nodded, crossing off an item on his notepad. 'That will be all for now, Sergeant.'

Once again the sergeant gave his exaggerated salute, which Phule started to return when another thought struck him.

'Oh . . . one more thing. Am I also correct in assuming you would not have taken your name, Escrima, from the Philippine stick-fighting form unless you were skilled at it?'

The modest smile and shrug flashed past again.

'Then I'd take it as a personal favor if you'd consent to teach it to the interested members of the company, myself included. I don't know that much about it, but any stick form that can take out Magellan and his men while they were armed with swords, and armored to boot, is worth studying.'

'Have a seat, Sergeant . . . Chocolate Harry, isn't it?'

'Just "Harry" will do, Captain,' the sergeant said, easing his massive bulk carefully into the indicated chair. '"C.H.," to my friends.'

'All right. We'll make it C.H.' – Phule nodded, jotting a quick note on his pad – 'seeing as how I think we're going to become fast friends over the next couple months.'

'Now, how do you figure that?' The sergeant frowned suspiciously. 'No offense . . . sir . . . but to my recollection officers aren't noted for chummin' around with us enlisted types.'

'Sorry. I'm getting ahead of myself,' the commander answered absently, flipping through his notes. 'That was assuming you're as crooked and conniving as I think you are.'

The supply sergeant's eyes narrowed, all but disappearing into his fleshy face as he leaned back in his chair.

'You know, Captain, that remark could be taken as more than a little racist. Are you sayin' that you think all us colored folk steal?'

As might be implied by his name, Chocolate Harry was black, though his skin tended toward a soft brown rather than the deep black sometimes associated with his race. He was also hairy, but it was in the form of a fierce, bristly beard, offsetting his close-cropped hairstyle. A pair of thick-lensed spectacles pushed up onto his forehead completed the picture he presented as he regarded his commander with a scowl that on a smaller person would have looked melodramatic.

'Hmmm?' Phule said, looking up from his notes at last. 'Oh. Not really, C.H. I was basing my assumption on the fact that your files show that you're well above average in intelligence. My thinking is that anyone with even half a brain in charge of supplies for this outfit would be supplementing his pay by at least dabbling in the black market. If I'm wrong, you of course have my apologies.'

Harry smiled broadly. 'Thank you, Cap'n. An apology from an officer is something a grunt like me don't get every day.'

'Excuse me, Sergeant,' the commander interrupted, returning the smile tooth for tooth, 'but I said "if I'm wrong." Before I'd feel right about extending that apology, I'd have to ask you to wait here while your files were confiscated and the supply warehouse padlocked so that an item-by-item physical inventory and audit could be performed to determine whether or not I was wrong.'

The supply sergeant's smile vanished like a mouse at a cat show, and he licked his lips nervously while his eyes darted from the commander to the door.

'That . . . won't be necessary, Captain,' he said carefully. 'I'm willing to admit, just between the two of us, of course, that there might be a few items that have been, shall we say, misplaced over the last few months. If you want, I can see if the missing equipment can be found again in the next couple of weeks.'

'That wasn't what I had in mind, C.H.' Phule smiled.

'Okay, then.' Harry hunched forward conspiratorially in his chair. 'I suppose you and I can work out some kind of profit-sharing agreement . . . '

The commander gave a short bark of laughter, cutting the sergeant short.

'Excuse me, Harry, but you're getting the wrong message here. I'm not trying to shut you down . . . or shake you down, for that matter. If anything, what I want is the exact opposite. I want you to expand your operation, and I think I can help you do that. You can start by clearing out most of the stock you've got in the warehouse right now.'

The supply sergeant scowled. 'How do you figure that, Captain? I mean, I sure do like your style, but it occurs to me that if we clean this outfit out, someone's bound to notice. You got some plan to hide the fact I'll be sittin' on an empty warehouse?'

'First of all, we're not going to try to hide it.' Phule grinned. 'We'll be doing this strictly by the book . . . specifically Section 954, paragraph 27, which states: "The supply sergeant may dispose of any surplus or outdated equipment by destroying or selling such equipment"; and Section 987, paragraph 8: "The commanding officer shall determine if any item of the company's equipment is suitable for repair or upgrade, or if it is to be deemed scrap and disposed of." Now, to my eye the bulk of our equipment is more suitable for a museum than a fighting force, so I figure your work is going to be cut out for you.'

Harry nodded. 'Very nice. I might even say "sweet" . . . 'cept for one thing. That still leaves me with an empty warehouse.'

'Not really. I think you'll find that the gear that'll be arriving over the next few weeks will more than fill the empty space. As I told the company, I've taken the liberty of upgrading the quality of our equipment . . . at my own expense, of course.'

'Of course,' the sergeant echoed, leaning back in his chair to study the commander through half-slitted eyes. 'That brings up another question completely, Captain. Now, if you're nearly as rich as you let on, I'm not exactly sure why it is you need me. I mean, what with you buyin' up the store for this outfit, why is it you want to fool around raising money havin' me sell off our surplus?'

Phule heaved a great sigh, as if losing patience with a child.

'C.H., you and I both know there are things you

can't buy in a store. What I mean is, my money and methods may be fine for normal equipment and supplies, but I'm expecting that from time to time, we may need a few items that can only be found on the black market. So I'm expecting you to get us a pipeline into the underground supply network by using the sale of our old equipment as a passport. Get my drift?'

'Read you loud and clear, Cap'n,' Harry said, his face splitting in a wide grin. 'You know, I ain't never called a white man "brother" before, but you just might qualify.'

'I'm afraid we'll have to settle for just "good buddies" for the time being,' Phule corrected hastily. 'You see, C.H., there are a few rules attached to this game – my rules, not the Legion's.'

'Uh-oh. Thought this was sounding a little too good to be true.'

'First of all,' the commander continued, ignoring the sergeant's theatric aside, 'I don't want you to sell anything that will come back to haunt us. If you make a deal for our automatic weapons, make sure it's after you've removed the selector switch that converts them to fully automatic – and that doesn't mean you have a sale on selector switches the next week. Our gear may be antique, but there's a lot of it I'd just as soon not have used against us . . . or the local police, for that matter. It'll be a bit difficult to play innocent if we're the only source on the planet for fully automatic hardware. That goes double for the new gear we're getting, including our wrist communicators. I suppose you can let a few of the regular units stray if it means opening the right doors, but the extra command units stay put. I don't want anyone but us to have the capacity to monitor the private lines. For that matter, if you think a bit, I'm sure you'll agree that it would be in your own best interest if no one could listen in to some of the private talks you and I will be having.'

The supply sergeant made a face. 'I suppose you're right, but it's gonna cramp my maneuvering a mite.'

'Rule number two: The monies from these sales get channeled into the company fund. Now, I don't mind if you do a little skimming for your trouble . . . in fact, I expect it and consider it only fair reward for devoting a portion of your personal time to helping further the company. Just do a reasonable job of doctoring the receipts for the files, and you'll hear no complaints from me. Remember, though, that I have a fair idea of what the going prices of things are, even on the black market. If I get wind of your taking more than a fair commission, I'll cut you off cold.'

'Cut me off from what, Captain?' Harry challenged. 'It wouldn't break my heart to get transferred out, you know.'

'I'm not talking about a transfer.' Phule smiled. 'I'd cut you off from your lessons. You see, C.H., right now you're a small-time chiseler and hustler. Stick with me, play the game my way, and I'll teach you to play in the big leagues, as well as show you how to build the kind of bankroll you'll need for seed money once your enlistment's up. Deal?'

'Have a seat, Brandy,' the commander said, waving his top sergeant into one of the visitor chairs. 'Sorry to keep you waiting, but for various reasons I wanted to save your interview for last.'

'No problem, sir.' The ranking noncom shrugged, sinking into the indicated seat. 'If there's one thing I've learned in the military, it's how to wait for officers.'

Phule ignored the blatant dig.

'Seeing as how it's late, and we're both tired, I'll try to keep this short and to the point.' He leaned back in his chair, crossing his arms over his chest as if hugging himself. 'Tell me, Brandy, in your opinion, what's the biggest problem facing me in this company?'

The top sergeant widened her eyes and raised her eyebrows as she pursed her lips in a silent whistle.

'That's a rough one,' she said, shifting her sprawl to a different position. 'I really don't know where to start. If you've got any smarts at all, you don't need me to tell you this company's the pits, from top to bottom, inside and out. As far as any one problem being bigger than the others . . . '

Her voice trailed off as she shook her head.

'To me, there's one problem that stands out like a beacon,' Phule said firmly. 'In fact, it's the only one I'm not sure I'll be able to handle.'

'What's that, sir?'

'You.'

Brandy pulled her head back, frowning.

'Me, sir?'

'That's right. Now, don't get me wrong. You're good, Brandy . . . head, shoulders, and waist above any of the other personnel I've inherited. From your record, and from my personal observations this last week, you're an excellent leader, easily as good or better than me.'

The commander shook his head slightly.

'The problem is that you're a cynic. If you had been around when the Wright brothers were designing their first plane, you would have been the one saying, "It'll never fly." Then, as it passed overhead on its maiden flight, your only comment would've been, "They'll never get it down!"'

A ghost of a smile flitted across the top sergeant's face.

'You got me there, Captain,' she admitted.

Her smile wasn't returned.

'That's the one thing I can't have in this company . . . not in the top sergeant slot, anyway. I'm going to try to turn this company around, starting with getting every Legionnaire under my command to develop a better opinion of his or her self. I can't do that if the main leader for the enlisted personnel keeps telling them that they're dirt and there's no point in even trying. I'm already figuring on a two-front war: with Headquarters and with the Legionnaires themselves. I can't afford to open a third front by fighting with you as well.'

The top sergeant gazed at him levelly. 'Are we talking about a transfer, sir?'

Phule grimaced. 'I'll admit the possibility has crossed my mind . . . and you're the only one I've seriously considered it for. I don't like it, though. It's too easy, too much like quitting without even trying. I admire your abilities, Brandy, as well as your leadership capacity. I'm hoping we can work together, work *with* each other, not in opposition. The only way I can see that, though, is if there are some major changes on your part.'

Brandy bit her lip thoughtfully before answering.

'To be honest with you, sir, I'm not sure I could change even if I wanted to. Old habits are hard to break, and I've been the way I am for a long time.'

'I'm not asking for guarantees,' the commander urged earnestly. 'For the time being, I'd be content if you were willing to give it a try. You see, Brandy . . . geez! I hate playing amateur psychologist, but . . . well, most of the cynics I've dealt with in the past, the hardcore "Who cares?" types, actually care a lot. It's just that at some point they've been hurt, and hurt bad. So bad, they won't let themselves even hope anymore for fear of being disappointed and hurt again. I don't know if that applies in your case, and don't really care. All that I'm asking is that you give things a chance before you shoot them down. Give the Legionnaires a chance . . . and give me a chance.'

Silence hung in the air for a moment as they both felt the awkwardness of two people sharing a sudden and unexpected closeness. It was Phule who finally pulled back, breaking the tension.

'Well, think it over, Sergeant. If, in the end, you figure it's not even worth a try, let me know and I'll arrange for your transfer.'

'Thank you, sir,' Brandy said, rising to her feet and saluting. 'I'll think about it.'

'And Brandy . . . '

'Yes, sir?'

'Think about giving yourself a chance, too.'

'Sir?'

Phule opened his eyes to find his butler standing in the doorway of his office.

'Yes, Beeker?'

'Excuse me for intruding, sir, but . . . what with the relocation scheduled for tomorrow . . . Well, sir, I thought you should try to get at least a few hours' sleep.'

The commander rose, yawning and stretching his cramped limbs.

'Right, as always, Beeker. What would I do without you?'

'I'm sure I don't know, sir. Did the meetings go well?'

Phule shrugged. 'Not as well as I hoped . . . better than I feared. There were a few moments, though. Brandy – that's the top sergeant – actually saluted me before she left.'

'Quite an achievement in itself, sir,' Beeker said, gently steering his charge through the door.

'And Rembrandt – that's the lieutenant who wants to be an artist – after my interview with her and Armstrong, she hung back for a moment and asked if I'd be willing to pose for her. I thought she meant for a portrait . . . took me a bit aback when I realized she wanted to do a nude study.'

'I see. Did you accept?'

'I told her I'd think about it. It's rather flattering, in a way, considering the number of subjects she has to choose from. Besides, it might be a nice gesture to help her with her art career . . . '

I really didn't think it was my place to inform my employer . . . Actually I didn't have the heart or the courage to tell him, and so left it for him to discover on his own. I had already had the opportunity to study Lieutenant Rembrandt's work, both finished paintings and works in progress. Without exception, she had devoted herself to landscapes . . . until now, that is.

4

Journal File #019

Moving the company into the settlement so our normal quarters could be remodeled was an enormous undertaking. The Legionnaires themselves traveled light, as they had little personal gear to deal with. Packing and storing the company's gear, however, especially the kitchen, proved to be a time-consuming task, even with everyone pitching in. Thus it was that we did not begin our actual trek into the settlement until nearly noon.

Wishing to impress both the company and the settlement, my employer had shunned the practice of transporting troops in trucks like cattle (though, after having observed them dine, I had a new appreciation of the appropriateness of this practice), choosing instead to hire a small fleet of hover limos to move his new charges. While this might be seen as an extravagant gesture, I have noted before that he is not of a particularly tight-fisted nature, especially when it comes to making an impression.

During the trip, the Legionnaires seemed to be in uncommonly high spirits, skylarking like schoolchildren on a field trip and playing with their newly issued wrist communicators. The ones I shared a ride with, however, took the opportunity to test the claim my employer had made the night before: that I could be spoken with on a confidential basis.

''Scuse me, Mr Beeker . . . '

The butler looked up from the screen of his portable computer to regard the Legionnaire who had addressed him with a look that was neither hostile nor warm.

'Just "Beeker" will suffice, sir. No other title is warranted or necessary.'

'Yeah. Whatever. I was just wondering . . . could you fill us in a little on the new commander? It sounds like you two have been together for a while.'

'Certainly, sir,' Beeker said, folding the screen and slipping the computer into his pocket. 'Of course, you realize that my relationship with my employer is of a confidential manner, and that as such I feel at liberty to voice my personal opinions only.'

'Say what?'

'What the man's saying,' Brandy put in from the other side of the limo, turning her attention from staring out the window to the conversation the other occupants were already listening to with rapt interest, 'is that he's not going to blab any secrets or details . . . just what he thinks himself.'

'Oh. Okay.'

'Please be assured, however, that I will treat whatever discussions we might have now or in the future with equal confidentiality.'

The Legionnaire turned helplessly to Brandy.

'He means he won't blab what you say, either.'

'Right. Well, Mr . . . All I want to know, Beeker, is if that guy's for real. I mean, he talks a good line and all, but how much of it's hot air? That's it, plain and simple . . . and I'd want you to try 'n' lay off the big words while you answer so's I can understand without havin' it translated.'

'I see,' Beeker said, tapping his finger against his leg thoughtfully. 'If I understand correctly, you're asking if my employer . . . your commander . . . can be trusted. To the best of my knowledge, he's always been scrupulously – excuse me, *painfully* – fair in all his dealings, both business and personal. As to his reliability . . . well, I don't think it's breaking any confidence to point out what the most casual observer would note in short order: that he's seriously unbalanced.'

For a moment, the Legionnaires in the limo were shocked into silence by the butler's statement. It was the top sergeant who found her voice first.

'What do you mean "unbalanced," Beeker? Are you saying the captain's loony?'

'Oh, I don't mean to say that he's dangerously insane or anything,' the butler corrected hastily. 'Perhaps I chose the wrong word in my efforts to keep my vocabulary simple. My employer is unbalanced only in the way that many successful business men and women are, in that he has a tendency toward the obsessive. It's not a matter of judging how his work fits into his life. His work *is* his life, and he views everything else in the universe in relation to that. This company of the Legion is his current pet project, and all his energies and resources are focused on advancing and defending it. Frankly it's my belief that you're all quite fortunate to be at the right place at the right time to be a part of his efforts. My experience has been that he rarely, if ever, fails once he sets his mind on something.'

'Excuse me, Beeker,' Brandy drawled, 'but I can't help but notice you specifically said his *current* pet project. What happens to us if he gets distracted by some other shiny toy?'

'Oh, I doubt very much that would happen. He's remarkably tenacious once he undertakes an endeavor. Unless, of course . . . '

Beeker let the sentence hang in the air.

'Unless what?'

'Well . . . your commander has near limitless energy and a drive that will sweep you along in its wake, even if you only choose to be passive to his plans and exercises. To discourage him – the only thing I can think of that might make him give up – would be active opposition from within the company on a massive scale. You Legionnaires would have to be adamant in your efforts to maintain your current images, individually and collectively.'

'I don't get it.'

'He means we'd have to work at being foul-ups before the commander would give up on us. Isn't that right, Brandy?'

'Hmmm? Oh. Right. No sweat there, Beeker. We may be a bit discouraged now, but we're at least going to *try* to keep up with your boy wonder . . . and anyone who doesn't is going to have to answer to me personally.'

In the spirited discussion that followed, no one noticed that the butler, though silent, was smiling.

The Plaza Hotel, though it had seen better days and tended to be upstaged by its newer, more modern brethren, still maintained an air of aloof dignity and elegance. The fountain in the park across the street was adorned with the graffiti of countless passing junior terrorists, and the park itself had long since been abandoned except for the street urchins who used its walks and benches for their daredevil glide-board antics by day and for their territorial disputes by night, but the hotel itself seemed to stoically ignore what was going on around it, like a harried mother of seven during summer vacation.

This beleaguered calm was shattered, however, as the first of the hover limos eased into the loading zone in front of the Plaza and disgorged its cargo of Legionnaires and luggage. Phule was in the lead vehicle, and left his charges to struggle with their personal gear as he descended on the front desk.

'May I help you, sir?' the desk clerk said, nervously eyeing the gathering mob visible through the front door.

'Yes, I'm Willard Phule. I believe you have a reservation for me . . . a hundred rooms and the penthouse?'

The desk clerk hesitated for a moment, then moved

to his computer terminal . . . coincidentally placing himself farther from Phule's reach.

'Yes, sir. I have it here. Willard Phule . . . the penthouse.'

'And a hundred rooms.'

'I . . . I'm sorry, sir. My records only show the penthouse.'

The commander's smile tightened slightly, but aside from that he showed no annoyance.

'Could you check again? I made the reservation a week ago.'

'Yes. I remember it coming in. It seems to have been canceled.'

'Canceled?' Phule's voice hardened. 'By whom?'

'You'll have to speak with the manager about that, sir. If you'll wait just a moment, I'll get him.'

Without waiting for a reply, the clerk bolted through the door behind the desk, leaving Phule to fidget impatiently as the lobby behind him began to fill with Legionnaires.

Lawrence (never Larry) Bombest might be younger than most wielding his title and power, but early in his career it was apparent that he was a born hotel manager. He ruled the Plaza with an iron fist, and though the employees chafed under his tyranny, they were nonetheless grateful of his unshakable certainty when crisis struck, as so often happens in the hotel business, and, as now, were quick to duck behind him in times of trouble. Many a wave of tired, angry traveler had broken against this rock without moving or altering it in the slightest, and he brought the sureness of a veteran with him as he emerged from his office and took in the situation at a glance.

'I am the hotel manager. What seems to be the trouble, sir?'

The commander squinted briefly at the manager's brass name badge.

'Yes, Mr. Bombast. My name is Willard Phule and

I'd like to know who canceled my reservation for a hundred rooms.'

Safely out of the line of fire and sight, the desk clerk struggled to hide a smile. Phule had inadvertently hit upon the staff's nickname for Bombest . . . Bombast . . . though, until now, no one had uttered it to his face.

'That's Bom*best*, sir . . . and I canceled that reservation myself.'

'May I ask why?'

'Certainly. I assumed there had been a typographical error on the part of whoever placed the reservation. It was done by computer rather than through our staff, and I've found that such errors are commonplace.' The manager gave a smug smile, which was not returned. 'Realizing the cost of a hundred of our rooms for a period of several weeks would be, shall we say, prohibitive, and, not being sure if the actual request was for one or ten rooms, I canceled the reservation as a courtesy. At the time I felt we could accommodate you on site according to your actual needs.'

'I see. I don't suppose you bothered to run a check on the credit card number that accompanied the reservation?'

'That is correct. As I said, the cost would be prohibitive.'

Phule made a magician's pass with his hand and dropped his credit card on the desk in front of the manager.

'I think *that* should settle the question of prohibitive cost.'

To Bombest's credit, he neither gaped nor cringed at the sight of the card, but rather made a show of turning it over to examine the signature on the back. It was a Dilithium Express card, reserved for the ultra-rich in the galaxy and normally only used to expedite the buying and selling of companies. Despite his outward calm, the manager began to experience a vague niggle of fear that he had bitten off more than he could chew.

'I see,' he said slowly.

'And now that I'm on site, as you put it, shall we proceed with accommodating my needs? What I need is the hundred rooms I reserved . . . as you can see.'

The commander indicated the now full lobby with a jerk of his head.

Bombest was fully aware of the crowd. Since seeing the Dilithium Express card, he had been weighing the potential windfall of business against the horror of admitting a full company of Legionnaires to his domain. Realizing that his salary would not be affected one way or the other, he reached his decision.

'I'm sorry, Mr. Phule. At this time, we don't have enough rooms available to grant your request. If you'd like, I could assist you in finding other accommodation more . . . appropriate to your party.'

The manager was fully prepared for the burst of anger that an announcement such as this invariably drew. He was, however, taken by surprise when Phule responded instead with a lazy smile.

'I don't want to argue with you on this, Bombast . . .'

'Bom*best*.'

' . . . since, you see, the same computer I used to place that reservation told me that of your hundred and fifty rooms, barely a dozen are currently occupied. Instead, I'll point out that there are three possible solutions to our little impasse. First, I could bring a complaint against you and the hotel under the law which states you can't refuse lodging to anyone on a basis of race, religion, sex, *or* occupation . . . but that's a lengthy, annoying process and doesn't satisfy my immediate need for rooms. Second, you can start handing out the keys like a good fellow. Third . . . '

The commander's smile broadened slightly.

' . . . I can buy this hotel and have you replaced with

someone who exercises better judgment when it comes to protecting the owner's interests.'

The casual reference to his legal vulnerabilities unnerved Bombest slightly, but he was also aware of the obvious lack of knowledge behind the third solution Phule had voiced, and rallied gamely behind that.

'What I meant, sir, was that, due to the low occupancy you referenced, we are currently understaffed to accommodate a party of your size in the manner the Plaza is famous for, and, rather than tarnish that reputation, I would suggest you would be happier at another hotel. As to the possibility of your actually purchasing the Plaza' – the manager allowed himself a slight smile – 'I'm afraid that's a rather hollow threat. You don't seem to be aware that we are not singly owned, but a part of a chain of hotels, which is, in turn, owned by a rather large conglomerate. I doubt you could interest them in entering into negotiations over a single unit.'

Phule shook his head in slow dismay.

'Actually Bombast . . . '

'Bom*best*.'

' . . . I'm afraid it's *you* that's not fully aware of the situation. Your chain is owned by the Webber Combine, and Reggie Page is the CEO – that's chief executive officer – at least until the next meeting of the board of directors, which happens to be in three weeks. Now, he's in a spot because he's already stretched the combine's credit to the limit for their new resort complex on Parna II, and the contractors have just gone on strike. That's the third disaster they've had in the last quarter, and if he doesn't come up with some ready cash to buy them off fast, the whole project, not to mention his own job, will go down the toilet. *That's* why I think he'd be interested if I offered to take this place off his hands.'

Bombest could feel his forehead growing damp, but Phule wasn't finished.

'I want to point out, though, that my mentioning this option wasn't a threat. Now, I could buy this place, but the paperwork involved would take at least twenty-four hours, which would mean that I'd have to move my people into another hotel until the deal was finalized. The problem there is that I've already told them they'll be staying *here*, and if I have to go back on that, if I get embarrassed in front of my new command because of your silly-ass games, then, *after* you're fired, I'll not only see to it that you never work on this planet again by purchasing any company you apply at, I'll block your leaving even if it means buying up every seat on every outbound ship for the next year. *That's* a threat. See the difference?'

'Y-yes, sir.'

Phule's smile returned to its original, relaxed dimensions.

'So, now that we've had our little chat, I'm sure you'll agree that the wisest course for everyone is for you to release those rooms to us, then see what you can do about bringing the staff up to the proper levels.'

Pompous and stubborn though he might be, Bombest was not stupid. Even a rock had to survive, and it was clear that it would not be in his – that is, the hotel's – best interest to enter into a personal feud with a megamillionaire. Making a quick management decision, he turned to the hovering desk clerk.

'We're going to need a hundred registration cards here, and two keys for each room . . . filling from the top floor down and bypassing the poolside units. Only issue the room keys *after* each card is filled out so that we have documentation on file as to who is occupying each room.'

He turned back to Phule.

'Will there be anything else, *sir*?'

'As a matter of fact, there is . . . if you'll just wait a moment. Armstrong! Rembrandt!'

The lieutenants elbowed their way through the crowd of Legionnaires to his side.

'Pair them off and oversee the room assignments. I want you and the cadre in the rooms nearest the penthouse . . . I'll be using that as a headquarters and operations while we're here. Make a list for our use as to who's where, but tell everyone not to unpack completely. We'll be changing the room assignments as partners are assigned.'

'Yes, sir.'

'Beeker!'

'Sir?'

The butler had already been standing by, being more familiar with Phule's operational habits.

'Deal with the valet before he faints. He is to show our people to their rooms, but he is not – I repeat, *not* – to help them with their gear other than to make any baggage carts available for their use. And Beek . . . be sure he's tipped adequately. Got it?'

'Very good, sir.'

'Now then, Bombest, we're going to need another hundred registration cards to fill out once our room assignments are finalized.'

'Ah . . . perhaps it would be easiest if we simply held off filling the original cards until you've had a chance to sort things out, Mr. Phule.'

'I appreciate the thought, Bombest, but that might take a week. No sense botching up your system just because we're still getting organized, is there?'

'No . . . I mean, yes . . . I mean, thank you, sir.'

'While I've got you here, though, there is one more thing. The park across the street . . . that belongs to the hotel, doesn't it?'

'Well, yes . . . but it's open to the public.'

'Good. I'm figuring we'll be using it from time to time for exercises and lessons. Could you hire someone to clean up the fountain . . . and charge it to my bill?'

'Certainly, sir . . . and, if I might add, that's very generous of you.'

Bombest was recovering his equilibrium now. Though still a bit shaken by their earlier confrontation, he was pleasantly surprised to find that the Legion commander was quite graceful, not to mention generous, in his triumph. Perhaps the occupation by this dangerous-looking group wouldn't be so bad after . . .

'*Mister* Bombest!'

The manager looked up to find Vincent, the restaurant's chef, striding across the lobby toward the desk, his face stormy.

'Please, Vincent! Keep your voice down. Now, what seems to be the –'

'There is a . . . *man* poking about in my kitchen! Dressed like one of *these*!' The chef shook an accusing finger at the uniformed Legionnaires who were clustered about in curiosity. 'I *demand* he be removed at once! I cannot work with *strangers* getting underfoot!'

Bombest felt suddenly trapped. He didn't want another fight with Phule so soon after their last clash, but he couldn't afford to offend the chef, either.

'Ah . . . Mr. Phule. Perhaps you could . . . '

'Please. I'm afraid there's been a misunderstanding,' the commander said, holding up a quieting hand. 'I told our mess sergeant that I wanted him to improve our food . . . but I meant once we had returned to our own base. Let me speak with him and explain . . . '

'Excuse me . . . please?'

The small group turned to discover that Sergeant Escrima had materialized in their midst.

'I wish to . . . how you say . . . apologize. I wanted only to see how kitchen was laid out here. Would have asked, but cook was not in the room. Please. Is my fault. Should not go into kitchen without asking cook first. Must apologize.'

'There. You see?' Bombest beamed, clapping his chef

on the shoulder. 'No harm done. The sergeant apologizes.'

'I should think so,' Vincent sniffed haughtily. 'Imagine . . . a no-talent Army Mixmaster . . . in *my* kitchen.'

Escrima's eyes glittered momentarily, but he held his smile. 'Please. Accept my . . . '

'Just a moment.' Phule was suddenly between the two men, his face hard. 'Sergeant Escrima was out of line, and he apologized. I *don't* think, however, that gives you any call or right to insult his ability as a cook. He may not be as skilled as you are, sir, but he certainly is not a no-talent bottle washer . . . nor is he in the Army. He's a Legionnaire. Might I suggest, sir, that you owe him an apology in return for your remarks?'

Bombest tried to catch the chef's eye, but Vincent still had his sails set.

'Hah! Before I would give such an apology, he would have to show me that I am wrong . . . that he can tell a mixing bowl from a toilet bowl.'

Remembering Phule's earlier response to such insolence, the hotel manager found himself wondering where he could find another chef on such short notice. This time, however, the commander had a different tactic in mind.

'Very well, then,' he said. 'Bombest, I'd like to rent your restaurant *and* kitchen for a full day . . . shall we say, day after tomorrow? Sergeant Escrima will require it to prepare the food for our company.'

'*My* kitchen?' the hotel chef shrieked. 'You cannot –'

Sensing disaster, the hotel manager broke in. 'I'm afraid, sir, the cost would be –'

'Five thousand dollars should cover it,' the commander finished. 'Of course, we'll provide our own supplies. The current kitchen help can have the day off, with pay, except . . . '

He turned to address the chef directly.

'You, sir. I shall personally pay you double for your normal day's wage, if and only if you are present in the kitchen for the entire day to sit and *quietly* observe how our mess sergeant conducts himself with food. You are also invited to join us for dinner, at which time you will be given an opportunity to tender your apology to Sergeant Escrima . . . if you feel he deserves it. Agreed?'

The chef opened and shut his mouth several times before nodding his silent consent.

'All right, then, Sergeant Escrima, make a list of the Legionnaires you want to assist you in the kitchen and give it to Brandy. C.H.!'

He didn't even have to raise his voice this time, as the supply sergeant had been loitering nearby throughout the entire exchange.

'Yes, Captain?'

'You're excused from normal duty tomorrow. Get a list from Sergeant Escrima as to what he needs in the way of supplies and get him whatever he asks for . . . top of the line. Got it?'

'Got it. Umm . . . Captain?' Harry dropped his voice and leaned close to the commander. 'Are you sure you want to do this? Truth to tell, our chow ain't been all that good.'

'I appreciate your concern, C.H.,' Phule murmured back, 'but I suspect Escrima's a better cook than you've seen so far. Even if he isn't, though, I'm not going to stand by and let an outsider mouth off at one of ours without doing my best to see he gets a chance to his licks in return.'

'Us against them, eh, Cap'n? Okay. I kin relate to that. I'll see what I can do.'

'Thanks, C.H., I'm counting on that.' Phule flashed the sergeant a quick grin. 'As to the "them against us," though . . . it may be true, but I wish I could offer you better odds.'

'Been up against worse all my life, Cap'n.' Harry

winked. 'No sense to start holdin' out for a better hand now.'

The commander waved a farewell as the supply sergeant headed off, then turned back to the front desk.

'Sorry to jump in like that, Bombest, but it seemed the best solution to an awkward situation.'

'No need to apologize, Mr. Phule. Your offer . . . and solution . . . were more than generous under the circumstances. Would you like the keys to the penthouse now? You could probably use a little quiet after all this.'

'You're right . . . but it's a luxury I can't afford. My butler, Beeker, will pick up the keys and see to getting my gear settled. Right now I have to pay a personal call on some key people here in the settlement.'

'The governor?'

Phule managed a weak smile.

'Actually I was thinking more of the chief of police.'

5

Journal File #021

Though it is seldom noted in action/adventure novels dealing with the military, one of the main tasks of a commander is serving as liaison between his or her force and the civilians they come in contact with. Similarly, such contacts in real life are rarely brought to the public's attention (normal military duty being, almost without exception, exceedingly dull) unless he or she has made a real hash out of dealing with the media, in which case the commander or force in question is inevitably portrayed as being bloodthirsty, stupid, or both.

Realizing the nature of the individuals we had just relocated into the settlement, a visit by my employer to the local constabulary was a wise, if not necessary, move . . . one which I would normally applaud. In this specific instance, however, there was an easily anticipated problem with such a tactic: the current chief of police.

The world of law enforcement is quite complex, but the individuals within it can usually be divided into two categories: administrators and policemen. The administrator of the local constabulary held the title of police commissioner as well as a seat on the Settlement Council. The chief of police, whom my employer chose to deal with, was responsible for coordinating and managing the day-to-day law enforcement on a 'street' level, and was, by anyone's definition, 'a cop.'

Much is made in literature of the instant camaraderie between two strong-willed men. In actuality, such a meeting is apt to produce the same results as attempting to add a second tiger to a hill: hatred on sight.

Chief Goetz was a bull of a man who would look more at home pacing the sidelines of a football game than sprawled behind a desk. His hair was close-shaved, some said in an unsuccessful effort to hide his receding hairline, and only accented the squashed pumpkin shape of a head that seemed to grow directly out of his shoulders. The rolled-up sleeves of his wilted white shirt were tight around biceps that showed no trace of fat, and, as a lingering tribute to his time on the beat, he had 'Miranda' tattooed across the knuckles of his beefy right hand. Even when he smiled, which was seldom, his scowl and clenched jaw failed to completely disappear . . . and he wasn't smiling now.

If anything, his expression held all the warmth and affection one normally reserves for the deposit left on one's new carpet by a wormy dog, which would be a generous interpretation of his feelings for the slim figure in black who had come to roost in his office.

'Let me see if I've got this straight, General . . . '

'Captain,' Phule corrected gently, but Goetz continued without acknowledging the interruption.

'You've moved some two hundred of your soldier boys into the settlement while the barracks and grounds the Legion rented are being remodeled . . . '

'That's right.'

'And in the meantime, they're going to be strutting and swaggering around *my* streets, in uniform, like trouble looking for a place to happen.'

'I wouldn't put it that way . . . '

'Well, *I* goddamn well would!' Goetz snarled, surging forward in his seat. 'Those tin soldiers of yours are going to be like red flags in the face of every street-tough bull who wants to see how he stacks up against a genuine army type.'

Phule let the army label slide for the moment.

'Really, Chief Goetz. My Legionnaires have been in town before. I don't see why there should be any difference now . . . '

'The difference is that there weren't two goddamn hundred of them before!' the chief roared. 'Before, they were outnumbered and stayed the hell away from rough-and-tumble with the locals! Now you've evened up the odds, so they're going to want to go anywhere and do anything they want, and you can bet your ass there's going to be trouble when they try.'

'I see.' Phule smiled thinly. 'I guess I overestimated the control the police have of the streets. The information I had gave no indication that the settlement was a hotbed of crime ready to explode.'

The police chief's face puffed out with red-purple storm clouds, the sight of which in the past had sent many of the men under his command to the locker rooms for a change of trousers.

'Now, just a goddamned minute!' he exploded. 'We've got the lowest crime rate of any . . . '

The storm blew over as quickly as it had appeared, leaving only a ruddy hue in its wake, and even that slowly faded as the police chief hung his head and stared at the files on his desk.

Phule waited patiently.

When Goetz raised his head again, his eyes shone darkly under heavy, suspicion-creased brows.

'You nearly had me going there, General,' he said through clenched teeth. 'Any particular reason you want to pull my chain so hard?'

'I just thought you should hear yourself, Chief.' The Legionnaire shrugged. 'By your own words, my troops haven't been able to go where they want or do what they want in the past. Since they have the same rights as any citizen to enjoy what the settlement has to offer, and their money is certainly welcome anywhere I know of in the settlement, I fail to see where my "evening the odds" is anything I should apologize for or correct . . . And it's "Captain," not "General." '

The police chief's lips pressed together in a tight grin.

'Sorry,' he said, without a hint of remorse in his voice. 'I never did pay much mind to rank among you soldier boys. Fact is, I pretty much ignore 'em altogether . . . unless they step out of line. If they do . . . well, then I treat 'em like I would anyone else disturbing the peace or otherwise breaking the law. Is that fair enough for you?'

'Well, Sergeant . . . '

'That's Chief!'

'Sorry.' Phule showed his teeth. 'I guess I assumed that since you didn't think rank was important . . . '

He let the sentence hang in midair.

Goetz glared at him for a moment.

'All right, *Captain*,' he growled finally, 'you've made your point.'

'Good. Now then, *Chief*, as I was saying, I'm afraid that my troops aren't to be treated *exactly* like any other lawbreaker. I believe there's a specific law regarding that, that they are to be turned over to the local commander – in this case, me – for whatever discipline is necessary rather than being bound over for civil trial.'

'There is?'

'Yes,' the commander said firmly. 'If you're not familiar with it, I could provide you with a copy of –'

'Oh, I'm familiar with it,' the chief said with a curt wave. 'It's just that usually, when we've taken one of your wayward lambs into custody, and called out to your base to ask someone to come pick him up, he's ended up sleeping it off in one of our cells. I'm just surprised at the sudden concern for proper procedure, is all.'

'Different commanders have different priorities,' Phule said. 'I'm sure the same thing is true in police work. All I can say is that while *I'm* in command of the Legionnaires stationed here, none of them are going to be left to rot in one of your cells . . . provided we're duly informed that they've been restrained, that is. I trust you'll see to it that word is passed to us on a timely basis?'

'Don't worry, we'll let you know.' Goetz smirked. 'Of course, whether or not it's on a timely basis will probably depend on whether or not anyone's answering the phone at your end.'

'We're using the penthouse at the Plaza as our headquarters while we're in the settlement,' Phule said scribbling quickly on a page in his notebook, which he tore off and tossed onto the chief's desk. 'That's the number, in case you don't have it already. If I'm not there to take your call, someone will who can relay the information to me immediately.'

Goetz made no move to pick the note up, but rather scowled at the Legionnaire.

'Excuse me for pointing out the obvious, *Captain*,' he said levelly, 'but weren't you just telling me I wouldn't have any trouble out of your crew? If that's the case, why are you so all fired eager to be sure we know what to do when we arrest one of them?'

'I believe I said I didn't expect there'd be any more trouble than usual,' the commander corrected. 'I'm not trying to kid you that there won't be *any* trouble, Chief. We both know there's bound to be some incidents once in a while. I'm just trying to establish a rapport between us to ease things when and if anything does happen.'

'Well, when and *if* anything happens, you can rest assured that . . . '

The phone on the desk exploded with sound, interrupting the chief in midsentence. Frowning, he snatched up the receiver.

'Goetz. What's the . . . I see. Well, put him on.'

The chief's eyes sought and held Phule's as he smiled into the phone.

'Chief of police . . . Yes, sir . . . I see . . . Just a moment.'

Covering the receiver with one hand, Goetz leaned

back in his chair and smirked at the Legionnaire in his office.

'What do you know, *Captain*? It seems we have an *incident*, as you put it, already.'

'What is it?'

'I've got the hotel manager of the Plaza on the line here. It seems a couple of your law-abiding troops are brawling in his lobby. Do you want to handle this, or should I send a few of my boys over to break it up?'

The commander held out his hand for the phone, which the chief passed him after a moment's hesitation.

'Phule here, Bombast. What seems to be the problem?'

'That's Bom – oh! Mr. Phule,' came the hotel manager's voice through the receiver. 'It's . . . ah . . . nothing really.'

'If it's nothing, why are you bothering the police?'

'I just . . . I didn't know how to reach you, sir, and a couple of your . . . troops are fighting in the lobby. Now, I'd like to be tolerant, but I have a responsibility to the owners if any damage is done, and my security can't . . . '

'Is one of them a woman?'

'Sir?'

'Come on, Bombast, you know the difference. Is one of them a woman . . . fairly short?'

'As a matter of fact, yes.'

'Can you hold for a moment?'

Phule covered the receiver with one hand while he counted slowly to ten.

'Bombast?'

'Yes, Mr. Phule?'

'Are they still fighting?'

'Well . . . no, sir. It seems to have stopped.'

'Then that's that. Oh, and Bombast?'

'Yes, Mr. Phule?'

'I don't think it's necessary to trouble the police with every little scuffle that occurs. If I'm not around, let one of the lieutenants or sergeants know and they'll handle it . . . and I'll personally guarantee any damages to the hotel. All right?'

'Y-yes, Mr. Phule.'

'Fine. Goodbye now.'

Shaking his head, the commander returned the chief's phone to its cradle.

'Sorry about that, Chief Goetz. I think it's taken care of now.'

'Nice of you to try so hard to keep our work load down.'

'Wasn't I supposed to handle that?' the Legionnaire said, raising his eyebrows. 'I thought you asked –'

'Now, what's all this "fool" stuff?' the chief broke in. 'I thought you said your name was Jester . . . excuse me, *Captain* Jester.'

'Captain Jester is my official name within the Space Legion,' Phule clarified. 'Unfortunately my credit cards are still in my civilian name, and I had to use that when I signed my company into the hotel.'

It was Chief Goetz's turn to raise his eyebrows.

'Your credit cards? Then you weren't kidding about taking personal responsibility for any damage done to the hotel? I was wondering how a down-at-the-heels outfit like the Space Legion could afford to use the Plaza for temporary housing, but I'm starting to see the light. Just what *is* your background, Captain?'

'In the Legion, it's generally considered poor manners to ask that, Chief.'

Goetz bared his teeth in a wolfish grin.

'Well, I don't happen to be *in* your Legion, Captain. I'm in charge of keeping order in this settlement, and that includes checking out suspicious characters who wander in . . . like people who start throwing around large hunks of credit with no visible income to explain it. *That* gives me the right to ask just about anything I damn well please, so I'm *asking* you again: What were you before the Legion dipped you in tar?'

Phule shrugged. 'The same as I am now. Wealthy. If you want to run a check, I'm sure you'll have no trouble confirming that my assets are legitimate. Incidentally that's spelled with a "*p-h*" . . . *P-h-u-l-e*, as in Phule-Proof Munitions.'

'Oh now, that's just swell!' Goetz spat. 'You know, Captain, if there's anything I hate more than soldiers who think they can bust up things without answering to civil law, it's rich boys who think they can buy their way out of anything. Well, let me tell you, *mister*, the law in this settlement isn't for sale. If your soldier boys keep their noses clean, they'll get no hassles from me or mine, but if they get out of line . . . '

'You'll turn them over to me without a mark on them, as we discussed earlier,' the Legionnaire finished. 'That *is* what we were saying when the phone rang, isn't it, Chief?'

'Oh, there won't be a scratch on them . . . unless, of course, they resist arrest.'

'If any of my troops get hurt resisting arrest,' Phule said coldly, 'I'll want to see the injuries done to the arresting officer . . . just to be sure they "resisted" *before* they were cuffed.'

Goetz's face purpled again.

'My men don't rough up suspects after they've been handcuffed, if that's what you're trying to say.'

'Then there shouldn't be any problems between us.' Phule smiled. 'Really, Chief, I didn't come in here to pick a fight with you *or* to try to bribe you or anyone on your force for special considerations. If you'll recall, the subject of money didn't come up at all until that call came in from the Plaza, and even then only when you questioned me about it directly. I just wanted to let you know we had moved into town, and that my company will be willing to help the police on an auxiliary basis if any trouble should arise.'

The police chief cocked his head to one side.

'If I understand you correctly, Captain, even though

you're new, the troops under your command are the same ones who have been stationed here for the last year?'

'That's right.'

'Then frankly I can't think of a situation desperate enough that I'd want to work with them' – he flashed his wolf's smile again – 'but I *do* appreciate your offering to help us poor flatfeet out. Now, get out of my office and let me get some work done.'

Phule was irritated with himself as he retraced his path to the Plaza. That the interview with the police chief had not gone as he hoped was an understatement. It would seem that rather than reaching an understanding with that notable, Phule had succeeded only in pouring oil on the troubled waters and setting them ablaze.

Reviewing the conversation, the commander tried to weigh which had contributed the most to his momentary loss of control: the chief's lack of regard for the Legionnaires, or the cheap shots that had been taken at his own 'rich boy' status. While he liked to think the former had been the major cause of his irritation, Phule had to concede that the latter had also been a factor in his inability to deal effectively with Goetz. The accusation that he tended to solve his problems by buying his way out of them had hit a little too close to home for comfort.

Pursing his lips, he set about once more shoring up his defenses to that particular line of attack. The speech he had made to the troops about being effective was a sincere attempt to pass along one of the few lessons he had embraced from his father's efforts to set him on 'the right path.' Results were what mattered, and it was only right that the individual use every tool and weapon at his or her disposal to obtain whatever results were deemed desirable or necessary in his or her life. Of course he used his money when it was effective to do so. That was no more unfair or unjust than athletes using their strength and coordination or attractive women using their beauty to their own advantage. The game of life was rough enough without forcing an extra handicap by deliberately turning one's back on the advantages one had been dealt by fate.

'Psst! Captain! Over here!'

Phule jerked his head up to find the company's supply sergeant beckoning to him urgently from the alley beside the hotel. He had been so engrossed in his thoughts that he hadn't even noticed Chocolate Harry's unmistakable bulk until specifically hailed. Now, however, he saw that there was a small gathering of Legionnaires nervously peering around the corner at the hotel entrance.

They looked so much like a bunch of school kids hiding after a prank gone bad that Phule had to hide his smile as he veered his steps to join them. Then he remembered his recent head-butting with Goetz, and it was much easier to look concerned.

'What's the trouble here, Harry? Is it the cops?'

'Worse than that, Captain,' the sergeant declared with a shake of his head, still craning his neck for a better view of the hotel door. 'There's a reporter in the lobby lookin' to talk to anybody from the Legion.'

The wave of relief that washed over Phule almost made him want to laugh. Immediately on its heels, however, came a feeling of genuine puzzlement. The presence of a reporter didn't seem to be much of a threat or a danger in itself, yet the Legionnaires around him displayed a concern that was too real for the commander to take lightly.

'We shouldn't be bunched up like this,' the commander said, taking command without having made a conscious decision. 'We're more likely to draw the eye than to avoid notice the way we are.'

'The captain's right,' Harry snarled loudly. 'We don't all gotta see what's goin' on . . . especially when there's nothin' happenin'. You . . . and you! Stay here and keep an eye peeled. The rest of you get back down the alley before half the world starts wonderin' what we're up to.'

The sergeant paused for a moment to be sure the others were following his instructions, before turning to Phule with a shake of his head.

'Sorry 'bout that, Captain. Guess we're a little rattled, is all. Good thing we got at least one level head around to remind us how to lay low.'

'Don't mention it, C.H.,' Phule said. 'I'm missing something here, though. What's the big sweat about having a reporter nosing around?'

Harry stiffened, his eyes narrowing for a moment. Then he shook his head and gave a humorless laugh.

'Damn!' he exclaimed in a wondering tone. 'It's real easy to forget that you're an officer, Captain. Let's just say that us enlisted types got some problems you brass hats don't and let it go at that.'

'Let's not,' the commander countered grimly. 'I told you before, C.H. We're all one crew, and what's a problem for some is a problem for all. Now, I may not be able to solve all the problems we're going to be up against, but I can't solve any unless I know what they are. So if you don't mind being tolerant for just a few minutes, I'd appreciate it if you'd take the time to explain to this dense officer exactly what the problem is here.'

The supply sergeant blinked in surprise, then shot one more nervous glance toward the hotel entrance before answering.

'Well, you see, Captain, you officers may come from pretty clean backgrounds, but for a lot of us, we joined the Legion to get away from some pretty rough situations. Some of us still have folks lookin' for us – folks who want real bad to get a piece of our hides. The last thing we want is to have some reporter puttin' out write-ups or pictures as to where we are now and what we're doing. You follow me? It's like hangin' a bull's-eye on our backs and hollerin', "Come and get 'em." '

'I see,' Phule said thoughtfully.

'That's the way it is, Cap'n,' Harry finished with an expansive shrug. 'Sometimes we just gotta back off . . .'

The commander's head came up with a snap.

'Don't say that, Sergeant,' he intoned coldly. 'The one thing you don't ever *gotta* do when you're under my command is back off.'

He turned away from the sergeant, raising his voice to address the group huddled at the far end of the alley.

'*Legionnaires! Assemble on me . . . Now! Lookouts too! All of you . . . Right now!*'

The fugitives eased forward, exchanging confused glances as they tried to puzzle out their commander's apparent bad mood.

'It's been brought to my attention that reporters make you nervous . . . that you're afraid your various pasts might catch up with you if word gets out as to your whereabouts. First of all, I'm telling you here and now, *Get used to reporters.* They're going to be around because a lot of what we're going to do will be news. Don't hide from them, learn how to talk with them so they report what *you* want them to report. Now that I'm aware of the problem, I'll be sure that there's opportunity for you to learn how to give and control interviews. In the meantime, just say "No comment" and refer them to one of the officers. What you *don't* do is let them or anyone else drive you away from your own area, whether it's a barracks or a hotel.'

He paused to sweep the assemblage with his eyes before continuing.

'That brings us to the second point. It seems that the group here thought I was talking to someone else when I gave my speech last night. Well, I wasn't. Some of you were running from people or a situation when you joined the Legion. I know that. Everyone in the company knows that. My reaction is as follows: So what? *If* a reporter pinpoints your new identity and location, or *if* any other slipup happens and your past comes looking for you, so what? You're part of the company now, and anyone who wants to get at you is going to have to come through *all* of us. *That's* what being in this company is all about. We're all family now, and that means that none of you ever have to face your problems alone again. Got that?'

There was a ripple of nods and mumbled 'Yes, sirs.'

'*I can't hear you*!'

'*YES, SIR*!'

Phule grinned at the shouted response.

'That's better. Now, let's go back to *our* hotel. I'll be talking to this reporter in the cocktail lounge, if any of you want to listen in. Haven't met a reporter *or* a Legionnaire yet who'd pass up a free drink.'

Scattered shouts of approval and mutual encouragement met this, as the Legionnaires abandoned their hiding post in the alley and headed for the hotel. Much of the banter had the overloud, overexuberant flair of individuals who weren't really sure of themselves and were drawing on each other for courage, but they *were* moving, and moving as a unit.

Phule waited until most of them had filed out of the alley before following, falling in step beside the supply sergeant.

'Well, C.H. What do you think now?'

'I dunno, Cap'n,' Harry answered with a slow shake of his head. 'What you say sounds well and good on paper, but I don't think you know what kinda hard cases some of us have nosin' around our trails. Truth to tell, I wouldn't bet much on our crew's chances if we really have to tangle with 'em someday. I mean, I'm probably one of the best in the company when it comes to mixin' it up, and I was the weak sister of my old ga – my old club.'

The commander politely ignored the inadvertent reference to the supply sergeant's past. He had suspected since meeting him that Harry had never been a lone wolf.

'Then I guess it's up to us to work the company until they're ready to take on all comers. If nothing else, we can field more firepower than most. Now all we have to do is coach the troops to keep it pointed downrange.'

Phule meant his comment as a joke, but instead of laughing, Harry nodded slowly.

'That'd be good for a start,' he said slowly. 'Won't be easy, though. Tell you what, Cap'n. If that offer is still open, I think I'll join you and that reporter for a drink. Maybe we can talk for a bit afterward.'

'Fine by me, C.H., but I thought you were nervous about being around a reporter.'

The sergeant nodded. 'I am, but what you said back in the alley made sense. Eventually the crew that's lookin' for me is gonna find me, and thinkin' about that makes me thirsty enough to ignore any reporter. 'Sides, how much can go wrong in one interview? Huh?'

'Sir? . . . Wake up, sir!'

Phule struggled up from the depth of slumber at the insistent sound of his butler's voice.

'I'm . . . awake,' he managed with some difficulty. 'God! What time is it, Beek? I feel like I just closed my eyes.'

'Actually, sir, it's been a little over two hours since you retired.'

'Really? Two whole hours.' Phule grimaced, forcing himself upright in bed. 'Can't imagine why I still feel sluggish.'

'It might have something to do with the quantity of alcohol you consumed before retiring, sir,' the butler supplied helpfully. 'You *were* more cheerful than usual when you came in.'

Like most guardians of dignity, Beeker did not approve of his charge drinking at all, and he made no effort to keep the edge of reprimand out of his voice.

'Chocolate Harry and I had a couple more rounds after the reporter left,' the commander said defensively, rubbing his forehead with the fingertips of both hands. 'I would have called it quits earlier, but Brandy rolled in and –'

'Excuse me for interrupting, sir,' the butler interrupted, 'but there's a call waiting for you in the other room.'

'A call?'

'Yes. On the holophone. It's from Legion Headquarters, which is why I deemed it necessary to wake you rather than simply taking a message.'

'Oh, swell. Just what I need first thing in the morning. Just a second while I get dressed.'

'If I might point out, sir, you're still dressed from last night. I commented on it when you retired, but you seemed rather eager to get to sleep.'

Sure enough, Phule found that he was still fully clothed. What's more, his uniform seemed to give less indication of the abuse it had suffered than did his mind and digestive tract. Running his hand quickly over his chin and upper lip, he decided that he would go without a shave rather than keep Headquarters waiting any more than they had, though he longed for the extra wake-up time that ritual would have given him.

'Well, I guess there's no point stalling,' he said, starting for the next room. 'Any clue as to what's up, Beek?'

'None . . . aside from the obvious indications that they seem to be a bit distraught.' The butler shrugged. Then his natural concern asserted itself, and he added, 'You should be aware, sir, that it was necessary for me to leave the line open when I came to rouse you, so you will be "on camera" as soon as you enter the room.'

Phule paused with his hand on the doorknob and grimaced.

'Terrific,' he said. 'Thanks for the warning, Beek.'

'I thought you'd like to know, sir. You're inclined toward rude gestures when surprised . . . especially early in the morning.'

The holophone was a device which projected a three-dimensional image of the caller into the room with the recipient, and sent one in return. While it was a disturbingly effective way to communicate, it was also expensive to operate, which was why the Legion usually relied on the more conventional com-type system for the routine sending of messages and reports. Com-type allowed data to be stored and sent in quick bursts during slack periods of interstellar communications, incoming messages being stored electronically by computer for review or printout at the recipient's discretion. The holophone was reserved for emergency use, when the sender wanted to be sure the recipient got the message, or wanted to interface directly with the person on the other end, like, say, for a reprimand or dressing-down. Consequently holophone calls were generally received with the same enthusiasm normally reserved for plagues or tax audits.

'Yes, Colonel Battleax,' Phule said, recognizing the projected figure in the room. 'What can I do for you this morning?'

The Legion's holophone equipment was a discontinued line purchased as surplus. With no service support for what was originally a dubious design, its performance was usually less than stellar, and today's transmission was no exception. The image had a tendency to double and/or fuzz, an effect which did nothing to improve Phule's disposition as he tried to maintain a pleasant air while focusing bleary eyes on the elusive phantom. If he had hoped his demeanor would be reciprocated, however, he could have spared himself the effort.

'Well, *Captain* Jester,' the colonel began without

greeting or preamble, 'you could start by explaining the article in today's news.'

'Article?' The commander frowned. 'I'm afraid you have me at a disadvantage, ma'am. It's still very early here and I haven't had a chance to see today's news.'

He shot a glance at his butler who had slipped into the room behind him. Beeker nodded in understanding and reached for his pocket com unit to call up the article in question.

'No? Well, let me read you some of the highlights . . . specifically the same highlights *my* commanding officer read me when bringing it to my attention.'

Battleax brought a notepad into view, bending her head to refer to it.

'Let's see . . . We'll start with the headline, which reads: "Playboy General?" And under that, the byline elaborates: "Munitions Heir Willard Phule to Lead Elite Force on Haskin's Planet." The article itself goes downhill from there.'

Off camera, Beeker paused in his efforts to roll his eyes in exaggerated exasperation. Phule ignored him with some effort, focusing instead on the thought of holding the reporter's throat in his hands.

'Yes. I can see where you'd be upset, ma'am. Let me assure the colonel, however, that at no time during the interview did I state or imply that I held the rank of general. I can only assume the reporter either misunderstood or was exaggerating for effect. I'll take it on myself to see that a correction is issued noting my correct rank as well as an apology to all generals, past, present, and future, for the error.'

'Oh, don't stop there, Captain. I'm dying to hear your explanation of the rest of the article.'

'The rest of what, ma'am?' Phule said, studying the screen of the hand com unit Beeker had passed him. 'I have the article in front of me now, and I'm not sure what else the colonel requires comment on.'

'Are you serious? For openers, why did you issue a press release at all?'

'That's easy.' The commander smiled. 'I didn't. It seems someone on the hotel staff leaked the word to the media when we checked in, and a reporter showed up looking for an interview. I don't know how much experience the colonel has had with the media, but I've always found that once the media is looking for a story, it's best to give them one. Otherwise, they're inclined to invent one of their own. If one volunteers a story, they'll only get *some* of the facts wrong – like my rank – rather than publishing a yarn that's *all* wrong. Realizing the rather spotty background of the Legionnaires I've been assigned to, I thought it would be wisest if the interview centered on myself rather than allow it to wander into areas we'd just as soon not have publicized.'

'Wait a minute. Let's get back to something you said a second ago, about the hotel staff alerting the media that you had arrived. Why did you give the reporter your real name instead of your Legion name?'

'She already had it . . . '

'*She*?'

'That's right. The reporter was a woman . . . a rather attractive one at that. Of course, I didn't make any attempt to point that out or take advantage of it during the interview.'

'Hmmm . . . That may have been the problem.'

'Ma'am?'

'Nothing. Go on with your story, Captain. I'm starting to see what happened, though. About your name?'

'Well, she was looking for me by name. This is actually a fairly common occurrence for me, Colonel. The media often has spotters in hotels to be on the lookout for celebrities, and like it or not, my family name is one which tends to draw media attention, even if it's just the gossip columns.'

'And why did you give your name to the hotel?'

'It was on my credit card, ma'am. The banking community is very conservative and will not issue credit cards for nicknames or aliases, and while the colonel knows I am financially well off, I rarely carry sufficient cash to register an entire company of Legionnaires at a good hotel. If I might point out, ma'am, while the Legion encourages and utilizes aliases, I'm not aware of any regulation which requires their use or forbids Legionnaires from using their given names.'

'Hmmm . . . An interesting point, Captain. Let's take a step back for a moment from your failure to use your Legion name and focus instead on this hotel thing. Why have you moved your company into a luxury hotel?'

'Again, Colonel, I'm not aware of any regulation forbidding a company commander to house his Legionnaires wherever he wishes, especially if he absorbs the expense personally.'

'I'm not questioning whether or not you had the right to do it,' Battleax put in. 'I'm asking *why* you did it.'

Phule glanced at the hand com unit again.

'I believe it's covered here in the article, ma'am. Our barracks are being remodeled, giving rise to the need for temporary housing for the company.'

'So that part of the article is correct?'

'Yes, ma'am.'

'Are you aware, Captain, that we lease those barracks and the land they're on from a local developer? If so, are you aware that we need the permission of the leaseholder before instituting any renovation or improvements to his property?'

'I am, ma'am. The fact is, Colonel, I purchased the buildings and land currently leased to the Legion from the local owner. As such, permissions to remodel are not a problem. For the record, however, I hasten to assure the colonel that I have no intention of raising the price should the Legion's contract here last long enough to require renewing that lease.'

'That's decent of you,' the colonel said wryly. 'This is all very interesting, Captain. Just between you and me, though, what do you plan to do with your new holding when and if we pull out of there?'

'Normally I'd hire someone locally to manage the property for me,' Phule explained. 'In this particular instance, however, there is already interest – in fact, a firm offer – to purchase the remodeled facility from me whenever I wish to dispose of it. It seems someone saw the architect's sketches and feels it would make an excellent country club.'

'This purchase would, of course, result in a profit for you.'

'Of course.'

'Why am I not surprised? Getting back to the article, Captain, perhaps you'd care to explain why it was necessary to move the company into the best hotel on the planet for their temporary housing? And while you're at it, how do you justify calling that outfit of yours an elite force?'

'That was another assumption on the reporter's part. I simply said I was here on "a special assignment", and she jumped to her own conclusions. As to the quality of our temporary housing . . . may I speak candidly, Colonel?'

'Please do. If you can clarify the situation without prolonging this rather expensive conversation, it would be appreciated . . . though from the sound of things, I should have called collect.'

'The remodeling of our quarters, the luxury hotel for temporary housing, and some of the other things you will doubtless be hearing about in the future are all a part of my plan to turn this company around. You see, these people have been *treated* like losers and been *told* they're losers for so long they have little choice but to *believe* that they're losers, and they act accordingly.

What I'm doing is treating them like they're the best, like top athletes being groomed for a competition. I'm betting that they'll respond by acting like winners because they'll *see* themselves as winners.'

'The theory being that if they don't look like soldiers and act like soldiers, how can we expect them to fight like soldiers? You're betting quite a bit on a theory, Captain.'

'I think it's a good risk,' Phule said firmly. 'And if it isn't . . . well, it's my money to risk, isn't it?'

'True enough.' Colonel Battleax pursed her lips thoughtfully. 'Very well, Captain. I'll give you your head on this one for a while. If your idea works, the Legion will benefit. If not, we're no worse off than when we started. Of course, now that your real name is known, if you foul up like you did on your last assignment, it'll be hard for you to disappear from sight.'

'Of course.'

'What I'm trying to say, Captain Jester, is I'm hoping you're aware that you're more vulnerable on this than the Legion is.'

There was genuine concern in the colonel's voice, which warmed Phule despite his early morning haziness.

'Of course,' he repeated. 'Thank you, Colonel.'

'Very well. I'll try to cover the ruckus at this end. You focus on shaping up those troops of yours. I have a hunch it's going to take all the time and concentration you can give it and then some. In the future, however, try to give me advance warning if the media is going to pounce on something you or your crew is doing. You're not the only one who doesn't like early morning surprises.'

'Yes, ma'am. I'll try to remember that.'

'Oh, and Captain . . . '

'Yes, ma'am?'

'The remodeling of your barracks. How long do you think that will take?'

'The estimate is two weeks, ma'am.'

A triumphant smile flashed across the colonel's face.

'I thought so. It might interest you to know, Captain, that that's the estimate my sister was given when she wanted a new porch put on her house. Battleax out!'

Phule waited until the projected image faded completely before heaving a big sigh of relief.

'That went better than I would have hoped,' he declared.

'Yes, sir,' Beeker responded. 'I notice you neglected to tell the colonel that you not only purchased the barracks and land but also the construction company that's doing the remodeling.'

'It didn't seem the right time, somehow.' The commander winked. 'Incidentally, remind me to get a clerk or something assigned to monitor the communications gear in here. You shouldn't have to do that on top of the rest of your duties.'

'Very good, sir . . . and thank you.'

'No thanks necessary, Beek. I just don't want to give you any more ammo than is necessary when it comes time to negotiate your next raise.'

Phule stretched and looked out the window.

'So . . . what's on the docket for today?'

'Quite a bit, sir . . . but as you pointed out when I wakened you, it's still early.'

'Well, I'm up now. Let's get to work. And give the officers and cadre a call – especially Chocolate Harry. No sense in letting them lounge abed when I'm working.'

6

Journal File #024

I will not attempt to capture the true feeling of what it was like for the company to stand guard duty in a swamp, though my employer's impressions of the duty the first day he joined them in that task would doubtless be of interest to some. This is not so much a lack of willingness or ability on my part to impart such details, but rather a simple lack of data, as I never actually accompanied the company into the swamp – a fact I became particularly appreciative of when I observed the condition of their uniforms at the end of the day.

Bombest had nearly resigned himself to the Legionnaires' presence in his hotel. There was no denying the welcome influx of rental monies during a normally slack period, and the troops themselves had proved to be far less raucous and destructive than he originally feared. He even made an honest effort to muster a certain amount of enthusiasm in his mind for their residence. What progress he had made along those lines, however, faded rapidly as he observed the Legionnaires' transports pull up to the front door late in the afternoon, disgorging what could only be described as 'mudmen' onto the sidewalk.

From the waist – or, in some cases, the armpits – up, they were recognizable as the hotel's latest guests. From the 'disaster line' down, however, any familiar detail of individual or uniform was lost in a coating of gray-green muck. As sticky as it looked, Bombest noted that the coating seemed to lack sufficient adhesion to fully remain on its hosts, disturbing quantities of it falling in flakes and globs onto the sidewalk and, with apparent inevitability, the lobby carpet.

'*Hold it right there*!'

The voice of the Legionnaires' commander, or, as Bombest tended to think of him, the Leader of the Pack, cracked like a whip, bringing the mud-encrusted figures to a complete, if puzzled, halt on the lobby's threshold.

The hotel manager watched with some astonishment as Phule, his uniform displaying the same dubious collection of swamp mire as his followers, squeezed through the front ranks and advanced on the registration desk with the cautious tread of one trying to ease over a mine field.

'Good afternoon, Bombest,' the commander said pleasantly upon reaching his destination. 'Could you call housekeeping for me and see if they have . . . Never mind. These will do nicely.'

So saying, he scooped up two of the stacks of the day's newspapers from the desk, the hard copies still preferred by many, piling them on top of each other, then slipping an arm under them as he fished some bills from the relatively clean shirt pocket of his uniform.

'Here . . . this should cover it. Oh, and Bombest?'

'Yes, Mr. Phule?' the manager responded absently as he tried to figure out how to count the money without soiling his hands. Delegation seemed the only answer.

'Do you know if everything's set up in the main ballroom?'

'In a way, sir. Yes. One of your sergeants thought it best if we erected the divider to allow some privacy between the men and women, and it was necessary to open one of the adjoining meeting rooms for additional space –'

'Yes, yes,' Phule interrupted. 'But they're set to go?'

'Yes, sir. If you wish, I'll inform them you've arrived.'

'No need, Bombest. Thanks, anyway,' the commander said as he began to retrace his steps toward the door.

'*Okay! Listen up!*'

The waiting Legionnaires lapsed into silence.

'I want the troops on point to take these papers and spread them out on the carpet between the door and the elevators. The rest of you move slowly and stay on the path as much as possible. Any extra papers are to be left by the elevators, and I want you to grab a handful to spread ahead of you as you hit your floors. Let's try to keep the mess to a minimum until we get cleaned up. Understand?'

'*YES, SIR!*'

'What's wrong with room service?'

The catcall from the rear was greeted with laughter and a few scattered rude replies until Phule waved the company into silence once more.

'Let me answer that question once and for all,' he announced. 'While we're guests at this hotel, there *is* a housekeeping service as well as a laundry service at our disposal. I have also contracted similar services for us once we move into our new barracks.'

A wave of enthusiastic cheers was cut short with another gesture.

'*However*, I remind you that this is a privilege, and it is *not* to be abused. If it comes to my attention that the personnel of these services are being forced to deal with any unnecessary unpleasantness or are putting in extra hours due to any laziness or inconsideration of anyone under my command, several things will happen. First, they will be paid a bonus commensurate to the work required. Second, the bonus will be deducted from your paychecks rather than included in the normal expenses I am covering personally. Finally, those services will be canceled and their work distributed among the company as additional duty until such time as I am convinced that you appreciate their efforts sufficiently to conduct yourselves with the appropriate courtesy and consideration. Do I make myself clear?'

'*Yes, sir!*'

'All right! I want you all to get upstairs and clean up, then report to the main ballroom for –'

A new eruption of catcalls interrupted the commander, though it was apparent that he was not the focus. Breaking off his briefing, he turned to see what had captured the company's attention.

'Hoooo-*eeee*!'

'Ain't that purdy?'

'Look out, girls!'

'How 'bout a kiss, Slick?'

Chocolate Harry stood framed in the hotel door, though 'stood' scarcely embraced the picture he presented. He was ramrod straight, despite his inflated-pear stature, and wore the smug smile of a rich baron surveying his peasants. The obvious reason for his self-pleasure, and the target of the catcalls, was his uniform.

In place of his normal faded and frayed uniform, Harry glowed in a velveteen jumpsuit of the purest midnight black. The change from his usual rough-and-tumble look was stunning, and the contrast between him and his mud-caked admirers made him look like he just stepped off a recruiting poster. Calf-high boots of what looked to be the supplest suede with low, broad heels added to his height as he drew himself up and fired a parade-ground salute at his company commander.

'Ready in the main ballroom, sir!'

Any annoyance Phule might have felt over his supply sergeant upstaging his announcement was quickly crowded aside by his amusement at Harry's obvious pleasure with the uniform. It was clear that the sergeant had been unable to resist the temptation to show off his new outfit, and had seized on the excuse of reporting in to parade it in front of the rest of the company. Stifling his smile, Phule returned the salute.

'Thank you, C.H. We'll be along momentarily. Tell everyone to stand by.'

'Yes, sir!'

Again the flashy salute, which the commander was obliged to return before turning back to the company.

'As I was saying, once you're cleaned up, report to the main ballroom. As you may have noticed, your new uniforms have arrived today, and there are tailors waiting for your final fittings. Carry on.'

His final words were nearly drowned out by a loud whoop of enthusiasm as the Legionnaires surged forward into the hotel, barely remembering their commander's order regarding the newspapers.

Following in their wake, Phule saw Chocolate Harry surrounded by a knot of Legionnaires admiring his uniform while waiting their turn at the elevators.

'Sergeant?'

'Yes, sir?'

The supply sergeant broke away from his admirers and hurried to Phule's side.

'Relax, C.H. The uniform looks great on you.'

'Thank you, sir. I mean . . . it do, don't it?'

Harry craned his neck around, trying to catch a reflection of himself in one of the lobby mirrors.

'I was under the impression that uniform was designed with sleeves, though.'

'That's the way it come out of the box,' the sergeant acknowledged, 'but I had a few words with the man in charge and convinced him they could come off. I like it better this way – easier to move in.'

He swung his arms back and forth, then flexed his substantial biceps as if to prove his point.

'I see what you mean, C.H. Maybe I'll try that with a couple of my uniforms.'

Phule suppressed the visions flashing in his mind of the confrontation between Harry and the uniform's designer.

'Do that, Cap'n. It works great. Whoop! Got to go now. It's gonna be real busy in there for a while.'

'Good. Carry on, Sergeant.'

The commander watched him go, then tiptoed over to the front desk with the exaggerated care of a villain in melodrama.

'Excuse me, Bombest?'

'Yes, Mr. Phule?'

'There'll be a Charlie Daniels coming by in a bit looking for me. If he stops by the desk, just have him come right up to my penthouse. I'd appreciate it.'

'Certainly, s – ah, would that by any chance be Charles Hamilton Daniels III?'

'That's the one. Send him up when he shows.'

'Mr. Daniels?'

The wiry figure in the penthouse door nodded in response to Beeker's inquiry.

'Yes, sir. Here to see Captain Jester.'

The butler hesitated only a fraction of a moment before stepping aside to admit the caller.

'Nice layout you got here,' the caller said, peering about as he ambled into the salon portion of the penthouse. 'Roomy, too.'

'Actually it's more room than I need . . . or am really comfortable with,' Phule responded as he emerged from the bedroom, still toweling his hair from the shower. 'I only rented it because we needed the space for our temporary headquarters.'

He gestured toward the tangle of communications gear at the far end of the suite where a Legionnaire sat idly sharpening a spring stiletto while minding the apparatus.

'Good.' Daniels nodded approvingly. 'Never did hold much with ostentatious displays of wealth. Either you got it or you don't, I always say.'

Their visitor was clearly into practicing what he preached, as his dress for the meeting consisted of faded blue jeans, a plain gray sweatshirt, and a pair of cowboy boots. It was only when one studied his half-open eyes that danced alertly from the wrinkles of his sun-reddened face that one had a glimmer of the truth: that far from being a down-at-the-heels laze-about, Charles Hamilton Daniels III was easily one of the richest men on the planet.

'Can I offer you a drink, Mr. Daniels?' Beeker said, clearly reassured that he had, indeed, admitted the right man to his employer's quarters.

'Well, if you got a couple fingers of brandy in that wet bar I see over there, I wouldn't say no . . . And it's "Charlie." I'm only "Mr. Daniels" to my lawyers – mine and other people's.'

'Very good, Mr. . . . Charlie.'

'I'll take care of that, Beeker,' Phule said, tossing his towel back into the bedroom and closing the door. 'I want you to run down to the main ballroom and keep an eye on things.'

'Yeah!' the Legionnaire on communications put in. 'Tell 'em I'll be down for my fitting as soon as someone gets up here to relieve me.'

The butler cocked a chilly eyebrow at him.

' . . . please,' the Legionnaire added hastily.

'Very good, sir.'

'Why don't you just go along with him now . . . Do-Wop, isn't it?' the commander suggested from the bar. 'I can cover the console while I chat with Charlie, here.'

'Thanks, Captain,' the Legionnaire responded, uncoiling from his chair and slipping his knife into a pocket before following the butler out the door.

'That's a relief,' Daniels commented, turning his head and craning his neck to see if Do-Wop was out of hearing. 'For a while, I thought we were going to have our chat with one of your boys sharpening his knife at me. That would kinda give you an edge, if you'll pardon the expression. Assuming you invited me up here to talk a little business, that is.'

'If that had occurred to me, I might have had him stay.' Phule smiled, passing his guest a snifter of warm brandy. 'I do appreciate your stopping by, though, Charlie. Normally I would have come to you, but I pretty much have my hands full trying to reorganize the company, and I didn't want to wait too long before talking with you.'

'No problem, son. What all's going on down in the ballroom, anyway, that's got everyone so het up?'

'The new uniforms for the company arrived today. They're a good crew, but right now they're acting like a bunch of kids squabbling over who gets to play with a new toy. Everyone wants to be the first to be fitted so they can show off their new outfits.'

Daniels nodded sagely.

'Is that it? There were a bunch of 'em running around the lobby when I came in. Gotta admit, though, the uniforms they were wearing sure didn't look like any government issue I've ever seen.'

He shot a sly, sidelong glance at Phule as he took a sip of his drink.

'Well, they aren't exactly standard uniforms,' the commander admitted uncomfortably. 'I had them designed especially for us – a full wardrobe, actually: field uniforms, dress uniforms, the works. You might know the designer. He's a local here . . . name of Olie VerDank.'

'Olie? You mean Helga's boy?'

'I . . . I guess so,' Phule said. 'He's the only designer in the settlement I know of with that name.'

'Good.' Daniels nodded. 'He's a talented fellah and could use the work – *and* the exposure. I'll tell you, I always thought men who designed clothes were a little . . . well, you know . . . until I met Olie. Shoulders like an ox, that one. Got a pretty little gal he married, too. He's got a bit of a temper, though, and don't much like to be told what to design. I'm a little surprised you got him to work for you.'

'I offered to match the profits of his fall line.' The commander shrugged, looking into his own drink as he stirred it with a finger. 'After that he didn't seem too inclined to argue.'

'I'd have to say that was a fair offer. More'n fair, actually,' Daniels said. 'Course, I imagine with a couple hundred of your troops all wanted to be fitted at the same time, he's busier than a one-legged man in an ass-kicking contest down there.'

Phule grinned openly at the colorful analogy before replying.

'It shouldn't be too bad. I've got a couple dozen tailors helping him – every one in the settlement, or, at least, every one I could find.'

Daniels snorted loudly. 'And I'm sure they all just love working together. You got style, son. I'll give you that. I believe there was some business you wanted to discuss with me, though?'

'That's right,' the commander said, leaning forward in his chair. 'I wanted to talk with you about today's performance in the swamp.'

'Don't know about your crew,' Charlie said, 'but we had us a pretty good day. Got three nice stones. In fact, I've got 'em with me if you'd like to see.'

He pulled a small cloth drawstring bag from his pocket and tossed it to Phule. The commander opened the bag and upended it, spilling three small pebbles into his hand.

'Very nice,' he said, trying to sound enthusiastic.

In reality, he found the stones to be immensely unimpressive. They were small, the largest being roughly the size of a marble, while the smallest was barely the size of a pea. A dull, mottled brown, they seemed no different from any pebbles one might find in a garden.

'Oh, they might not look like much now,' Daniels commented, seeming to read Phule's thoughts, 'but they polish up real nice with a little work. This is what they end up lookin' like.'

He held out his hand to display the ring he was wearing. The stone in the ring was larger than those Phule was holding, measuring nearly a full inch long. It was the same brown as the raw stones, but shone with a rich luster, and streaks of dazzling blue and red danced in its depths as Daniels moved his hand, making it look like the product of a successful breeding between tigereye and fire opal.

'*Very* nice,' Phule murmured, and meant it this time. He had never seen anything quite like it before, and for a moment was unable to take his eyes from the play of colors in the ring.

'Thought you might like to see what we've been panning for while your crew stood guard. Course, what keeps the price up is their scarcity. That little stone you're holding will probably sell for enough to pay the bill for your Legionnaires for three months.'

'Really?' The commander was genuinly impressed. He carefully eased the stones back into their bag and returned it to Daniels. 'I'll admit I had no idea they were so valuable. Umm . . . it might be wise not to mention their worth in front of my troops. I mean, I trust them, but . . . '

'No sense in puttin' needless temptation in their way. Right?' Charlie grinned. 'Son, I appreciate the advice, but we already figured that out for ourselves. 'Sides, even if someone was to make off with a few of these beauties, it wouldn't do 'em much good. Everyone around here knows who we are, and any stranger who tried to sell one of these stones would stand out like a gorilla in a beauty contest. They couldn't sell 'em local, and we wouldn't let a ship or a shuttle get cleared for lift-off while there was one missing.'

'Good.' Phule nodded. 'Then there's no problem. Actually, though, what I wanted to talk to you about was the way my crew stood duty today.'

Daniels squinted his eyes in thought for a moment, then shook his head and took another sip of his drink.

'Okay. I can't recall 'em being any different today than usual, but then again, I'll admit I wasn't payin' much attention.'

'Neither were they,' Phule said flatly. 'At least, not to anything except their scanners.'

'Their scanners?'

'That's right. You know, the ones programmed to alert them if anything dangerous entered the area?'

'I know what you're talking about. Fact is, we provided 'em. It's another one of those conditions the insurance folks dreamed up especially for our operation. I'm just not sure why you have a problem with 'em.'

Phule surged to his feet and started pacing the room.

'The problem is that they're relying too much on them, from what I can see. If they malfunctioned – or, more important, if anything wandered up that *wasn't* covered by the programmed data – we'd never notice until someone got bitten, or whatever.'

Daniel's face wrinkled in a scowl.

'Never thought of it, but you've got a point there, son.'

'Even more important,' the commander continued. 'I don't like the idea of my troops being so dependent on machines to do their thinking for them. Now, I use computers all the time myself, but I'll still match the human mind against one every time when it comes to judgment calls.'

'So what exactly is it that you propose instead?'

'I want to implement a training course to familiarize every Legionnaire under my command with the dangerous life-forms in the area. Once that's done' – Phule hesitated, then took a deep breath and continued with a rush – 'I want to turn the machines off so that the crew are relying on their own observation and judgment to do their job. Realizing that if anything goes wrong the miners will be the ones to suffer, I wanted your approval as the head of the combine that hired us before putting my plan into motion.'

'Heck,' Daniels said, 'I've got no problem with that, though I might have if you hadn't bothered to check with us first. There's not that much dangerous out there, anyway. Like I said, it was more to keep the insurance folks happy than anything else. Fact is, we used to get by without scanners *or* guards before folks zeroed in on us and started insisting we get civilized. You just go on ahead with your training. I'll take care of lettin' the other miners know what's goin' on.'

'Thank you, Charlie.' The commander smiled, relieved that his proposal had been accepted so easily. 'Now then, as to the potential impact on your insurance rates . . . '

'Don't worry about that, either,' the miner insisted. 'Just tell your crew to keep those scanners handy even when they're turned off. Then, if we ever have problems or have to file a claim, we'll see about arranging a "temporary equipment malfunction" or something. Much as those insurance types like to think up regulations for us, ain't seen one yet actually come out into the swamp to see if we're following instructions.'

'I'd rather not start dabbling in insurance fraud,' Phule said carefully, 'but if instead we –'

The insistent beep of his wrist communicator interrupted him, and he broke off speaking to answer the call.

'Captain Jester speaking.'

'Beeker here, sir. Sorry to intrude, but you might want to come down here when you have a moment.'

'What's the problem, Beek?'

'Well, there seems to be some difficulty fitting the Sinthians with their new uniforms. Specifically the tailors are arguing with the designer that it can't be done.'

Phule grimaced. 'All right. I'll be down as soon as

I finish here . . . figure about fifteen minutes. Jester out.'

'Which ones are the Sinthians?' Daniels said curiously.

'Hmm? Oh. Sorry, Charlie, a little distracted there. The Sinthians are . . . well, you must have seen them on duty. They're the nonhumans with the eyestalks and the spindly arms.'

'The little fellahs? Sure, I know 'em. Nice little guys once you get the hang of listenin' to 'em. Tell you what, Captain. Can I talk to that Beeker fellah on your communicator for a second?'

The commander only hesitated a second before agreeing.

'Certainly, Charlie. Just a second here.'

He quickly punched Beeker's com number into his wrist communicator.

'Beeker here.'

'Beeker, this is Jester again. Charlie has something he'd like to say to you.'

He extended his arm to Daniels, pointing at the microphone with his other hand.

'You there, Beeker?' the miner called, unconsciously raising his voice as if trying to cover the distance with volume.

'Yes, sir.'

'Do you happen to know if one of the tailors you've got down there is named Giuseppe?'

'I'm not sure, sir. If you'll hold for a moment, I'll –'

'Short little guy. His face looks like a raisin with a moustache.'

'Yes, sir. He's here.'

'Well, you go over there and tell him that Charlie Daniels says that if he can't manage to fit uniforms on those little aliens – or a bowling ball, or a pile of gelatin, for that matter – well, then, I guess I've been braggin' about the wrong tailor to the commander up here. You tell him that for me.'

'Very good, sir.'

Daniels leaned back and winked at Phule.

'There. I guess that ought to do it.'

'Jester out,' the commander said into the communicator, signing off before shutting the unit down. 'Thanks, Charlie.'

'Glad I could help,' the miner said, setting his glass down and rising to his feet. 'Don't you go worrying about our insurance, either. I figure we'll be able to work something out if it ever comes to that. Seems to me like you're going to have all you can handle just worryin' about that crew of yours. On that little chore, I wish you luck!'

Of course, my employer did considerably more than simply worry about the Legionnaires under him. Particularly in those early days of his command, he pushed himself mercilessly in his efforts to learn about the individuals that made up the company. As an example, the same day that started early with the call from Headquarters and that he first stood duty with the company and *issued their new uniforms* and *met with Charlie Daniels about the use of the scanners, rather than call it a day, and a busy one at that, my employer summoned his junior officers for a late night meeting.*

'To get started,' the commander said, leaning forward in his chair, 'let me reiterate that the reason for this meeting is to gain further insight and understanding into the individual Legionnaires we command by pooling our thoughts and observations. While the Legionnaires themselves can pick and choose whom to avoid and whom to be friends with during off-duty hours, as officers we are not allowed that privilege. We have to work with and utilize every individual in the company, whether we like him or her personally or not, and to do that we have to know whom and what it is we're dealing with. Is that understood?'

'Yes, sir!'

Phule hid his wince at the stiff response by rubbing his eyes as if tired – a gesture he did not have to fake. While he had tried to make his lieutenants comfortable on the penthouse sofa, and it was obvious they were more at ease with each other than when he had first spoken with them, it was equally obvious that they were still tense and nervous in the presence of their commanding officer.

'Also, let me apologize for the hour. I know it's late, but I wanted to do the first pass on the list while our memories were still fresh from today's duty, particularly mine.'

He flashed a quick grin at the lieutenants, which was not returned. The commander sighed inwardly and abandoned his efforts to lighten the mood of the meeting. He'd just have to rely on time and familiarity to loosen the lieutenants up.

'All right. I notice you have quite a few notes, Lieutenant Rembrandt. Let's start with your observations.'

Rembrandt stiffened slightly and shot a quick glance around the room as if either hoping he was addressing someone else or looking for an escape route.

'Me, sir? I . . . Where would you like me to begin?'

Phule shrugged. 'Your choice. We're going to discuss everyone sooner or later, so it really doesn't matter whom we start with . . . And Lieutenant?'

'Sir?'

'Try to relax a little. This is just an informal chat to kick around our thoughts. Okay?'

Rembrandt drew a slow, deep breath, then nodded.

'Well, I should probably admit that a lot of information I have, I got from talking to Brandy, the first sergeant. I . . . I'm still trying to get a handle on a lot of the troops myself, and I thought it would be a good starting point.'

The commander nodded. 'Sound thinking. The non-coms work the closest with the Legionnaires, so we should listen to what they have to say whenever they're willing to share their thoughts. Go ahead.'

'Probably the best approach would be to start with some of our more unusual Legionnaires,' Rembrandt began, starting to relax a bit. 'It's my guess that we'll be spending a lot of time trying to figure out what to do with or about them, so we might as well start early.'

She paused to flip through her notes, then settled on a page.

'Proceeding on that basis, the one I personally have the biggest problem getting a fix on is one of the wimps. She has –'

'One of the what?'

The words burst from Phule's lips before he actually had time to think. Both the lieutenants started visibly, and the commander mentally cursed himself. So much for a relaxed meeting.

'The . . . the wimps, sir. That's how Brandy refers to them, anyway. When we were talking, she separated the problem Legionnaires into two groups: the wimps and the hard cases.'

'I see.'

The commander seesawed mentally for a few moments as the lieutenants watched him in silence. Finally he shook his head and sighed.

'It's tempting to let it go to keep the meeting relaxed,' he said, 'and I *do* want you both to feel comfortable speaking freely. You touched a nerve, though, Rembrandt, and I can't just ignore it. I don't want any of the company's leadership, officer or noncom, to fall into the habit of referring to the company or any subgroup in it by derogatory terms. It tends to influence our own views and attitudes, and even if we manage to resist that trap ourselves, anyone overhearing us will think, with some justification, that we hold the Legionnaires in contempt. I want you – both of you – to actively resist the temptation of forming that habit and to work at breaking whatever habits along those lines you've gotten into. Everyone in the company deserves our respect, and if we have trouble giving it, it's because we haven't studied them long enough, *not* because there's something wrong with them. Agreed?'

The lieutenants nodded slowly.

'Good. For that matter, Rembrandt, I want you to talk to Brandy about *her* speech patterns. She's probably the worst violator of all of us.'

'Me, sir?' Rembrandt paled. It was clear she did not relish the thought of confronting the company's formidable first sergeant.

'I'll take care of it for you, Remmie,' Armstrong volunteered, jotting a quick note on his pad.

'Thank you, Lieutenant Armstrong,' Phule said levelly, 'but I'd rather have Lieutenant Rembrandt handle it herself.'

'Yes, sir. I understand.'

Phule studied Armstrong's stiff posture, then shook his head.

'No, Lieutenant, I don't think you do. I said thank you and I meant it. I really *do* appreciate your offer. It shows that the two of you are starting to help each other out, and normally I'd encourage it.'

He leaned forward earnestly.

'It's not that I don't think you could handle talking to Brandy, it's that I specifically think Rembrandt should do it . . . for two reasons. First, she was the one who mentioned the labels Brandy's using. If you – or I, for that matter – approach Brandy on something Rembrandt said, it leaves the impression that she's reporting things to us for disciplinary action, which would undermine her efforts to establish herself as an authority figure. I need two junior officers, not one junior officer and an informer. Second, Rembrandt, it's important to *you* to address these problems yourself. Sure, Brandy's intimidating and I don't think anyone in the room would relish the idea of butting heads with her, but if I let you hide behind either Armstrong or me, you're never going to grit your teeth and take the plunge yourself, which means you'll never build the confidence you need to be an effective officer. That's why I want you to be the one to talk to Brandy.'

He made eye contact with the lieutenants one at a time, and they nodded their agreement.

'As to *how* to talk to Brandy, if you'll accept a little unasked-for advice, I'd suggest that you simply avoid approaching it as a confrontation. Oh, I know you'll be nervous, but make it casual and conversational. It's my guess she'll go along with it without realizing her habits have been a subject for conversation among us. The less we have to resort to orders and threats, the smoother this company will run.'

'I'll try, Captain.'

'Good.' The commander nodded briskly. 'Enough said on *that* subject. Now then, before I interrupted you, you were starting to say something about the Legionnaire you have the most trouble getting a fix on?'

'Oh. Right,' Rembrandt said, rummaging in her notes again. 'The one I was thinking of was Rose.'

'Rose?' Armstrong snorted. 'You mean Shrinking Violet.'

'That's what the other Legionnaires call her,' Rembrandt agreed.

Phule frowned. 'I don't think I've met her yet.'

'Not surprising,' Rembrandt said. 'If you had, you'd probably remember her. Rose, or Shrinking Violet, has to be the shyest person I've ever met in my life bar none. It's impossible to carry on a conversation with her. All she does is mumble and look the other way.'

'I've given up trying to talk to her,' Armstrong put in, 'and from what I can see, so has everyone else in the company. I mean, she's a good-looking woman, and when she arrived a lot of the guys tried to get to know her better, but you get tired of being treated like you're Jack the Ripper.'

'It's the same with the women,' Rembrandt said. '*Everybody* seems to make her nervous. Heck, it's easier to deal with the nonhumans. At least they'll meet you halfway.'

'Interesting,' the commander murmured thoughtfully. 'I'll have to try to talk with her myself.'

Armstrong grimaced. 'Lots of luck, Captain. If you can get her to say half a dozen words, it'll be more than she's said since she arrived.'

'Speaking of the nonhumans,' Phule said, 'I wanted to bounce a thought off the two of you. Specifically I want to split the two Sinthians when we assign team pairs. I figure it's hard for humans to relate to and interact with nonhumans. If we team the two of them, it will only make them that much harder to approach. The only problem is, I'm not sure how the Sinthians will react to being separated. What are your thoughts?'

'I don't think you have to worry about them complaining, Captain.' Armstrong grinned, winking at Rembrandt. 'Do you, Remmie?'

'Well,' his partner replied in a mock drawl, 'I don't expect it'll be a problem.'

The commander glanced back and forth at the two of them.

'I get the feeling I'm missing a joke here.'

'The truth is, Captain,' Rembrandt supplied, 'the two of them don't get along particularly well.'

'They don't?'

'The way it is, sir,' Armstrong said, 'is that apparently there's a real class prejudice problem on their home world. Both of them headed off-world to get away from conditions.'

'Their names kinda say it all,' Rembrandt continued. 'One of them, Spartacus, is a product of the lower class, while Louie, which I believe is short for Louis the XIV, is rooted in the aristocracy. Both of them joined the Legion thinking they would never have to deal with someone from the hated "other class," and you can imagine how overjoyed they were when they both got assigned to this outfit.'

'I see. How much does their mutual dislike affect their performance?'

'Actually they're pretty civilized about it,' Rembrandt said. 'It's not like they get violent or anything. They just avoid each other when possible, and maybe glare and mutter a bit when they can't. At least, I *think* that's what they're doing. Between their eyestalks and the translators, it's a little hard to tell.'

'The bottom line, though, Captain, is that I don't think they'll object to being assigned other partners.' Armstrong grinned.

'Fair enough.' Phule ticked off an item on his list. 'All right. Who's next?'

The mood of the meeting had relaxed considerably when the commander finally called a halt to the proceedings. All three officers were punchy with fatigue and tended to giggle disproportionately at the lamest attempt at humor.

Phule was pleased with the results as he ushered his junior officers to the door. The long meeting had drawn them closer together, where it could just as easily have put them at each other's throats.

'Sorry again about losing track of the time,' he told them. 'Tell you what. Sleep late tomorrow and we'll pick it up again at noon.'

The two lieutenants groaned dramatically.

'And hey! Nice work . . . both of you.'

'"Nice work," he says,' Armstrong said, making a face at his partner. 'I didn't think we were going to get a pat on the back until we fell over from exhaustion. Of course, tomorrow we get to pick up where we left off.'

'He's just saying that because we knew some things he didn't,' Rembrandt countered owlishly. 'Once he's squeezed us dry, we'll be cast aside and forgotten.'

Phule joined in their laughter.

'Go on, get some sleep. Both of you. You're going to need your strength before I get done with you.'

'Seriously, Captain, what's the rush?' Rembrandt said, propping herself against the wall. 'What happened to our relaxed, informal sessions of note comparing?'

'You put your finger on it a minute ago,' the commander told her. 'You two know some things about the troops that I don't. I want to get as much information out of you as I can before we run everybody through the confidence course day after tomorrow – well, tomorrow, actually.'

He glanced up from his watch to find the lieutenants staring at him, all trace of humor gone.

'What's wrong?'

Armstrong cleared his throat.

'Excuse me, Captain. Did you say we were running the confidence course the day after tomorrow?'

'That's right. Didn't I mention it to you?'

Phule tried to focus his mind to separate what he had and hadn't said during the last several hours.

'No, you didn't.'

'Sorry. I thought I had. I told the construction crew to give top priority to completing the new confidence course, and the word is that they finished work on it today.'

'You mean you expect *our* company to run a confidence course?' Rembrandt seemed to be hoping she had heard wrong.

'Of course. We've got them looking like soldiers. It's about time we started working toward getting them to act and feel like soldiers, don't you agree?'

For the first time that night there was no automatic chorus of assent. Instead, the two lieutenants just stood looking at him as if he had grown another head.

7

Journal File #087

For those of you who are like me, which is to say dyed-in-the-wool civilians, and therefore unfamiliar with the stuffy quaintness of military jargon, you should at least be made aware that it is a fantasy language all its own, specifically designed to hide its activities and attitudes beneath officious blandness. (My own personal favorite is referring to casualties as inoperative combat units.) Such is the case with the so-called confidence course.

What it is, is a path strewn with obstacles at regular intervals which the soldiers are to traverse in the least possible amount of time. In short, it's what normal people would refer to as an obstacle course. It is no accident, however, that military personnel are never referred to as 'normal people.' Somewhere in their hidden past (you notice no one in the military ever writes about it until after they've retired, or shortly before) it was decided to change the image of the old obstacle course. Rather than change the course, they opted to change the name. The theory was that it would be more acceptable to those it was inflicted upon if they understood its function, which is 'to increase the soldier's self-confidence by demonstrating to him (or her) that he (or she) can function successfully under adverse conditions.' This, of course, assumes that said soldier is able to successfully negotiate the prescribed course.

Personally I would have questioned the wisdom of my employer's use of the confidence course as a means of establishing or reestablishing the self-esteem of the individuals under his command . . . had I been asked. After reviewing their files, not to mention experiencing the dubious pleasure of viewing and meeting them in person, I would have had serious doubts as to their ability to successfully tie their own shoelaces, much less negotiate an obstacle – excuse me, confidence course. From what I have gleaned of their comments on their first attempts at this exercise, my appraisal was not far from accurate.

Uncomfortable silence reigned in the small group of observers watching the company run the confidence course . . . or attempting to. Of the four, only the commanding officer seemed to be studying the scene with a neutral intensity. Brandy, the Amazonian first sergeant, stood in a relaxed parade rest, openly sneering her disdain at the antics on the course, while the two lieutenants alternated between averting their eyes in embarrassment and exchanging uneasy glances, united by their mutual discomfort, at least temporarily.

Surely the captain had known what would happen when he ordered this exercise . . . hadn't he? He had every warning that his troops habitually performed at a level far below even the loose standards of the Legion. Still, he had given no indication that his expectations were anything but high. He had even issued new orders modifying the conditions under which the course would be run. Rather than the time being recorded for each individual as they were run through in small groups of half a dozen, the unit would be judged and rated on their performance as a whole. That is, the timer would be started, and not stopped until the last Legionnaire crossed the finish line. What was even worse, he insisted that the Legionnaires run the course in full combat gear, complete with weapons and packs, an announcement met with a mixture of horror and grumbling by the company. Already aghast at the idea of having to run the course at all, the new conditions robbed them of whatever energy and enthusiasm they might have been able to muster. For the moment, at least, their minds were one, even if the binding thought was the delightful fantasy of lynching their new CO.

The result was, predictably, chaos. While most of the company could manage at least a few of the obstacles, none could negotiate all of them with any semblance of poise or skill, the vast majority floundering even when they cast dignity to the winds. In no time at all, the course was littered with knots and clumps of Legionnaires bunched together at the more difficult obstacles or simply muttering together darkly while glaring at the knoll where the observers stood.

Even though Armstrong and Rembrandt had anticipated all this and gone to some lengths to point it out to their new commander, they were still haunted by a vague uneasiness. Phule had read them the riot act upon taking command, pointing out that the company was their personal responsibility. While he shared that responsibility, it was doubtful he would acknowledge any hand in the development of the Legionnaires prior to his arrival. In short, despite the apparent camaraderie they had experienced during the skull sessions regarding the individual Legionnaires, the lieutenants saw themselves as holding the bag for the company's current condition. Though more than a little resentful of this burden, they were still plagued by small voices of guilt as they watched the fiasco on the course.

Should they have run the company through this course more often themselves under normal conditions? Perhaps if they had insisted on daily calisthenics in an effort to improve the physical conditioning of the Legionnaires, today's showing might not be so grim. Of course, they were aware that if they had tried to implement such a program, they would have probably been shot in the back accidentally at the first opportunity (a possibility that still existed, and made them more than a little uneasy when Phule issued weapons and ammo to the Legionnaires for today's effort). The fact remained, however, that they hadn't even tried.

Well, the past was past and there was nothing they could do now except watch glumly as the situation on the course deteriorated. Trying to shut out the overall horror, they began focusing on individual activities.

Super Gnat, the little tomboy Legionnaire, was just approaching the three-meter board wall. This was a particularly challenging obstacle, one that daunted all but the most athletic Legionnaires. Because of this, there was a small path around it to enable the downhearted to bypass this test after a few tries before they became terminally depressed. Needless to say, the bulk of the company chose this route after a token run at the board, and many didn't even bother pretending to try. Not so with Super Gnat.

Putting on a quick burst of speed, she threw herself at the wall, only to hit barely halfway to the top with an impact that could be heard by, and drew winces from, the watchers at the nearby knoll. It was a sincere, if futile, effort. One which easily should have earned her the walk-around so flagrantly taken by so many of the others. It seemed, however, that Super Gnat was of a different mind.

Picking herself up from the dust, she paused only long enough to resettle her gear, then hurled herself at the obstacle again with a savagery that, if anything, surpassed that of her first effort . . . with the same unfortunate results. Again she charged the barricade, and again the sound of her body hitting the wall floated up the knoll to the observers. And again . . .

Other Legionnaires streamed past her, but still she continued her dogged assault on the wall. The lieutenants grimaced and winced sympathetically with each impact, and even the hard-hearted Brandy shook her head in wonder over the little Legionnaire's tenacity. Phule's reaction, however, was as different as it was unexpected.

With a smooth stride that had him off the knoll before the others knew he had started moving, the

CO approached the obstacle himself. Timing his silent approach to match Super Gnat's rush, he stooped and put an impersonal hand under her rump, boosting her up and over the wall with her next jump. Though doubtlessly surprised at the assist, the Legionnaire did not so much as pause for a backward glance, but scurried off toward the next obstacle, blissfully unaware of whose hand it was that had propelled her to success.

The remaining trio on the knoll watched her go, then turned their gaze to their commander, only to be met with an angry, challenging glare as he rejoined them.

'If that's a loser,' Phule snarled, 'then I'm a bad credit risk!'

This time the first sergeant joined the exchange of startled glances as they all groped for something to say. Fortunately they were spared the effort as the CO continued, with a more level voice now.

'All right, Top,' he said. 'I think we've seen enough. Call 'em in. It's lecture time.'

Brandy needed no more encouragement than that. Though still skeptical of the changes Phule was introducing, she secretly liked the wrist communicators and was glad of the opportunity to use hers. Depressing the General Broadcast button with her fingertip, she addressed the company through the speaker.

'Abort exercise! Repeat. Abort! All personnel assemble at the reviewing knoll! I mean *now*, Legionnaires! *Let's move it!*'

A few weak cheers drifted up from the course as she ended her announcement. Most of the company, however, broke off their efforts and trudged toward the knoll with downcast eyes. They had looked bad, and they all knew it. While clinging to their righteous indignation over what had been expected of them, no one relished the inevitable tongue-lashing that was to come.

Though Brandy made sure her face was set in an expression of grim annoyance as the company gathered, inwardly she was more than a little elated. It was clear to her that today's performance more than justified her low opinion that Phule had tried to dismiss as cynicism. If anything, she was looking forward to hearing him enumerate the shortcomings of the rabble he had been defending so staunchly.

'I don't have to tell you that was a pretty miserable showing,' the CO announced as the last few stragglers joined the group. 'I'm just wondering if anyone has the smarts or the courage to tell me what's wrong.'

'We stink on ice!'

It was the now obligatory voice from the back of the crowd that was raised, though everyone seemed to be in agreement with it. Phule, it seemed, was not about to let it go at that, however.

'Who said that?' he demanded, peering in the direction the voice had come from.

Before his gaze, the mass of Legionnaires melted away, leaving one dark-haired, rat-faced individual to meet the challenge alone.

'I guess I did . . . sir,' he admitted uncomfortably.

'It's Do-Wop, isn't it?' the commander said, recognizing the Legionnaire who had done communications a few days before.

'Yes, sir!'

'Actually it's De Wop,' someone whispered loudly, and a snicker rippled through the assemblage as the singled-out party flushed with annoyance and embarrassment.

Phule ignored it all.

'Well, Do-Wop, I admire someone who speaks their mind . . . but you're wrong. Dead wrong.'

The company frowned in bewilderment, except the first sergeant, who scowled openly as he continued.

'What's wrong is that you're down there, and we're' – his gesture encompassed all four observers on the knoll – 'up here! I told you before that it's our job to work with you, to find ways to make you effective, not to stand up here and shake our heads while you flounder around getting discouraged by trial-and-error learning. If anything, I owe you an apology for putting you through that first round, but I felt it was necessary to prove a point. You have my promise it's the last time you'll face an exercise alone.'

The company responded with thunderstruck silence as Phule came down off the knoll to join them on their own level, the rest of the observers trailing uneasily in his wake. Their expressions ranged from confused to disgusted, but there was little they could do but follow Phule's lead.

'Okay now,' the CO said, motioning for those in the front rows to kneel down so those behind could see and hear. 'I told you before, we're a team. All of us. The first mistake was that you were trying to run this course as individuals. There are obstacles out there, as well as in anything we'll ever want to do, that can flat out beat any one of us. But together, working as a team to help each other and to think out any problem, there's nothing we can't do. Nothing! Accept that as a given. Burn it into your minds and hearts that we can do *anything*. Then all that remains is working out the how, and that's where the team comes in.'

The company was hanging on his words, caught up in his certainty and wanting him to be right.

'Let's get down to some specifics here and see how this works. The three-meter wall is a problem.'

He pointed at the offending obstacle, and the Legionnaires nodded, a few grimacing wryly.

'It's obvious just from looking at it that if you've got the height and the strength, you can go over it. But if you don't, you're stuck. That may be true for a pack of individuals, but we're not. We're a team, and we don't leave teammates behind or let them get stuck just because they aren't tall. Forget getting *you* over it and start thinking about getting *us* over it. If someone was to get on top and stay there to give a hand up to those coming after him, everyone could get over a lot easier.

Better still, if some of you heavyweights were to make a staircase with your shoulders, we could go over this thing without breaking stride. Again, the idea is to maximize what you can do, not to let yourself get defeated by what you can't do.'

There were smiles in the ranks now. The irrepressible energy of the captain was having its effect, and the Legionnaires were starting to believe they could beat the system.

'Another example,' Phule continued. 'Some of you are slower than others. The Sinthians in particular are not built for speed. Well, being slow is nothing to be ashamed of, especially when it's a factor of your physical build. They should no more have to suffer from not being fast than the rest of us have to be embarrassed by not being able to fly. It's a problem to be dealt with. We help them deal with it because they're our teammates. If there's a situation like this course, where time is important and we don't want them to fall behind, help them along. Carry them if you have to, even if it means doubling up on some of the field packs. Remember, our goal is to be efficient, and we'll do whatever is necessary to get the job done. Now, let's take a look at some of these other obstacles . . . '

He strode off in the direction of the series of obstacles commonly referred to as 'The Pits', with the rest of the company crowding along behind him. Reaching the first station, he turned back to the Legionnaires, and this time the front ranks dropped down without his signaling to them.

The obstacle consisted of a trench about four meters across filled nearly to the top with an evil-looking mixture of slime, algae, and muddy water. There was a framework constructed over the trench from which three heavy ropes hung. The Legionnaires were to swing across the trench on the ropes and continue on their way, a maneuver which was, in reality, much more difficult than it looked.

'I noticed that there was always a bottleneck at this station,' Phule said. 'While some of you had the right idea in giving your buddies a push to get their swing started, the real problem is that three ropes aren't enough to keep the traffic moving.'

He paused and peered into the trench at the water.

'Now, I know you're all proud of your new uniforms, but these are supposed to be combat conditions, and combat is no time to worry about keeping your clothes clean. Does anyone know how deep this trench is?'

The Legionnaires looked at each other, but the CO didn't bother waiting for an answer.

'The most valuable thing in combat besides initiative is information. Intelligence. Sergeant Brandy!'

'Sir?'

'Would you demonstrate for the company the fastest way to find out how deep this trench is?'

The company blinked in astonishment at the captain's audacity, but the much-feared top sergeant only hesitated the barest heartbeat before springing into action. Crisp uniform, spit-shined boots, and all, she took one long stride and leaped boldly into the trench. Then, finding that the muck barely reached the bottoms of her substantial breasts, she waded to the far side with as much dignity as she could muster, looking not unlike the *Bismarck* coming into port.

Lieutenant Armstrong, who had always envied the top sergeant's poise, did not bother to hide his grin as he elbowed Rembrandt in glee. Unfortunately Phule noticed the exchange.

'Lieutenants?'

'Sir?'

The junior officers cringed inside as their commander nodded pointedly at the trench, but they were compelled to match the sergeant's example. Two sets of officer's uniforms hit the muck as the company looked on with delight.

'As you can see,' the CO commented calmly, 'it's

actually quicker to simply wade through this obstacle than to stand in line for a rope. Now, if you'll follow me, we'll take a look at the next problem. Remember how deep this is and lend a hand to your shorter teammates.'

With that, he turned and stepped off the edge of the trench himself, accepting a hand up from Brandy as he reached the other side. The company charged into the trench like lemmings behind him, eager to see what else their commander had up his sleeve.

The next station was much like the last, except that the trench was wider and spanned by three logs. This time, Phule didn't hesitate, but hopped immediately onto one of the logs and crossed to the far side, beckoning for the waterlogged Armstrong to join him.

'This one isn't too difficult,' he called from the other side, 'if you're reasonably agile. Of course, some of us aren't reasonably agile, and even for those that are, keeping your balance takes time. So again, we simply modify the world to fit our needs . . . Tusk-anini! Could you get the other end of this?'

At nearly seven feet, the big Volton was easily the strongest, most imposing figure among the Legionnaires, even if his stringy dark hair, protruding tusks, and misshapen head didn't give him the appearance of a cross between a warthog and Frankenstein's monster. Stepping forward, he grasped one end of the log as Phule and Armstrong got the other, and together they rolled it sideways until it rested against the center span. A few more moments, and the third log was shoved into place next to the others.

'This is easier to cross,' Phule declared, walking out to the center of the makeshift bridge and jiggling it with his feet to check its steadiness, 'but it's still a little wobbly if we're all going to cross it in a hurry. Anyone have any rope in your packs?'

Nobody did.

'Well, I know you all have knives. They were issued

to you, and while they aren't the best-quality cutlery, they'll do for the moment. Do-Wop?'

'Here, Captain!'

'Grab a partner and go get us some rope to tie these logs together with.'

'Sir?'

'Think, soldier! I believe you'll find some back at the last station. That is, of course, if you don't feel it will compromise your well-known principles to stoop to liberating something for the company's benefit.'

Whoops and cheers went up from the Legionnaires at this, as Do-Wop could normally be relied on to requisition anything that wasn't nailed down solidly – and chained, to boot.

'While we're waiting,' Phule called, waving them into grinning silence, 'let's kick around some ideas of how to beat the next obstacle. Anyone have any ideas?'

As fate would have it, Bombest was not only on duty but in the lobby when the company blew into the hotel after their bout with the confidence course.

Do-Wop was the first in, though it was difficult to recognize him through the slime and drying mud that were caked on his uniform. He was in undeniably high spirits, though, as he tossed a wad of wet currency on the front desk and scooped up an entire stack of newspapers from the counter.

'Hey, Super Gnat!' he called at the next figure through the door, recognizable only by her height, or lack thereof. 'Give me a hand with this! You know what the captain said. If those baboons track up the lobby, we'll all have to pay for the cleanup out of our wages.'

The manager watched with interest as the two of them laid a path with newspapers between the front door and the elevators, barely in time as the first wave of Legionnaires burst into view.

'Did you see Brandy's face when the captain said . . .'

'I'll tell you, I never thought I'd live to see . . .'

'Hey, Bombast! Better call the laundry service and have 'em send someone over for a pickup. We've got a little overtime for them!'

The hotel manager did his best to smile along with the general laughter that followed this comment despite the use of the hated nickname, but it came out looking like a thin-lipped grimace.

'Me, I'm ready for a drink or five.'

'Get cleaned up first. Can't have the civvies see us looking like this!'

One figure detached itself from the jubilant mass and approached the front desk.

'Say, Bombest! Could you send someone to open up the pool area? I think the crew is going to want to play a bit, and it's probably better for all of us if they do it in the pool instead of the bar and the restaurant.'

The manager did not even try to keep the look of horror off his face this time. If it hadn't spoken, Bombest would never have recognized the mud-encrusted figure before him as Phule. His mind flatly refused to accept that anyone of Phule's social standing and training would stoop to wallowing in the muck with the common troops.

'The pool?' he echoed weakly, unable to tear his eyes away from the commander's soiled condition.

Phule caught his look, but misinterpreted it.

'Don't worry, Bombest.' He grinned. 'I'm sure everyone will shower before hitting the pool.' He gestured at the newspaper-littered lobby. 'If they're too cheap to pay to have the carpet vacuumed, they sure aren't about to spring to have a ring around the pool scrubbed off.'

'I suppose not.'

'Oh, and could you have room service send about three trolleys of beer to each of our floors? On my bill, of course.'

'It's all on your bill, Mr. Phule,' Bombest commented, beginning to recover his composure.

The commander had been starting to turn away, but instead he leaned on the desk, chatty in his enthusiasm.

'I know, Bombest, but this is special. Be sure they're told that it's with the commander's compliments. I'll tell you, I wish you could have seen them today. I'll have to check on it, but I don't think any outfit has run the confidence course in less time than they did.'

'They do seem to be in high spirits,' the manager agreed, wishing to maintain the friendly tone of the conversation.

'They should be. Do you know we ran that course over a dozen times today? They'd still be going at it if I hadn't called it a day.'

'Why did you do that? I mean . . . it is still fairly early.'

'The course has to be rebuilt first,' Phule said proudly, his grin flashing through the dirt on his face. 'That reminds me. I've got to call the construction crew and see if they can get someone out there today to get started on it.'

'It . . . sounds like they're doing well.'

'That they are. I am worried about the Sinthians, though. They're just not able to keep up without help. I've got to come up with some way to help them move faster before they get completely dispirited.'

Bombest was groping for an appropriate answer when he noticed two figures approaching their conversation.

'Willard? Is that you?'

Phule turned, smiling as he recognized the reporter whose interview had resulted in the call from Headquarters. She was barely into her twenties with soft, curly brown hair and a curvaceous body that even the conservative lines of her office suit couldn't hide.

'Hi, Jennie. Surprised you recognized me like this.'

'I almost didn't, but Sidney here said he thought it

was you. It's not that easy to fool a holophotographer.' The reporter grinned, gesturing at her partner. 'He specializes in spotting celebrities that are trying to travel in disguise.'

'Yes. I can see where that would be a handy skill,' the commander said, forcing a smile. He had never been that fond of the sharp-eyed holophotographers that flocked around public figures like vultures around a staggering animal. In particular, he found he disliked the easy, broad-shouldered, wavy-haired good looks of the photographer who stood so close to Jennie. He exuded a relaxed air that intense people such as Phule always envied but could never hope to master. 'Pleased to meet you, Sidney.'

He bared his teeth as they shook hands.

'So. What can I do for you today, Jennie? I don't think we can top that last article you wrote until we learn to walk on water.'

Any sarcasm hidden in his question was lost in the reporter's enthusiasm.

'Well, our editor has assigned us to do a series of weekly articles on you, complete with pictures . . . if you're willing, that is. I was hoping we could talk with you and get a few shots, or set a time at your convenience.'

'I see. Unfortunately I'm not really presentable at the moment.' Phule gestured pointedly at his soiled condition. 'We've been running the confidence course today . . .'

'Really? That could make a good lead right there . . .'

' . . . and besides,' the commander continued, 'I'd rather you did a few stories on the company itself. I'm sure the public would find it more interesting than a series on me alone.'

'I . . . suppose,' the reporter said hesitantly, seemingly reluctant to pass up her chance to spend time with the commander. 'We could try putting in some stuff about how other people view you and your activities.'

'Fine. Then it's settled. We'll see what we can do about lining you up with . . . Do-Wop! Brandy!'

He waved at the two figures en route from the elevator to the lounge, and they wandered over to join the conversation.

'These two are interested in doing a story on our confidence course training session,' he explained. 'I was wondering if the two of you would be willing to fill them in.'

'With holos?' Do-Wop exclaimed, spotting the holophotographer's equipment. 'Hey, neat! Sure thing, Captain.'

'Um . . . the trouble here is that they don't look like they've been through anything,' the reporter commented tactfully.

The two Legionnaires had already showered and changed, and except for their damp hair there was no trace of their recent ordeal.

'No problem' Do-Wop insisted hastily. 'We can just duck up and change back into our other uniforms and –'

'Better still,' Brandy said levelly, eyeing the holophotographer, whose good looks had not escaped her notice, 'we could just go across the street to the park and take a quick dip in the fountain to wet ourselves down. I'm not sure the public wants to see how really dirty we get on the course.'

The holophotographer ran an appraising look over the top sergeant's generous figure and nudged the reporter with his elbow.

'That'll do just fine,' he declared. 'Shall we go?'

As the group headed out of the hotel, Phule snagged the photographer and drew him aside.

'Umm . . . Sidney? We both know that Jennie there has enough enthusiasm to carry a whole brigade along with her once she gets rolling. I'm counting on you to keep a bit more level head on your shoulders.'

'What do you mean . . . ?'

'Let's just say it would be wise for you to check with the various Legionnaires before taking, much less publishing, holos of them. Some of them joined the Legion to leave their past behind them.'

'Really?' The photographer started to look around, but Phule wasn't finished.

'And if they didn't shove your gear down your throat when you tried to take the pictures, I'd be inclined to take a *personal* interest in your career, as long as it lasted. Do we understand each other?'

Sidney met the commander's gaze, and what he saw there made him decide that this was not the time to extol the virtues of freedom of the press.

'Understood, Mr. Phule,' he said, giving a quick salute that wasn't entirely mockery.

Phule paid only distant attention to the antics of the photo session. Instead, he found himself watching the neighborhood rat pack of kids who interrupted their glide-board frolicking to investigate the gathering. After the reporter shooed them away from the shooting for the fifth time, this time threatening to call the police, the kids resumed their normal games, perhaps more energetically because of the nearby holophotographer.

Though best on hard, flat surfaces like sidewalks, the glide boards could work on anything, and the kids prided themselves in demonstrating their expertise in the face of adversity. They rode them over the tops of the park benches and across the uneven grass. Their favorite maneuver was to skim down one particular slope into a dip, then use their momentum to jump their boards over the hedge, coincidentally landing in the fountain the photographer was using for his backdrop. The boards were even faster over water, however, and they had no difficulty in gliding across the fountain and disappearing before the news team could do more than raise their voices in protest.

Phule watched them intently for a while, then drifted over toward where they were gathering to plot their next move. The kids watched his approach, ready to bolt for the safety of the alleys, but he smiled and beckoned to them, so they held their ground until he was in talking distance.

'Whatcha want, mister?' the apparent leader challenged. 'Looks like you could use a dip in the fountain yourself.'

Phule grinned ruefully along with the titters of laughter. He hadn't had a chance to clean himself up yet, and if anything he looked worse than the urchins.

'I was just wondering if you could tell me a little about your boards,' he said. 'Are they hard to operate?'

The kids glanced at each other, torn between their love of their boards and the temptation to tease an adult. The boards won.

'They're a little tricky at first,' the spokesman admitted. 'You've got to learn to keep your center of balance low or they'll toss you off.'

'With a little practice . . . '

'With a lot of practice . . . '

'You can make 'em do just about anything . . . '

'You want to give it a try?'

'Once you get the hang of it . . . '

Now that the barrier was broken, the information came in a torrent as the kids all tried to talk about their passion at once. Phule listened for a few moments, then waved them into silence.

'What I really want to know,' he said in a conspiratorial voice that brought the kids crowding closer, 'is if you think you could teach a Sinthian to ride one of these things . . . Have any of you ever met a Sinthian?'

8

Journal File #091

Their success on the confidence course, not to mention their pride in their new 'uniforms,' seemed to mark a turning point in the attitudes of the Legionnaires. As a whole and as individuals, the company began to embrace their new commander's belief that 'we can do anything *if we work together and are not too picky about* how *we do it!'*

Like children looking for excuses to show off a new toy, the Legionnaires abandoned their previous habit of clinging to their home base during their off-duty hours, and instead were soon seen throughout the settlement looking for new challenges to apply their 'togetherness' techniques to, whether it was called for or not! Many of the local citizens grew to believe that this extroverted crew was an entirely new force which had been imported, as most of their 'projects' could be viewed as 'good deeds' or 'civic improvements.' Unfortunately, however, not all of their pastimes fell on the proper side of legality, a fact which kept my employer quite busy intervening between them and the local authorities.

Aside from this, the bulk of his time was occupied in a sincere effort to get better acquainted with the individuals under his command in preparation for the assigning of the company into two-man teams. Of course, his efforts only revealed what I had suspected since he first received this assignment: that Legionnaires relegated to an Omega Company are not the easiest individuals in the universe to deal with.

'Mind if I join you?'

Super Gnat looked up from her breakfast to find the company commander standing over her table. With a shrug, she waved him into the facing chair.

The smallest member of the company was not unattractive, though no one would call her beautiful. An obvious band of freckles across her cheekbones and nose combined with her heart-shaped face and short brown hair to give an impression of a pixie – a robust young farm pixie, not the cuter, more sophisticated Tinker Bell variety.

Phule stirred his coffee slowly as he tried to organize his thoughts into words.

'I've been meaning to talk to you for some time,' he began, but the Gnat stopped him, holding up a restraining hand while she finished chewing and swallowing her current mouthful.

'Let me save you a little time here, Captain. It's about my fightin'. Right?'

'Well . . . yes. You do seem to be involved in more than your share of . . . scuffles.'

'Scuffles.' The little Legionnaire sighed. 'If I was bigger, they'd be called brawls. Oh well. Let me explain something to you, sir.'

She readdressed her food as she spoke.

'I was the littlest of nine kids in our family – not the youngest, the littlest. Our folks both worked and weren't around much, so us kids were left pretty much to sort things out for ourselves, and like most kids, we weren't big on democracy or diplomacy. If you didn't stand up for yourself, nobody else would and you ended up at the bottom of the heap. Of course, me bein' the smallest, I had to fight more than most just to keep my share of the grief and housework from getting too big. You know what it's like to have a sister five years younger than you try to push you around?'

Phule was caught flat-footed by the question and groped for an answer. Fortunately none seemed to be required, as Super Gnat continued.

'Anyway, I sort of got in the habit of going for anyone who tried to hassle me. You see, when you're my size, you can't wait for the other person to swing first, or it's all over before it starts. You gotta go for them first if you want to get your licks in. Even then it doesn't always work, but at least that way you've got a chance.'

She paused to sip her coffee, then wiped her mouth decisively with the napkin.

'I guess what I'm saying, sir, is that what you sees is what you gets. I can appreciate that my fighting all the time is disruptive, but it's an old habit and I personally wouldn't make book on its changing. If it really bothers you, I could transfer out. Lord knows it won't be the first time.'

Despite his poise, Phule was a bit taken aback by the frankness of this little Legionnaire. While he was concerned about the conduct of the company, he found himself warming to the Gnat.

'I . . . really don't think that will be necessary,' he said, dismissing the possibility offhand. 'Tell me, doesn't it bother you that you always get beaten? Why do you keep picking fights you can't win?'

For the first time since the start of their conversation, Super Gnat looked uncomfortable.

'Well, you see, sir, the way I was raised, I've always figured the important thing is to stand up for yourself and what you believe in whatever the odds. If you only fight when you can win . . . well, then you're just a bully takin' advantage of weaker folks. I guess growin' up the way I did, I never had much use for bullies, so I'm kinda sensitive about bein' one myself.'

The commander was impressed. Enough so that the idea of the Gnat as a bully wasn't even outlandish.

'But you *would* like to win more often? Or at least some of the time?'

'Of course I would,' she said. 'Don't get me wrong, Captain. Just because I'm not choosy about my fights doesn't mean I've got a thing for losin'. You got any suggestions on that score, I'd appreciate 'em.'

'Well, I was thinking you might look into the martial arts . . . you know, like karate. A lot of them are designed by and for small people, and . . . '

He broke off when he realized Super Gnat was beaming at him with an impish grin.

'You don't have to tell me about the martial arts, sir. You see, I've got belt ratin's in three schools a karate – Korean, Japanese, and Okinawan – plus judo and some a the Chinese forms. The trouble there is that you've got to keep a level head for the forms to work, and when I get mad – and I gotta be mad to fight – it all just kinda slips away and I'm back to bein' a scrapper.'

'Three schools,' Phule echoed weakly.

'That's right. My first husband, he owned a string of dojos, so it was real easy for me to get lessons. Now, if you'll excuse me, sir, I'm supposed to be helpin' in the kitchen just now.'

She departed, leaving Phule gaping after her.

'Have you got a minute, Captain?'

Surprised, Phule looked up to find Chocolate Harry framed in the doorway of the penthouse. Actually the pear-shaped black supply sergeant did more than fill the doorway: He dominated it and the room with his bulk.

'Sure. Come on in, C.H. What can I do for you?'

Though deliberately casual in tone and manner, the commander was curious as to what had dragged Harry away from his normal lair in the supply rooms. They had not spoken more than in passing since the new uniforms were issued, and while the supply sergeant had been more than efficient in handling his expanded duties, Phule was curious as to his true reactions to the revitalization of the company.

Harry eased into the room, peering around through

the thick lenses of his glasses as if he expected to find an intruder – or a bargain – lurking in the corners. Finally he ran a hand over his close-cropped hair and began.

'Well, sir,' he said, that surprisingly wheezy voice of his emerging mysteriously from his dense, bristly beard. 'I've been doing some thinkin'. You know the problems we've been havin' comin' up with weapons for Spartacus and Louie?'

Phule nodded carefully. Along with the problems of locomotion, the Sinthians had other difficulties in interfacing with the troops, not the least of which were armaments. Their spindly arms had enough wiry strength to handle most of the firearms in the company's arsenal, but there was a problem with their eyestalks. It seemed that the sighting devices designed for eyes mounted side by side on a head, like on a human face, were somehow beyond the Sinthian's physiology. They were issued weapons along with the rest of the company when they went out on exercises, but were under strict orders not to fire a round until they had demonstrated an ability to place their shots at least in the vicinity of their intended target.

'Have you got an answer, C.H.?'

'Mebbe so.' The sergeant fidgeted. 'You see, before I signed up, I was a member of . . . a club. Pretty rough-and-tumble folks. Anyway, we had one guy, blind as a bat, who was one of the meanest dudes we had in a fight. What it was, was he got hold of a sawed-off shotgun and used that when things got rough. He didn't have to be real accurate, just so long as he got the general direction right. I was thinkin' . . . you know, with the Sinthians . . . '

Phule considered this. A sawed-off shotgun was a classic close-combat weapon, especially as an adaptation to some of the new belt-fed models. There was no denying its effectiveness, though it was not usually issued in the military. Of course, the police still used them for really nasty situations, so it wasn't entirely unprecedented. Then again, this was Harry's first independent effort to help the company, and the commander was loath to discourage him.

'That's an excellent idea, C.H.,' he said, reaching his decision. 'As a matter of fact, we're going to be getting a visit from a sales rep of old Phule-Proof Munitions in the next few days. We'll have to see what he has in stock that can be modified to our purposes.'

'That's great, Cap'n. Wouldn't mind browsing through their selection myself. Ain't often I've had a chance to see the new stuff instead of hand-me-downs and black market rejects.'

'Oh, you'll be involved in the selections, Sergeant.' The commander smiled. 'Never fear on that score. Getting back to the shotguns, though. I only see one possible problem with issuing them to the Sinthians. Specifically it will be of the utmost importance that they're pointed at least in the right general direction when they fire. That'll mean being sure they're teamed with someone reliable, and not that many of our more solid Legionnaires have expressed a willingness to accept them as partners. It seems that everyone's afraid that their slowness would be a liability on combat. That may change if the glide-board idea works out, but in the meantime . . . '

'Shoot, that's no problem, Captain.' The sergeant beamed, his teeth showing through his fierce beard. 'I'd have room for one of 'em – mebbe both – in the sidecar of my hawg. I can keep an eye on 'em myself!'

'Your what?'

'Mah hawg . . . my hover cycle. I'll tell you, Captain, I never have been able to figure out why the military doesn't use 'em in combat. They worked fine for us in civilian life, and they can go anywhere one of those glide boards can.'

Phule had a vague feeling that he had just been

maneuvered into letting Chocolate Harry ride his hover cycle into combat. Still, if it was efficient . . .

'Tell you what, C.H. Bring your . . . hawg . . . by after duty hours tomorrow. I want to take a look at it myself.'

'Right, Cap'n!'

'Oh, and C.H., while we're on the subject of the nonhumans in the company, what weapon do you think would be best for Tusk-anini?'

'Tusk?' The sergeant blinked. 'Heck, Cap'n. It don't matter none what you have him carry. He ain't gonna shoot it, anyway.'

'I beg your pardon?'

'I thought you knew, Cap'n. The Voltron may look like some kinda big stomper, but he's a strict pacifist. Won't even raise his voice to anyone, much less a weapon.'

It was late when the commander leaned back, stretching from the litter of notes on the table in his bedroom, and decided to call it a day. No sooner had he reached his decision, however, than he realized he was hungry. He had worked through the dinner hour (again) and knew that the hotel restaurant was long closed, as was the bar. Still, now that his concentration was broken, an emptiness in the vicinity of his stomach reminded him that he should feed it *something* or he'd have trouble getting to sleep.

There was a vending machine which dispensed snacks, but that was two floors down (apparently people living in penthouse suites weren't supposed to patronize vending machines), but he had dismissed Beeker several hours ago, and was loath to call on the services of the Legionnaire who would be on communications duty in the main room with no justification other than his own laziness. It seemed he had no choice but to stir his stumps and run the errand himself.

Having reached that decision, Phule felt the momentary tug of politeness and chose to exit his lair through the duty area.

'I'm going down for some noshies,' he announced, opening the connecting door while feeling in his pocket for some change. 'Can I get you anything while I'm at it?'

The Legionnaire on duty started and looked up from her magazine as if he had shot at her, then ducked her head, shaking it in a quick negative, but not quite fast enough to hide the fact that her face had colored with a blush like a tomato on a seed catalog before she did.

The commander paused, studying the woman as his memory flashed data from files and conversations across his mind.

That's right. This was the Legionnaire named Rose the lieutenants had been talking about. As they had noted, she was attractive enough, with ash-blond hair and the kind of figure usually described as willowy. Of course, her tendency to try to crawl back inside her uniform like a turtle when spoken to did nothing to enhance her appearance.

Brandy had suggested skipping over her when her name came up on the duty roster, but Phule insisted on letting her take her turn at communications like everyone else. Now, looking at her bowed head and averted eyes, he wondered if he shouldn't have been more flexible. From the way she was acting, if a call came in she'd probably faint rather than answer it.

'Say, have you got change for a dollar?' he said, trying once more even if it meant ignoring the coins in his pocket.

The total reaction to his question consisted of a deepening of Rose's blush and another quick shake of her head.

Tenaciously the commander wandered closer, trying to edge into her line of vision.

'While we're talking, I'm curious about your reactions to my reorganization of the company. Do you see it as an improvement or just a waste of everyone's time?'

Rose turned her head away from him, but finally spoke.

'Mmphl gump hmm ol.'

Phule blinked a couple of time, then leaned closer.

'Excuse me . . . what was that again? I couldn't quite hear you.'

The Legionnaire seemed to collapse in on herself, answering only with a feeble shake of her head and a shrug.

The captain abandoned his efforts, realizing that to push further would be, at best, a cruelty.

'Well, I'll be off now,' he said, heading for the door. 'I'll only be a few minutes if anyone calls in.'

Rose relaxed a bit as he retreated, acknowledging his departure with nothing more than a vigorous nod.

As soon as he closed the door behind him, Phule puffed out his cheeks in a long exhale as if he had been holding his breath. He realized, with no small surprise, that dealing with someone as shy as Rose had the effect of making *him* nervous. The bashful Legionnaire's painful bashfulness made him immensely self-conscious, and throughout the 'conversation' he had found himself trying to figure out what he was saying or doing to make her so uncomfortable. All in all, he came out of it feeling like he was the one who shot Bambi's mother.

Lost in thought, Phule decided to take the stairs down to the vending-machine floor instead of waiting for an elevator.

It was easy to see why the lieutenants – and probably anyone else she had been assigned to – thought of her as a problem case. He would try to talk to Rose again, sometime when he wasn't so tired. Maybe if he was more alert he would be able to find a way to put her at her ease. As it was, it was hard to relax around someone who constantly reacted to you as if you were some kind of a monster.

As if on cue, a nightmare rose off the steps at his feet, stopping his descent – and his heart – in midstride.

'*Wha* . . . Oh! Jeez, Tusk-anini. You scared the . . . I didn't see you there.'

'Not apologize, Captain. Many scared by me when expected. You not expect see me, so scared.'

The big Voltron shook his head, though Phule noted he rotated it around his nose like a dog instead of pivoting his chin back and forth on his neck as a human would. There was no denying this nonhuman Legionnaire cut a formidable, if not terrifying figure under the best of circumstances, much less when encountered unexpectedly in a stairwell late at night.

Nearly seven feet tall with a massive, barrel chest, Tusk-anini towered over all but the tallest of humans, and even those had to look up to meet his black, marblelike eyes. His brown-olive skin more closely resembled an animal hide than human flesh in color and texture, particularly when complemented by substantial amounts of dull-black hair. Crowning the entire effect was a misshapen face only a mother – or, one assumes, another Voltron – could love. It was elongated and protruded into an unmistakable snout, and his two tusklike canines jutted from his lower jaw on either side of his nose, presumably the feature the Legionnaire took his name from.

'Incidentally I'm sorry we haven't spoken before,' the commander said, still struggling to regain his composure.

'Again, no apologize, Captain. Know you busy. Do good job, too. Will help any way you want.'

Phule only listened to the Voltron's response with half an ear, the rest of his attention being claimed by the stack of books in the stairwell.

'What were you doing here, anyway, Tusk-anini? Reading?'

The Legionnaire nodded, his head moving in exaggerated up-and-down motions like a horse fighting a bit.

'I no need much sleep, so read lots. Came here so roommate not have to sleep with light on in room.'

Phule squatted down to examine the books and looked up with new speculation in his eyes.

'These are pretty heavy reading. How come you brought so many?'

'Will read whole stack tonight.'

'The whole stack?'

Again the Voltron tossed his head in agreement.

'Read fast. Humans have much knowledge. Joined Legion learn human knowledge. Want be teacher after duty tour over.'

The commander hastily revised his estimation of the Voltron. It was so easy to assume that because he was big and spoke broken English, his intelligence was somewhat lower than that of the average Legionnaire. Once one was thinking about it, though, the fact that the Voltron had mastered an alien tongue well enough to speak it, however clumsily, rather than resort to the translators used by the Sinthians, said something about his mental ability . . . and his pride! It was obviously a matter of some pride to Tusk-anini that he could speak a human tongue at all, even if he did it so crudely he gave the impression of being stupid.

'Why don't you use the duty room of my penthouse?' Phule said, his mind racing over this new discovery. 'You'd be more comfortable, and I think the light's a lot better for reading.'

'Thank you, Captain. Most gen . . . erous.'

The Voltron stumbled a bit over the word, but began to gather up his books.

'Let me give you a hand there. You know, Tusk-anini, if you were serious about helping – above and beyond the call of duty, that is – there *is* something you might be able to give me a hand on.'

'What that?'

'I get lots of communications from Headquarters: copies of reports and modifications to the rules and regulations. Most of it is pointless paper shuffling, but I end up having to read it all to find the few items that *do* affect us, especially the changes in regulations. Now, if you could read through those for me, and pull the really important items for me to look at . . .'

The beep of Phule's wrist communicator interrupted his explanation. For a long moment he debated ignoring it to continue his conversation with Tusk-anini. Then he remembered that Rose would have to deal with it if he didn't, and reached for the activator button.

'You got Com Central here,' came a voice from the unit's speaker. 'What desperate situation can we alleviate for you this evening?'

The commander froze with his sign-on unuttered on his lips. Apparently whoever was calling in was also thrown by the response, as there was a pregnant pause before a reply came on the air.

'Is . . . is Captain Jester there?'

That voice was clearly recognizable to the commander as Brandy's, which meant the other voice had to be . . .

'The Great White Father, or Big Daddy, as he's sometimes known, is not available at the moment, Top. He's done tippee-toed off to feed his face, thereby giving lie to the belief that the man never eats or goes to the bathroom.'

'Who . . . who *is* this?' the voice of the company's first sergeant demanded.

'You got Rose at this end, Super Sarge . . . that's Rose as in Rose-alie? I am faithfully and alertly monitoring our dazzling communications network this evening, as is my sworn duty according to the duty roster you signed and posted this very morning.'

'That Rose?' Tusk-anini rumbled, but Phule waved him into silence as he listened for the next exchange.

'Rose?' Brandy's surprise was clear in her voice. 'I don't . . . Well, tell the captain when he gets back that I want to talk to him.'

'Hold on a second there, Brandy-Dandy. Before I tell him any such thing, perhaps you might want to reconsider your request? The Main Man is tryin' to keep going on potato chips and two hours' sleep, and I was kinda hoping he'd have a chance to fall on his face and die for a couple hours when he got back – that is, if there isn't an emergency hangnail or something to keep him up all night. You don't suppose that just maybe this busy old universe of ours could stagger along without him until morning, do you?'

'Rose, have you been drinking?'

Phule fought back a snicker and kept listening.

'Not a drop that wasn't as pure as a maiden's virtue, O Ramrod of the Masses . . . and don't you go trying to change the subject. Is it absolutely, positively cross-your-heart-and-kiss-your-elbow necessary that you talk to the Cheez Whiz tonight, or can I maybe leave him a love note for when he wakes up?'

'Well, Rose-alie. Since you put it that way, I suppose it can wait until the dawn's early light. I can work around it for now.'

'Whoa back there, Brandy-wine. You know, you've been keeping the pedal to the metal yourself there lately. Now, realizing that you have to be in tippee-top sergeant shape to kick some sense into our merry band when the officers aren't looking, don't you think it might be a good idea to catch a few winks yourself while the tide's out?'

'What are you? My mother?'

'Just your average loyal Legionnaire trying to do her best to help the wheels of our mighty war machine turning smoothly instead of goin' flat. While there may not be much that I can do personally to assist our fearless leader, I feel it behooves me to try to see to it that those who *can* make a difference stay on their feet and function at something approximating maximum efficiency. Get my drift, or am I goin' too fast for you?'

Brandy's laugh was clear over the communicator.

'All right. You win. I'll get some sleep and pick it up from here tomorrow. Good night now . . . Mother. Brandy out.'

'That Rose?' Tusk-anini said, repeating his earlier question as the communicator went dead.

'It sure as hell was.' Phule grinned. 'Come on up when you're ready, Tusk-anini. I've *got* to talk to that woman!'

The commander flew back up the stairs, nearly breaking down the door of the penthouse in his enthusiasm and eagerness.

'I overheard that last exchange, Rose,' he exclaimed, bursting into the room. 'You were fantastic!'

'Uggle mpt.'

Stunned, the captain stopped in his tracks and stared at the Legionnaire who a moment before had been verbally the height of confidence and wit. Head bowed and blushing, she was the same as she had been when he left the room.

'I . . . I'm sorry. Didn't mean to shout,' he said carefully. 'I just wanted to compliment you on your handling of Brandy's call.'

Rose blushed and shrugged, but kept her eyes averted.

'Well, I guess I'll follow your advice and get some sleep now. Oh. I told Tusk-anini he could do his reading up here. He'll be up in a few minutes.'

That got him a nod, but no more. After a moment's hesitation, he retreated through the connecting door into his bedroom.

Once within his sanctum, Phule leaned back against the now closed door and thought hard for several long minutes. Finally, with careful deliberation, he raised his hand and punched the proper key on his wrist communicator.

'This is the all-night voice of Com Central,' came the now familiar voice. 'How may we help you decide what to do with the rest of your life?'

'Rose? Captain Jester here,' Phule said, sinking into a chair with a smile.

'Why you High-ranking Rascal. Didn't you promise me you were going to go beddie-bye?'

'Truth to tell, Rosie, I just couldn't doze off until I told you one more time how much I appreciate your golden tones brightening the airwaves.'

'Well, thank you, Captain. My lonely night here at Com Central is brightened considerably by your tribute.'

'And also,' Phule continued quickly, 'I've just *got* to know why you're so much different than when we meet face-to-face.'

'Hmmm . . . I suppose I can light that one little match of enlightenment for you, since things are so slow tonight – but only if you promise to go right to bed when I'm done.'

'You've got a deal. So, what's the story?'

'Not much to tell, really. I had a terrible stutter when I was a kid. I mean, it could take me fifteen minutes just to say "Hello" to someone. The kids at school used to tease me something awful about it, so I got so's I wouldn't say anything just to keep them from laughing at me.'

The commander nodded his understanding, so wrapped up in Rose's tale he didn't pause to think that she couldn't see his reaction.

'Anyway, finally somebody got around to running some tests on me. They slapped some earphones on my head and turned up the tone until I couldn't hear myself talk, and you know what? Like that, I could talk as normal as anybody! It seemed the problem was that I was scared of the sound of my own voice! Once I found that out, things got a bit better, but I still had trouble talking in front of other people. So what I did was I got me a job in a little-bitty radio station, and let me tell you, I did everything. I was the DJ, the news and weather person, the ad person. Mostly, though, I did phone-in conversations with the listeners. Everything was fine, just as long as I didn't have to talk to folks face-to-face. I practically lived at that station for five years . . . until it got bought out and the new owner automated the whole shebang and fired me.'

'And so you joined the Legion,' Phule finished for her thoughtfully.

'Well, there were a few things I did first, but that's about the size of it. Now, don't you go feeling sorry for me, Big Daddy. I'm a grown girl now and I made up my own mind to join.'

'Actually,' the commander said, 'I was thinking seriously of offering you permanent duty at Com Central – that is, if you can forgo the pleasure of standing duty in the swamp.'

'Now, that's a thought. Let me mull it over and get back to you on that one. Meantime, I believe you were going to get some sleep? Seems to me I recall someone making me a promise to that effect a little while back.'

'Okay. I'll do it.' Phule grinned. 'Nice chatting with you . . . Mother. Jester out.'

Clicking off his communicator, the commander rose, stretched, and headed for the bed. All in all, it had been a pretty good day. It looked like he had found himself a new clerk *and* a communications specialist. If things worked out, he'd have to see about getting them each an extra stripe.

It wasn't until he had disrobed down to his shorts that he remembered that he never *had* gotten anything to eat.

9

Journal #104

The assigning of partners within the company was a milestone event. Though it actually occurred over the space of several weeks, the effects were apparent almost immediately.

While great care had been taken in deciding who would be paired with whom, and for the most part the choices accepted by the Legionnaires, it was expected that there would be some complaints and protests. Needless to say, in this, at least, my employer was not to be disappointed.

'Excuse me, Captain. Have you got a minute?'

Phule glanced up from his coffee to find two of his Legionnaires, Do-Wop and Sushi, fidgeting at his table. It seemed that his relaxing morning cup of coffee was not going to be so peaceful.

'Certainly. Would you like to have a seat?'

'This shouldn't take long,' Do-Wop said, shaking his head. He was of medium height and weight, with a coarse complexion and black curly hair that always looked like it needed washing. 'We were wondering if it was possible to be assigned different partners. I mean, there are still some of the crew who haven't been assigned . . . '

'Both of you feel this way?' the commander interrupted.

'That is correct, Captain,' Sushi confirmed crisply. A full head shorter than Do-Wop, he was a slightly built Oriental who dressed and held himself with meticulous precision. 'Our personalities and values are incompatible. I'm afraid that any permanent association between the two of us would prove to be detrimental to the smooth operation of the company.'

'I see.' Phule nodded grimly. 'Sit down, both of you.'

This time, it was a command, not an invitation, that was voiced, and the Legionnaires grudgingly selected chairs.

'Now then, tell me more about these incompatible values you're experiencing.'

The two men glanced at each other, each apparently reluctant to be the first to voice his complaints. It was Do-Wop who finally took the plunge.

'He's always talkin' down to me,' came the complaint. 'Just because he knows a lot of big words . . . '

The commander held up a restraining hand.

'I really don't think that the size of your partner's vocabulary should be a factor here.'

'It's not just that,' Do-Wop said, flushing slightly. 'He called me a crook – to my face!'

'I said you were a petty thief – and you are!' Sushi corrected sharply. 'Anyone who would jeopardize the unity of the company for nickel-and-dime – '

'There! You see?' the other appealed to his commander. 'How am I supposed to team up with someone who – '

'*Just a moment!*'

Phule's voice cracked like a whip, cutting through the argument and cowing both men into silence. He waited for a moment until they had leaned back in their chairs, then turned to Sushi.

'I'd like a little clarification here,' he said. 'How *exactly* would you define a *petty* thief?'

The Oriental glanced at the captain, then turned his gaze toward the ceiling.

'A petty thief is one who, in his criminal activities, takes risks disproportionate to the potential rewards.'

'Criminal activities!'

'Sit down, Do-Wop,' Phule ordered, keeping his eyes

on Sushi. 'If you can keep your mouth shut and listen, you just might learn something.'

The curly-haired Legionnaire sank slowly back into his chair, and the commander continued his line of questioning.

'If I understand you correctly, Sushi, your objection to Do-Wop is not the fact that he steals, but rather the scale he operates on.'

A faint smile played across Sushi's lips.

'That's right, Captain.'

'So tell us, what kind of reward do *you* figure would justify . . . what was that phrase? Oh yes . . . criminal activity?'

'Not less than a quarter of a million,' the Oriental said firmly and without hesitation.

Do-Wop's head came up like a shot.

'A quarter of a . . . Oh bullshit!'

The other two men ignored him.

'Of course,' Phule said levelly, 'eight or nine million would be even better.

'Of course.' Sushi nodded, locking gazes with his commander.

Do-Wop's head swiveled back and forth as he frowned at each of them in turn.

'What the hell are you guys talking about?' he demanded at last.

The Oriental broke off the staring match, shaking his head with a sigh.

'What Captain Jester is speaking of with polite circuitousness is something he has been careful not to acknowledge since he took command of our unit. Specifically that he and I have met prior to our enlistment . . . under social business situations.'

'You two know each other?'

'What is more,' Sushi continued, 'he is leaving it up to me whether or not to mention that I left the business community under a cloud of suspicion – a matter of embezzlement involving several million dollars.'

'It was never proven,' Phule said.

The Oriental smiled. 'Computers are marvelous devices, aren't they?'

'Wait a minute!' Do-Wop exploded. 'Are you trying to tell me you got nine million dollars?'

'I don't actually *have* it.' Sushi grimaced. 'It was eaten up by a series of . . . shall we say, bad investments.'

'Bad investments?'

'It's another term for gambling debts,' Phule informed him.

'Excuse me. Captain?'

The company's first sergeant had approached the table during their discussion.

'Uh . . . can it wait, Brandy?' Phule said, leaning back from the conversation. 'We're kind of in the middle of something here.'

'It'll just take a second,' the sergeant assured him, plowing on. 'Some of the troops were asking about that honor guard job, and I was wondering if there was any kind of an update.'

'I've got an appointment to see the governor next week,' the commander informed her. 'In the meantime, I've got to try to come up with some kind of leverage to make him see things our way.'

'Got it. Thanks, Captain. Sorry to interrupt.'

The distraction dealt with, Phule turned back to the situation at hand. Sushi was looking into the distance with the studied inscrutable expression of the Orient, while Do-Wop was staring at him with something akin to awe.

'All right. Listen up, now. Both of you. I didn't just pull names out of a hat when I made you two partners. The way I see it, you can both learn from each other.

'Sushi, you need to loosen up a little, and Do-Wop here is just the man to show you how to do things for the fun of it. And Do-Wop, maybe working with Sushi will help you to . . . raise your goals in life a little.

Anyway, I'd appreciate it if you'd both give this partnership a try for a while before deciding it won't work.'

'Hey! Are you saying you think I'm a thief, Captain?' Do-Wop bristled.

The commander fixed him with his coolest stare.

'I haven't wanted to mention it, Do-Wop, but there *have* been a number of reports of missing personal items in the company.'

'You can't blame that on me! The locks in this hotel are the pits! I could go through any of 'em without breaking a stride.'

'Really?' The commander seemed suddenly interested. 'Do you think you could teach the other Legionnaires how to do that?'

'Piece of cake.' The Legionnaire beamed. 'Like I said, anyone could do it.'

'Fine,' Phule said. 'Then I'll make an announcement and have any interested parties report to you for lessons tomorrow.'

'My pleasure, Captain.'

'Outside your room.'

Do-Wop blanched.

'My room?'

'That's right. I want you to teach them how to handle a variety of locks – doors, suitcases, the works – and you can use the locks on *your* room and personal effects to do it.'

'But . . . '

'Of course, if there's anything in your gear that might have "strayed" in over the last few weeks, it might be advisable to have it "stray" right back to its owners before you begin the lessons. Don't you agree?'

Do-Wop opened and shut his mouth several times like a beached fish, but no words came out.

'Come on, partner.' Sushi laughed, clapping him on the shoulder. 'I think we've been outflanked on this round. Looks like we'd better do a little lost-and-found work this afternoon.'

Not all the pairings were turbulent, but some were notably unusual. Perhaps the strangest of all came about after one particular off-duty incident in the hotel cocktail lounge.

While the Legionnaires tended to dominate the watering hole, there was always a smattering of civilians in attendance. Some were drawn by the media coverage the company had been getting and came to covertly gawk at the troops, while others were surprised to find so many uniforms in what they thought was a civilized lounge and simply refused to yield ground. For the most part, however, the two groups tended to steadfastly ignore each other.

Not that the Legionnaires were unaware of the civilians, mind you. Much of the loud banter and all of the roughhousing that had been developing within the group lately was left upstairs when they came in to drink. They were all still harboring painful memories of not being allowed in the premises before Phule's arrival and their subsequent relocation into the Plaza, and by unspoken agreement were on their best behavior when relaxing in the hotel lounge.

This particular evening, however, there was trouble in the air. A trio of civilian males were perched at the bar, and seemed to have their minds set on causing a disturbance. They were at that awkward age: too young to be responsible, but too big not to be taken seriously. The best guess was that they were students, possibly athletes, from the university on the other side of the settlement. Their clothes marked them as that, being too expensive for your average street tough. Then again, street toughs usually have a certain survival instinct, however loud they might appear at times. Long before reaching maturity they have lost any childhood belief in their own invulnerability and trust to their wits to avoid situations clearly hazardous to their health. Not so with the threesome in question.

They were into the forced hilarity so easily recognized in a group looking for attention, trouble, or both. They would put their heads together and whisper, all the while keeping their eyes on a specific table or person, then suddenly explode into gales of laughter, unnaturally loud so as to set them rocking dangerously back and forth on their stools. When no one came over to them to demand 'What's so funny?' they'd settle on another victim and repeat the process, a little louder this time.

The Legionnaires steadfastly ignored the theatrics, but without exchanging words all knew that something was going to have to be done about the interlopers. The problem was, no one seemed willing to make the first move. Not that they were afraid of the youths. While the noisemakers were healthy enough specimens that they might have given the Legionnaires a run for their money in a one-to-one tussle, the company had them outnumbered sufficiently that it would have been an easy matter to simply overwhelm them and toss them out onto the street . . . and serious consideration was being given to doing just that. Unfortunately none of the Legionnaires was eager to start the ball.

To gang up on the troublemakers, particularly with other civilians looking on, could only draw criticism on the company. If they challenged the intruders with even numbers, the age and 'military experience' of the Legionnaires would still cast them as the bullies of the situation, and if, in that situation, they lost the brawl, the loss of face would be untenable. What was worse, the company commander and his butler were in the lounge, holed up at a back table as they pored over their pocket computers. While the Legionnaires were reluctant to start a fight in front of civilians, they definitely didn't want to be the perpetrators of a military–civilian brawl under the appraising eyes of their own superior officer.

Consequently the company tightened their grips on their drinks and refused to acknowledge the taunting from the bar, all the while hoping that the management or the captain himself would intercede before things got too bad. Unfortunately the latter was in huddled conversation with Beeker, and both seemed oblivious to what was going on at the other end of the room.

Then Super Gnat walked in.

For a moment, the Legionnaires were frozen in silent terror. If it had been a western, someone would have shouted, 'Somebody fetch the marshal! There's gonna be trouble!' Since it was real life, however, they did the next best thing.

'Hey, Super Gnat!'

'Over here, Gnat!'

'Got an open chair here!'

The little Legionnaire stopped in her tracks, startled by the sudden eruption of invitations as her teammates tried desperately to head off the inevitable. Of course, it was all in vain.

'HELL, I'D BUY HER A DRINK, BUT SHE'S NOT TALL ENOUGH TO REACH THE TOP OF THE BAR!'

'HAW! HAW! HAW!'

Silence hung heavy in the room as the Gnat slowly turned her head to look in the direction of the noise.

'OH, LOOK! NOW SHE'S MAD! WHATCHA GONNA DO ABOUT IT, RUNT?'

The company was torn as the little Legionnaire's head sank into her shoulders and she began to stalk grimly across the room toward her tormentors. There was a tradition of not interfering in someone else's fight, but, for all her comic fierceness, Super Gnat was family, and no one wanted to stand by and watch her get hurt. There was no doubt in anyone's mind what the outcome of the brawl would be, since it was doubtful that the Gnat could take any one of the loudmouths, much less all three, as was clearly her intent.

There was a quiet scrape of chairs as the individual Legionnaires struggled with their decision. The only thing that was clear was that if the interlopers did serious damage to the Gnat, they were going to have trouble getting out of the lounge in one piece – public relations be hanged!

Suddenly a huge figure loomed out of the candlelit darkness and interposed its bulk between the civilians and the approaching Super Gnat.

'Ummm . . . Gnat?' Tusk-anini rumbled in his voice that was at once rasping and melodic. 'Captain says tell you . . . if you bust up place, you pay . . . all damages.'

The little Legionnaire pivoted around, her eyes seeking the company commander to protest such a charge. While she looked for Phule, her opponents looked at the figure between them and their intended prey.

As has been noted before, Voltrons are impressive if encountered by the light of day and one is expecting it. In a dimly lit cocktail lounge with a low ceiling, it can give the impression that part of the wall decided to walk up to your stool . . . if a wall had a large, misshapen head complete with tusks, and matted dark hair that ran down the back of its neck.

The three troublemakers tried to stand up, only to discover they already had performed that act without thinking when the apparition appeared. Which is to say, they became aware that they weren't sitting down . . . Tusk-anini was really that big!

'Umm . . . are you with her?' one of them managed at last.

'What he's trying to ask,' inserted another, 'is whether we have to fight you if we take her on?'

The Voltron reacted to this by retreating a step in shocked surprise.

'Her? No . . . she no need my help. She meaner than me . . . lot meaner!'

As one, the trio swallowed hard and looked at the Super Gnat again.

'Want advice?' Tusk-anini pressed eagerly. 'Leave now. If no, then somebody get hurt . . . maybe bad.'

There was no mistaking the open sincerity and concern in the Voltron's voice, though his normal peaceful nature was harder to detect. Suddenly aware of their own mortality, the cowed youths threw some money on the bar and beat a hasty retreat, evacuating the premises before the Gnat managed to catch Phule's eye, the latter notable being engrossed in conversation again.

After the 'Super Gnat in the Lounge' episode, it was only natural that she and Tusk-anini be teamed as partners. The full effect that the fiery little Gnat and the gentle giant would have on each other was not even suspected until several days later. Unlike the lounge incident, there was no foreshadowing or warning of the explosion before it happened.

The Legionnaires had taken to using the Plaza restaurant as an after-hours gathering place for reading, quiet conversation, and any other activity requiring more space than a hotel room, and more light than was provided in the lounge. There were usually a couple dozen people there, and that was what Brandy was looking for when she stopped in for a late night cup of coffee and a little relaxing conversation before turning in.

Scanning the room with her mug in hand, her eye fell on Tusk-anini poring over a stack of papers.

'Hey, Tusk!' she said, plopping down at his table. 'How're things shaping up between you and the runt? Won't she let you work in the room?'

The Voltron raised his head and regarded her with his black marble eyes.

'Brandy. No call partner runt. She no like.'

Taken aback, the first sergeant tried to laugh off the rebuff.

'Hell . . . no offense meant. I know the runt's sensitive about her height, but – '

'NO CALL PARTNER RUNT!'

The Voltron rose angrily to his feet, and Brandy was aware of heads turning in their direction.

'Cool down, Tusk,' she cautioned. 'What's bothering you, anyway?'

'SHE HEAR YOU, SHE GET MAD. YOU HAVE TO FIGHT HER. MAYBE HURT. YOU NO CALL HER RUNT!'

The whole room was watching the confrontation of the company's Gargantuans now, and the top sergeant was suddenly aware of her status and authority being challenged.

'Look, Tusk-anini!' she snarled. 'Nobody tells me how to talk – not even the captain! If I want to call the Gnat a runt, I will . . . and nothing you can do or say – '

The Voltron's bunched-up fist thudded down on top of her head, surprising her and knocking her sprawling backward off her chair.

The others in the room watched in stunned silence as their most pacifistic teammate loomed over the fallen sergeant, trembling with rage.

'I WARN YOU, BRANDY. NO CALL PARTNER RUNT!'

It had been a long time since anyone had challenged Brandy physically, but some things you never forget. Shaking her head to clear it, she groped about and found a chair leg.

'I believe this is my dance!' she hissed, and came off the floor at the Voltron.

Phule sighed and checked his uniform when the flurry of pounding erupted on the door of his suite.

'Come in, Super Gnat,' he called as the assault began anew.

The smallest company member exploded into the room, red-faced and oblivious to the verbal clue that she was expected.

'Captain! Did you know that my partner's down in

our room with a bandage on his head? That the doc says he might even have a minor concussion?'

'I'm aware of that.'

'And did you know that bitch Brandy did it to him?'

'I'd heard that, too.'

'Well, what are you going to do about it?'

Phule regarded her levelly.

'Nothing.'

'*Nothing?* But she – '

'Since I figure doing nothing is better than seeing your partner brought up on charges.'

Super Gnat blinked, hesitating in her tirade.

'Charges? I don't understand, Captain.'

'Sit down, Gnat,' Phule instructed calmly. 'If I take official notice of what happened, then I'll have to acknowledge all the eyewitness accounts of Tusk-anini launching an attack on Sergeant Brandy . . . an attack that ended when she knocked him cold defending herself. I don't want to have to do that, so unless that bitch, as you called her, decides to press charges, I'm willing to pretend the whole thing never happened.'

The Gnat frowned fiercely for a moment, then shook her head.

'I can't believe it, Captain. They've got to be lying. Tusk-anini is the gentlest soul in this whole company. What'd he want to take off after Brandy for?'

'Let me ask you a question,' the commander said slowly. 'Would you want to tangle with Brandy?'

The little Legionnaire twisted her mouth into a grimace.

'That's one I'd walk around if there was any way,' she admitted. 'Even if I kept my head and remembered what I learned in those classes I was tellin' you about, she'd probably peel me like a grape. That's one mean lady.'

Phule nodded sagely.

'That's what the fight was about.'

'Sir?'

'It seems that Brandy was referring to you in less than complimentary terms, and your partner was afraid that if she talked like that in front of you, you'd take her on and probably get hurt.'

'Shoot. You can say that again. Why, she could . . .'

The Gnat broke off in midsentence as the implications sank in.

'Wait a minute. Are you sayin' old Tusk took her on because of me?'

'That's what the witnesses say. It seems he figured he had a better chance against Brandy than you would. Of course, he doesn't have your training. He tried to do it on guts and enthusiasm.'

Super Gnat shook her head ruefully.

'That don't cut it in heavy traffic,' she said. 'Believe me, I know!'

'He was doing what he thought he had to, to protect his partner,' Phule said. 'I might suggest that you consider doing the same.'

'Sir?'

'Think about it, Gnat. Your partner, who never raised a hand in anger before, is getting into fights to protect you from your temper. If you can't control yourself for your own sake, you might think about him before you fly off the handle next time.'

A quiet knock at the door interrupted them. At Phule's summons, the company's first sergeant eased into the room.

'Evening, Captain. Hi, Gnat.'

Super Gnat assumed the relaxed warmth of an icicle, but Phule was unruffled.

'Good evening, Top,' he said. 'I assume you're here about Tusk-anini?'

'Oh no . . . well, in a way, I guess. Actually I was looking for Super Gnat. The troops said she was headed this way.'

'You found me.'

'Well, the way it is, Gnat, I think I owe you an apology.'

'An apology?'

'Yeah. I've been thinking about what happened, and the truth of the matter is, I was out of line. Not that I meant any harm, mind you, but I guess I never stopped to consider how much the teasing really bothers you. Heck, if anyone should know what it's like to be needled about size, it's me. Anyway, I should know better, so I want to apologize. I'll try to watch it in the future.'

'I appreciate that, Brandy. I really do. I think Tusk is the one you should be apologizing to, though.'

Brandy flashed a quick grin.

'I was down there first. He kept insisting I owed you the apology, not him.'

'Oh.'

'Anyway, I'm apologizing to you both. No hard feelings?'

Super Gnat accepted the extended hand and they both shook solemnly.

'Well, that's all I wanted. Maybe when you get done here you can come on down to my room, Gnat. I have a few tips on handling size jokes I'd like to share with you over a brew.'

'I'm pretty much done here,' the little Legionnaire said, raising her eyebrows in question at the commander.

'Just one more thing while you're here, Gnat. Sorry to jump subjects on you, but what's your opinion of Sergeant Escrima's classes on stick fighting?'

Super Gnat chewed her lip slightly before answering.

'Truth to tell, Captain, I don't think they're doin' much good at all. The sergeant knows his stuff, but he's not that good an instructor. He just plain goes too darn fast for most of the folks to figure out what he's doin' . . . 'cept the ones like me who have had some martial arts training before and are just watching for the variations.'

'That's the way I see it, too,' Phule said. 'If you're agreeable, I'd like you to take over the classes.'

'Me? Shoot, I don't know that much about stick forms.'

'What I want you to do is to take private lessons from Escrima, then teach what you learn to the rest of the company. If nothing else, it might keep them from teasing you quite so much if they see what you can do in a formal class situation.'

'I'll give it a try, Captain,' the Gnat said doubtfully, then her face split in a quick grin. 'Tell you what. I'll do it if you give me some private lessons in fencing. Deal?

'Deal,' the commander said. 'Now, both of you get out of here and let me get some work done.'

10

Journal #111

While the changes in the Legionnaires' views of themselves and each other were remarkable, the reversal of the attitudes toward the company on the part of the local citizens was as, or more, noteworthy. Perhaps the most radical change was on the part of the head of the police, Chief Goetz.

'Really appreciate your stopping by, Chief,' the company commander said, shaking that notable's hand crisply as they met in the Plaza lobby.

'Well, I figured if you were nice enough to invite me along for this special weapons demo you were getting, the least I could do was offer you a ride,' Goetz said. 'Oh, by the way, I never got around to thanking you for including me in that spread your chef cooked up. It was delicious . . . even if I'm not sure what I was eating half the time.'

'To tell you the truth,' Phule said, grinning, 'neither did I. I figured it would be rude to ask, if not flat-out dangerous to your health. Escrima has a record of being more than a little touchy about his cooking. It *did* taste great, though, didn't it?'

'It certainly did,' the chief agreed. 'I was particularly fond of the roast pig. Of course, I was struck by the coincidence of the report that hit my desk of three pigs that turned up missing from the university's animal husbandry department the day before.'

Phule cursed mentally. He hadn't found out until the day *after* the feast that Chocolate Harry had been more than a little loose in his acquisition of supplies for Escrima's efforts. If he had known, he would have refrained from inviting the chief of police, or at least insisted that the pigs be carved into less recognizable bits before serving. Until now, however, he had thought the dish had passed unnoticed.

'If you'll just give us a few days,' he said stiffly, 'I'm sure we can produce the receipts for those particular items.'

'A few days?' Geotz's eyebrows shot up. 'That supply sergeant of yours must be slipping if it'd take him more than a couple hours to crank out some forged sales slips.'

'Now, look, Chief . . . '

'Relax, Captain,' the policeman said with a sudden, impish grin. 'I'm just pulling your chain a little. Those university students liberate enough stuff from the settlement for their fraternity initiations and scavenger hunts and what all, I'm sure it would take more than a couple of pigs to even up the score. I just wanted you to know we weren't totally . . . What in the hell is *that*?'

Phule looked where the chief was pointing and flashed a sudden smile.

'That? Oh, that's just one of our mobilization experiments. It's working out surprisingly well.'

The object of their attention was Spartacus. The blue-collared Sinthian was poised on his glide board at the top of the long, curved flight of stairs that led from the Plaza's mezzanine to the main lobby. As they watched, he shifted his weight forward, plunging the board down the stairs. Neither the curve of his course nor the frightening acceleration seemed to bother the Sinthian as he rode the glide board down a level and across the lobby, skillfully weaving it around a group of Legionnaires who were standing there in conversation. The Legionnaires didn't bother to look around as he swept past, ignoring him, as did the hotel staff at the main desk.

'Seems like folks are pretty used to these goings-on,'

Goetz said dryly, noting the lack of reaction in the lobby.

'If we encourage him, he just starts showing off,' Phule said. 'When that happens, things usually get broken. He's really very good on that thing, though . . . practically lives on it. I'm surprised you haven't seen him before. He's usually in the park across the street every evening matching stunts with the kids that hang out there.

'Excuse me, Captain?'

Phule glanced around, then drew himself up and returned the smart salute being given him by the company's supply sergeant, who had managed to approach unnoticed.

'Good morning, C.H. We were just talking about you a second ago. What's the problem?'

'No problem, Captain. It's getting on toward time for the weapons demo, and I thought I'd offer you a lift on my hawg.'

'Not this time, Sergeant. Chief Goetz here is already giving me a ride . . . Oh, excuse me. You two have met, haven't you?'

Harry's eyes slid sideways to meet the policeman's stare.

'I . . . I've sure heard about Chief Goetz.'

'And I've heard about you, Sergeant,' Goetz returned with a tight-lipped smile. 'Don't let us keep you. I'm sure you and I will be . . . talking someday.'

'Harry *does* have a point, though,' Phule interceded quickly. 'We should get going ourselves.'

The new facilities for the Legionnaires were nearing completion, and everyone was looking forward to moving back in with eager anticipation. One of the first things to be completed, after the confidence course, that is, was the firing range, and that was where the company assembled for the demonstration.

The sales rep from Phule-Proof Munitions had an

impressive array of weaponry, and a snappy line of patter to go with it, as he worked his way down the display. Aside from his tendency to refer to the company commander as 'Willie,' a practice which invariably caused Phule to wince and everyone else, particularly the chief of police, to smile, the salesman's knowledge and skills of his little bundles of death quickly earned the attention and respect of the entire assemblage.

The high point of the demonstration came when the Legionnaires were invited to come down from their bleachers and try some of the weapons themselves. For a while, the sergeants had their hands full keeping the troops' enthusiasm from turning them into a mob, but eventually things got sorted out and soon the air was filled with the *crack* and *boom* of firing as the Legionnaires gleefully shredded and blew apart assorted targets.

'Quite an assortment,' Chief Goetz said, plopping down on a bleacher seat next to the commander.

'Yes. I thought you'd find it interesting. Especially some of the plastic and rubber "Mercy Loads" they've been developing.'

The policeman grimaced. 'Of course, it's nice if the suspect is wearing some kind of eye protection when you open up on him. If I had my way, we'd stick with either holding our fire or shooting for keeps rather than trying to kid ourselves that we can hit someone without hurting them. I've noticed my troops shoot a lot better on the range than they do on the street. Truth is, under pressure they're almost as bad shots as your crew seem to be normally.'

It was apparent that the Legionnaires were far from crack shots. Whatever damage was being done to the targets was more the result of the massive amount of firepower being launched downrange than from any degree of precision in its placement.

Now it was Phule's turn to grimace.

'I've seen worse, though it's hard to recall offhand anytime I've seen more lousy shots gathered in one place. More important, I've *taught* worse marksmen how to shoot. I almost canceled this demonstration until I had more time to work with the troops, but this is one of Phule-Proof's touring demos, and it was either nail it when it was available or wait a couple months until another one was in the area. Now it's going to be a pain to keep the troops away from the full automatics and laser sights long enough to drum the basics into their heads.'

Goetz nodded, not taking his eyes off the firing line.

'Sounds like we're in agreement there, Captain. If you don't teach 'em right to start with, they'll always rely on firepower and gimmicks instead of learning how to shoot.'

The commander cranked his head around and stared at the police chief for several moments.

'Maybe I shouldn't ask this, Chief,' he said at last, 'but I can't help but notice that your attitude toward me and my Legionnaires has mellowed considerably since our first meeting.'

'Well, I'll tell you, Mr. Phule. I may be hardheaded from time to time, but mostly I try to keep an open mind. Most of my beat patrolmen have been pretty open with their praise for your troops. It seems that *somebody* in your outfit has taken to monitoring the police band, and a few of your boys have shown up at some of the stickier calls we've had over the last few weeks. The way I hear it, they don't interfere or get in the way, but we both know there are times when having a couple extra uniforms around, no matter what color they are, goes a long way toward keeping a crowd from getting too rambunctious.'

'That fits,' the commander said. 'I've always felt that most people have a basically good self-image. Once my troops are convinced that they *can* make a difference, it's not surprising that they try to make a difference for the better.'

The chief held up a restraining hand.

'Now, don't get me wrong. Nobody's kidding anybody that your crew was in the choir over the stable at the first Christmas, but they've earned enough goodwill in the department to have me cut them – and you – a little bit of slack.'

'Not enough slack, I notice, to keep you from filing reports with Legion Headquarters every time one of my crew puts on a command performance at the station,' Phule observed wryly.

Goetz sighed and shrugged.

'That's the result of a direct request from your Headquarters, son. Came in about the same time you arrived. I don't mean to butt into your business, but it would appear that somebody in the Legion's upper echelons doesn't like you much. Leastwise, they're watching real close for you to make a mistake.'

The commander frowned. 'I didn't realize that. Appreciate the warning, though.'

'Warning?' The chief's face was a picture of innocence. 'I was just responding to an official request for information from one of the residents in the community I am sworn to serve and protect.'

'Got it.' Phule nodded. 'Thanks, anyway . . . unofficially. I wonder if it would be possible for you to – '

'*Captain!*'

There was no denying the urgency in the voice that hailed him.

'Excuse me, Chief. What is it. Tusk-anini?'

'Spartacus going to shoot gun!'

A quick glance at the firing line was sufficient to confirm the information. The Sinthian was perched on his glide board, a shotgun tucked under his spindly arm, as Chocolate Harry explained the weapon to him with vastly exaggerated gestures.

'So I see,' the commander said. 'It seems, however, that the situation is being handled by – '

'Not know Newton's third law physics?'

Phule frowned. 'What law?'

'Isn't that the one that . . . ' Chief Goetz started, but the sentence was never finished.

KA-BOOM!

The Sinthian's skill on his glide board was such that instead of being knocked off the device by the shotgun's recoil, he spun violently around and around like a top . . . though, if asked, those in the near vicinity might have preferred the former option. Anyone who had not recent occasion to refer to or recall Newton's third law of physics was now graphically reminded that, indeed, for every action there is an equal and opposite reaction! Educated or not, good marksmen or not, there was nothing wrong with the Legionnaires' sense of survival, and in a twinkling everyone present was either crouched behind cover or flat on the ground, including the observers in the bleachers.

Fortunately Spartacus was only firing single loads while testing the shotgun, so the mayhem was more comical than anything. Had he been utilizing the belt-feed auto-loader option, the results might not have been so humorous.

'Seems to me,' Chief Goetz drawled, raising his head to look at Phule, 'the kick on that weapon's a tad strong for that fellah – at least while he's standing on that board, anyway.'

'The same thing just occurred to me,' the commander said, peering over the bleacher seat he was flattened behind. 'It's a problem, though. The Sinthians' eyestalks keep them from using a weapon with enough accuracy to be effective. That's why we were trying them on shotguns. I'd say to hell with it and issue them fully automatic weapons, but I'm afraid that would only compound the recoil problem.'

'What you need is something that doesn't have much

of a kick.' Goetz frowned. 'Have you thought of trying them on splat guns?'

'Splat guns?'

'Compressed-air guns that shoot little paint balls. Some of the guys in the department use 'em in a weekend war-game club they belong to.'

'Oh. Those things.' Phule shook his head. 'I always thought they were more expensive toys than weapons.'

'Some of those "toys" are fully automatic and have a muzzle velocity of over four hundred feet per second,' the chief informed him.

'Really?' The commander raised his eyebrows in surprise. 'I didn't know that. Still, I'm not sure what good it would do to hit someone with a paint ball in combat, no matter how fast it was going.'

'Well' – Goetz grinned wolfishly, easing himself back onto his bleacher seat – 'I just might be able to run down a source for some HE paint ball loads.'

'High explosives?' Phule was definitely interested now. 'Are those legal?'

'It may come as a surprise to you, Mr Phule, but every so often the police are aware of items available that do not conform exactly to the letter of the law.'

'Uh-huh. And what is this information going to cost me?'

'Consider it a favor,' the chief said. 'Of course, it might be nice if you did me a little favor in return – like, say, maybe loaning the department that cook of yours for our annual banquet that's coming up next month?'

'I think we could clear that under Community Relations.' The commander grinned. 'In the meantime, I want to see if there isn't *some* way we can get those completely legal shotguns to work for us.'

'If you don't mind,' Goetz said, sliding off the seat to lie prone once more, I'll watch your experiments from here.'

As it turned out, Spartacus declined to make a second attempt at handling the weapon, preferring to stay with his beloved glide board rather than abandon it for firepower.

Undaunted, Chocolate Harry pressed the shotgun on Louie, the aristocratic Sinthian. Unable to match Spartacus' expertise on the glide board, Louie had long since abandoned his efforts to master the device, claiming it was beneath him, so the unstable footing provided by that vehicle did not present a problem. Anchored firmly on the ground, or, eventually, in the sidecar of Harry's hawg, he was more than able to control the weapon, or at least approximate control sufficiently for Phule to allow him to continue using it.

As a crowning touch, one of the Legionnaires found an antique German helmet and cut holes in the top for Louie's eyestalks. The picture they presented, Chocolate Harry astride his massive hover cycle with Louie perched in the sidecar, eyestalks protruding from the top of an old helmet and clutching his belt-fed shotgun, made more than one citizen stop in their tracks for a second look. In fact, Chief Goetz commented at one point that the appearance of that particular team at the scene of a crime was a greater deterrent than an entire squad of patrolmen.

Strangely enough, his new acceptance by the company seemed to ease Louie's distaste for his lower-class fellow Sinthian, to a point where he actually entered into a business partnership with Spartacus to introduce the glide boards to their home planet. Spartacus recorded a series of demonstration and instructional tapes, while Louie used his family's contacts and influence to cut red tape for the necessary licenses and business permits. The entire company chipped in for the start-up funding, a gesture nobody regretted, as it was to earn them profits in the future far in excess to their initial investment.

As the teams and partnerships among the Legionnaires solidified, so, too, did their acceptance of themselves and each other. Countless feuds and disagreements were set aside as a new feeling of unity flourished within the company. Simply put, as each individual conquered his or her own feelings of inferiority or inadequacy, he or she in turn grew more tolerant of the shortcomings of the others.

For some, however, acceptance did not come so easily, occasionally pushing them to extreme measures.

It was the company's last night at the Plaza. The construction on their new facilities was complete, and orders had been passed to pack in preparation for relocation in the morning. By unspoken agreement, as they completed their packing most of the Legionnaires gathered in the Plaza lounge for a minor going-away celebration. Of course, there were not enough seats to accommodate the whole company at once, but the mood was jovial and most of the individuals were content to lean against the walls or sit on the floor in groups, or wander casually from conversation to conversation. As is common in such social, military gatherings, more than a few conversations turned into one-downmanship competitions as individual Legionnaires complained and bragged about who had stood the worst duty in the course of their careers.

'. . . you think swamps are bad?' Brandy grinned, gesturing for attention with her drink. 'Listen, once I was assigned to a crew that had to guard – get this – a bloody *iceberg*! Never did find out why, but it was impossible to stay warm with the gear we were issued, unless you found someone to be *real* close to, if you get my drift. After a few weeks of freezing your tutu off, I'll tell you, some of the *ugliest* Legionnaires started looking pretty good!'

The knot of Legionnaires laughed appreciatively but briefly, as each leaned forward in eagerness to be next.

'Talk about hard duty,' Super Gnat proclaimed, beating the others off the line. 'My second assignment or was it my third? . . . whatever! Anyway, the CO had a real thing against short people, and, of course, the only way I get to play basketball is if they use me for the ball. So she calls me into her office one day and says – '

'I'll tell you what rough duty is!'

Annoyed at the interruption in midstory, the group glanced up to find Lieutenant Armstrong weaving his way unsteadily in their direction.

'It . . . isn't a matter of *where* you stand duty or *what* you've gotta do. When you're serving under a freaking ghost . . . and that ghost is your . . . father *and* one of the most highly decorated soldiers ever, then you . . . gotta spend your whole life trying to prove you're one tenth as good as everyone says he was. *That's* rough duty! I only wish the sonofabitch had stayed alive long enough to make a mistake.'

The Legionnaires glanced at each other uncomfortably as Armstrong tried to get his lips and glass coordinated.

'Umm . . . don't you think it's time you got some sleep, Lieutenant?' Brandy said carefully, breaking the silence.

Armstrong peered at her owlishly, blinking fiercely as he tried to get his eyes in focus.

'You're . . . right, Sergeant Brandy. Mustn't say or do anything unbecom . . . unbecoming an officer I . . . think I'll get some fresh air first, though. Good . . . night, everybody.'

The lieutenant drew himself erect and attempted a salute that came close to missing before lurching off toward the street door, steadying himself occasionally with a hand on the wall.

The group watched him go in silence.

'An officer and a gentleman . . . God help us,' someone said, raising his drink in a mock toast.

'Umm . . . I hate to say it,' Super Gnat drawled, 'but it's awful late for him to be walking the streets in that condition.'

'So what? He's a jerk!'

'Yeah, but he's *our* jerk. I'd just as soon not see anything happen to him while he's wearing the same uniform I am. C'mon, Gnat. Let's give the man a fighter escort until he crashes.'

Leaning against the wall, unnoticed behind a potted plant, Phule smiled to himself at the exchange. More and more, the Legionnaires were starting to watch out for each other. Some of it was camaraderie, some a general defense of the company's reputation, but it all added up to *esprit de corps*. If this kept up, then eventually . . .

The beep of his wrist communicator interrupted his thoughts.

'Mother?' he said, keying the unit on. 'What are you doing upstairs? Come on down and – '

'I think we got a problem, Big Daddy,' the communications specialist announced, cutting him short. 'The chief of police is on the line for you. Says it's urgent.'

Phule experienced a sinking feeling in his stomach that had nothing to do with drinking.

'Patch him through.'

'Here he is. You're on, Chief.'

'Willard? You'd better get down here, pronto. A couple of your boys are in a jam, and there's no way I can cover for them.'

'What's the charge?' the commander said, knowing full well what the answer was going to be.

'It seems they were caught red-handed on a breaking-and-entering,' the police chief informed him. 'That might not be so bad, but it was the governor's house they were breaking into, and he caught them himself!'

11

Journal #112

While it may seem that my employer has a greater tendency than most to 'buy his way' out of problems and dilemmas, I have noticed that he invariably draws the line when it comes to dealing with politicians. This is not, as it might be supposed, the result of any distaste on his part for the influence of 'special interest groups,' nor does he subscribe to the 'An honest politician is one who, once he's bought, stays bought!' school of thought. Rather, it stems from a stubborn belief on his part that elected officials should not have to be 'paid extra' to do their jobs.

As he puts it, 'Waitresses and card dealers are paid minimum wage in anticipation *of their income being supplemented by tips, so if one doesn't tip them, one is, in effect, robbing them of their livelihood. Public officials, on the other hand, are* expected *to live within their salaries, so any effort on their part to obtain additional earnings for the simple performance of their duties is extortion at its worst and should be a jailable offense!'*

Needless to say, this attitude does nothing toward increasing his popularity with the politicians he comes in contact with.

Governor Wingas, or Wind-gust, as he was known to his rivals, could not suppress a feeling of smug excitement as the commander was ushered into his study. Ever since reading in the media that there was a megamillionaire in residence in the settlement, the governor had been racking his brain for a way to entice a fat 'campaign contribution' out of that noteworthy.

All party and luncheon invitations had gone unanswered, however, as had his personal notes soliciting contributions and hinting vaguely at 'beneficial legislation' for the Legionnaires.

Now, at long last, he was not only getting a chance to meet the munitions heir, but that chance was coming under circumstances that could only be viewed as 'favorable for negotiation.' In layman's terms, with two Legionnaires under lock and key, he had their commander over a barrel and had no intention of settling cheaply . . . or easily.

'So, we finally meet, Mr. Phule . . . or should I call you Captain Jester? The governor smiled, leaning back in the leather chair behind his desk as the commander settled in one of the guest chairs.

'Make it "Captain Jester," ' Phule said, not returning the smile. 'This isn't a social call. I'm here on official Legion business.'

'That's right.' Wingas nodded, enjoying himself. 'You're the one who doesn't accept social invitations. Well, then, shall we get down to business? What can I do for you . . . as if I didn't know. Frankly I expected you sooner than this.'

'I had some other stops to make first,' the commander returned flatly. 'As to what you can do for me, I'm here to ask you to drop the charges against the two Legionnaires currently residing in jail.'

The governor shook his head.

'I couldn't do that. The men are criminals. I caught them myself outside the window of this very room. No, sir. I can't see letting them go free to steal again . . . unless, of course, you can give me . . . shall we say, a *reason* to show leniency?'

'I can give you two reasons, Governor,' Phule said through tight lips, 'though I expect only one will really matter to you. First of all, the men weren't breaking into your home . . . '

'Perhaps you didn't hear me, Captain.' The governor smiled. 'I caught them myself!'

'. . . they were breaking *out* of your home,' the commander finished, as if he hadn't been interrupted. 'You see, my Legionnaires are very eager to have a chance at that honor guard job you've given to the Regular Army, and those two men, Do-Wop and Sushi, broke in here trying to find something I could use as leverage to force you to give us that chance.'

Phule paused to shake his head.

'In some ways, it's my fault. I talked about looking for leverage while they were listening, and they took it on themselves to try to get it for me. Anyway, they brought what they found to me, and I ordered them to put it back. They did, and you caught them as they were *leaving*. In short, there was no crime, which should be all the justification you need to drop the charges.'

'No crime!' the governor snorted. 'Even if I believed this yarn of yours, Captain – which I don't – they *still* broke into my home. Twice, from what you say.'

The commander flashed a tight smile, his first since entering the room.

'Make up your mind, Governor. Either you believe me or you don't. In case you're having trouble making up your mind, however . . . ' He stretched out a hand, pointing at the governor's desk. 'Bottom drawer on the left, in a file labeled "Old Business." *That's* what they were replacing. Convinced?'

The governor's smile dropped away like supporters after a losing election.

'If you mean . . . '

'Frankly, Governor,' Phule continued, 'I don't care what your sexual preferences are, or whom or what you practice them with – though I usually confine my own leanings to our own species – much less whether or not you keep pictures for souvenirs. All I want is my men back. Of course, if their case *should* go to court, I'd be obligated to testify in their behalf including describing in lurid, graphic, the-media-will-love-it detail the pictures they were supposed to have stolen.'

'You couldn't prove a thing,' the governor snapped, paling. 'Unless . . . are you saying you kept copies of those pictures?'

'I could bluff and say yes,' Phule said, 'but the truth is, I didn't. Like I say, Governor, I had no intention of using that information, which is why I told my men to put them back. Still, a politician's reputation is a delicate thing, isn't it? The faintest shadow of scandal can ruin it, whether it's ever actually proved or not. The question as I see it, is whether or not prosecuting my men is worth jeopardizing your political career.'

Wingas glared at Phule for several moments, then snatched up his phone and angrily punched in a number.

'Chief Goetz, please. Governor Wingas calling . . . Hello, Chief? This is the governor. I . . . She's fine, thank you . . . Look, Chief, I've decided to drop the charges against those two Legionnaires you're holding . . . That's right. Let them go . . . Never mind why! Just do it!'

He slammed the phone down with a bang and stared out the window, waiting for his temper to cool before turning to the commander once more.

'All right, Captain Jester. That's settled. Now, if there's nothing else, I'll ask you to excuse me. I believe I have some pictures to burn.'

To his surprise, the Legionnaire made no motion to rise.

'As a matter of fact, while I'm here, there *is* another matter I'd like to discuss with you, Governor.'

'There is?'

'That's right. The honor guard job I mentioned earlier?'

'Oh yes. The one you weren't going to use the pictures as leverage to get.'

With admirable speed, the governor put his anger

behind him. Politics was no place for anyone who couldn't change gears swiftly, or who yielded to the self-indulgent pleasure of holding a grudge against someone who was a potential ally or contributor. For a moment, Wingas allowed himself to hope that there might be a contribution in this, after all!

'What it is, Governor Wingas,' Phule said, 'is I think we may be in a situation where we might be of mutual benefit to each other.'

The governor's hopes solidified into reality. He had heard enough pitches for favoritism that he easily recognized the roundabout approach. It was strange, but people rarely came right out with their requests . . . or offers. You simply had to wait them out while they worked themselves up to their final approach. The only question left in his mind at this point was how large a contribution Phule was prepared to offer. That, and how long it was going to take him to get to the bottom line.

'That's what politics is all about,' he said cagily.

The commander was looking pointedly around the room, his eyes dwelling on the leather-bound books and original artwork that festooned the walls.

'This certainly is a nice place you have here, Governor.'

'Thank you. We . . . '

'Though probably not as nice as that town house over by Altair where your wife is living.'

Despite his resolve to be patient, the governor felt a stab of annoyance at the mention of his personal holding . . . and of his wife.

Yes, yes. Now then, just how large a campaign contribution are we talking about here?'

'Contribution?' Phule frowned. 'I think there's some mistake here, Governor. I wasn't talking about making a contribution to your . . . campaign. Not when you're already living beyond your means.'

Wingas purpled. 'Who says I'm living beyond my means?' he demanded.

'Not "who," Governor,' the commander said. 'More like "what" – specifically your current loan application. Frankly, if you don't get it, I'd be surprised if you stayed out of bankruptcy for the rest of the year.'

'That's just a consolidation loan, so I can . . . Hey! Wait a minute! That information is supposed to be confidential! What right have you got to go poking around my personal finances?'

'Oh, the information is confidential, all right,' Phule assured him. 'I just happen to be on the board of the bank that's reviewing your application, and in that capacity I'm supposed to use my best judgment in appraising the risk involved in major loans, which I'm afraid your loan qualifies as.'

The governor slumped back in his chair as if he had been struck.

'Are you trying to tell me that unless I give the Legion the honor guard contract, you'll veto my loan approval?'

'Let's just say it would be difficult not to factor it into my assessment of your judgment and reliability.' The commander smiled.

'I see.'

'However, I'd like to clarify something you just said. I'm not asking you to hand the Legion the contract on a platter. Just give them an equal chance with the Regular Army to *earn* the assignment.'

Wingas cocked his head to one side, looking at Phule through narrowed eyes.

'If you don't mind my asking, Captain, why not just push for the assignment flat out? I'm not in much of a position to argue with you.'

'That's a fair question, Governor,' the commander said. 'You see, I'm trying to build my company's confidence in itself. If they can earn that contract in a fair competition with the Regular Army, or even make a decent showing for themselves, their confidence should increase. Buying the contract, or pressuring you into giving it to them, would tend to have the opposite effect. It would give every indication that I believed the only way they could get the job is if I bought it for them. The truth is, I have every confidence in my troops that in an open, fair competition, they can perform as well or better than anything the Regular Army can offer.'

'Interesting,' the governor murmured thoughtfully. He stared out the window, then shook his head.

'Nope. I can't do it. Since you've got a gun to my head, Captain, I might as well be honest with you. Normally I'd take your money, then get back to you with a message that I had been outmaneuvered. The way things are, though, you'd probably take it as a double cross and shit all over my loan application. The actual situation is that I *can't* help your boys, even enough to give them a chance. I've already signed the contract with the Regular Army for the job, and I can't get out of it if I wanted to.'

'Oh, I expected that, Governor,' Phule said easily. 'I believe there is *one* loophole that you could wiggle out of . . . if you were so inclined, that is.'

'What's that?'

'Why, the settlement ordinance that forbids the unilateral contracting of services without the review of competitive bids, of course.'

'I'm sorry, I don't recall any such – '

'As a matter of fact, I happen to have a copy of the ordinance right here, sir.'

The commander produced a sheet of paper from his pocket and set it on the desk in front of the governor.

'You'll notice that it's signed by the members on the Settlement Council *and* that it's dated a week before your contract with the Regular Army . . . sir.'

Wingas made no move to pick up the document. Instead, he narrowed his eyes suspiciously at Phule.

'Captain . . . why do I find myself thinking that if I were to call for the original of this document, I'd find that some of the signatures on it would still be wet?'

'I believe I *did* mention that I had to make a couple extra stops before I called on you this evening,' the commander pointed out levelly.

The governor threw up his hands in theatric surrender.

'All right! I give up! When the Army gets here, we'll set up a competition where you and your thugs will have chance at the contract! Is that all, or do you want my dog, too? I don't have a daughter.'

'That will be all, Governor Wingas,' Phule said, rising and reclaiming the paper from the governor's desk. 'Needless to say, I'm glad we had this little talk. I was sure we'd be able to work things out.'

'Captain Jester!'

The governor's voice stopped him with his hand on the doorknob.

'Sir?'

'Have you ever considered running for public office?'

'Me, Sir? No.'

'Good.'

12

Journal #121

In reviewing my entries thus far, I notice they give the impression that my employer was always on top of things and anticipated every contingency. Such was not the case. He was certainly exceptional when it came to adapting quickly to situations or covering when surprised, but surprised he was . . . more often than he would ever care to admit.

I can state this unequivocally, as it was my privilege to be present on more than one occasion when he was clearly (to my eye) caught flat-footed.

The company's new facility, or The Club, as the Legionnaires took to calling it, was certainly no comedown from the comfort they had enjoyed during their stay at the Plaza. In addition to the already referenced confidence course and firing range, it had its own swimming pool and sauna, a moderate-sized gymnasium, and enough rooms to accommodate a small convention. As it evolved, however, the main gathering point for the Legionnaires was the combination dining hall, meeting room, and cocktail lounge. With its comfortable sofas and fireplaces amid the widely scattered tables, it proved to be ideal for socializing during off-duty hours, which in turn made it the pivotal point for dispensing or collecting information or gossip that wasn't available through normal channels.

Phule paused for a moment before seating himself for breakfast, surveying again the bustle of activity in the dining hall. To his eye, it was apparent that there was something afoot this morning. The Legionnaires were huddled together in groups at various tables around the room, their heads close together as they murmured back and forth while poring over something. Occasional snickers erupted, and more than a few speculative glances were directed his way . . . and there was obvious nudging with elbows as his presence was noted.

That the commander found this conduct puzzling and more than a little curious went without saying. Their general manner was that of school kids sneaking a peek at a frog which had been smuggled into class, all the while wondering what the teacher would do when she discovered its presence. The trouble was, for the life of him he couldn't imagine what would inspire this behavior in his own motley crew. Finally he gave up trying to speculate and sank into a chair at his butler's table.

'Good morning, Beeker,' he said absently, still peering around the room. Were it not for his preoccupation, he might have noticed that his butler never glanced up from the Port-A-Brain he was bent over.

'Morning, sir.'

'Tell me, Beek . . . the troops tell you things they won't tell me . . . if it isn't a breach of confidence, do you have any idea what has everybody wound up this morning?'

'I believe I could make a fairly accurate guess.'

Phule broke off his surveillance and turned his gaze to Beeker, only to find himself studying the top of that notable's head.

'Well?' he prodded.

The butler tore his eyes from the computer screen to meet his employer's gaze with ill-concealed amusement.

'I believe it also explains the sizable donation Brandy made to the company fund . . . the one you found so puzzling.'

'Look, Beek. Are you going to tell me or – '

'I believe it involves this . . . sir,' Beeker said deadpan as he swiveled the computer screen around to share with the commander.

The screen displayed a page from a magazine, but the reduced size did not affect the impact of the banner headlines superimposed on the picture:

HELL'S BELLES

THE GIRLS OF PHULE'S COMPANY COME IN SMALL, MEDIUM, AND (VERY) LARGE!!

Sprawled across the page, in what might be politely referred to as their 'natural splendor,' were the all too recognizable figures of Brandy, Super Gnat, and . . . Mother!

Becker watched his employer's face intently for any sign of surprise or alarm, but Phule's expression was as noncommittal as it was when reviewing the profit/loss statement of a company he was considering acquiring. The only clue that there was anything abnormal in his reaction was the length of time he spent studying the display, and it would require someone as familiar with his normal patterns as Beeker to spot even that. Phule was usually able to assimilate information and make decisions at a glance, yet in this situation he stared at the screen as if it was a busted flush he could change by willpower alone.

'I could download it and run an enlarged hard copy if you'd like . . . sir,' the butler said at last, unable to restrain the urge to bait Phule out of his silence.

'I'm well aware of that, Beeker,' was the calm reply as Phule continued to keep his eyes glued to the screen.

'It would be no trouble at all,' Beeker pressed relentlessly. 'I've already had several requests for just that from your Legionnaires, so one or two copies more or less wouldn't – '

'Is this local or interstellar?'

'What do you think . . . sir?'

Phule raised his eyes at last to stare sightlessly at the far wall for several moments before answering.

'I think . . . '

'Oh! You've seen it! Hi, Beeker!'

The butler rose politely to greet the company's first sergeant.

'Good morning, Brandy. Yes, the captain and I were just discussing it, as a matter of fact.'

'Really? What do you think, sir? Not bad for an old girl, huh?'

'It's . . . you look good, Brandy,' Phule managed through a strangely tight smile. 'You all do.'

'I think so, too.' The sergeant beamed. 'I'll admit I was a little worried at first, displaying this old heap side by side with the newer models' – she jiggled a little to illustrate her point – 'but the proofs turned out great, so I gave it my go-ahead.'

The butler nodded sagely.

'Oh yes. The extra copies you asked for will be ready this afternoon.' He smiled.

'That's swell! How much will I owe you for those.'

'Nothing. Consider it to be with my – or more accurately, with the captain's – compliments. After all, it's his printer I'm using.'

'Hey, thanks, Captain. Well, got to go . . . my public awaits.'

Phule finally broke his self-imposed silence.

'Ah . . . Brandy?'

'Yes, sir?'

He started to speak twice before managing to settle his mind on one question.

'How did you get Mother to go along with this.'

'Go along with it? It was her idea! Well . . . later!'

The two men watched as she strode off to join one of the huddles, waving merrily at the whistles and catcalls that erupted at her approach.

'It was Mother's idea . . . sir,' Beeker repeated blandly.

Phule smiled vacantly at the room.

'Jesus wept!' he said, uttering through clenched teeth the closest thing to a profanity that had passed his lips in years. 'Do you realize – '

The beeper on his wrist communicator interrupted him in midsentence – the shrill Emergency Page that's pitched to grate against the nerves of any intelligent being in the known universe. Phule silenced it the only way the circuits would allow, by opening communication.

'Yes, Mother?'

'I really do hate to interrupt you at breakfast, Big Daddy, but there's a Colonel Battleax on the holo from HQ. She wants to talk to you real bad.'

'On the way,' Phule said, rising from his seat. 'Jester out.'

'Like the lady said,' Beeker quipped, 'your public awaits!'

Following the pattern set during their penthouse HQ days, the communications equipment had been installed in a room next to the commander's office. The new location had not improved the quality of the holo projections received, however, or the content of their messages.

'What kind of a silly-ass stunt is this, Captain?'

The image of Colonel Battleax hovered a few feet above the carpet, though in her vibrant anger it might not have been an error in transmission. The disheveled condition of her uniform, even more than her distraught manner, was an indication that she was transmitting without her usual preliminary preparations.

'Silly-ass stunt?'

'Don't give me that, Jester! I'm talking about the pictorial on your girls in this god-awful T&A magazine!'

'Oh . . . that!' Phule said, mentally blessing the marvels of modern magazine distribution. 'Yes, ma'am. What seems to be the problem?'

'What's the problem? Don't you realize what this does to the dignity of the Legion?'

'Excuse me, ma'am . . . dignity? Are we talking about the same Legion?'

'You know perfectly well what I mean, Jester!'

Years of experience in keeping a calm front in the face of disaster rose to Phule's assistance.

'I'm not at all sure I do. I believe it was the colonel herself who said in our last conversation that she was tired of reading media reports of my company in barroom brawls. More to the point, it's my understanding that the Legionnaires were off duty and on their own time for the photo session in question, and Legion regulations clearly limit the extent to which a commander can interfere with his troops during their off-duty hours . . . Articles 147 to 162, I believe.'

The colonel's image glowered down on him.

'All right, Jester. If we're going to play those games, Article 181 specifically forbids Legionnaires from accepting wages, gratuities, or any other form of individual payment for employment or services while enlisted in the Legion – off duty or not!'

'But Article 214 expressly allows Legionnaires to perform work or service on their own hours, providing the proceeds from those labors are paid directly to or forwarded to their assigned company rather than retained as private gain. I can reassure the colonel that the payment for the Legionnaires' appearance in the magazine in question was duly surrendered to the company fund, as is required by the tenants of that article.'

'I'm familiar with that article as well, Jester,' Battleax shot back, 'and I'm somehow not surprised you have it memorized. To my recollection, however, the rest of that article goes on to state that the approval of the company commander is required for such off-duty activity. Are you telling me that you approved this appearance?'

Phule started to cross his fingers behind his back, then recalled the requirement of not lying, or at least not saying anything that might later be proved a lie. With that in mind, he uncrossed his fingers and phrased his answer very carefully.

'Colonel Battleax . . . ma'am . . . frankly it's *their* bodies. I don't feel I have the right to order them not to display them, any more than it would be my right to order them *to* display them.'

The colonel's image pursed its lips for a moment, then seemed to deflate with a long exhale.

'I see. All right, Captain. You're off the hook again. I hope you realize, though, exactly how much I'm going to enjoy explaining this here at HQ.'

'I realize that, ma'am,' Phule replied, stoically repressing a smile at the mental image, 'and I'd like to say that I and the rest of the company appreciate the colonel's efforts in our behalf.'

'Well, you can tell that menagerie of yours for me that they can show their appreciation by trying to give me a few *less* items to explain. Okay?'

'Yes, ma'am. I'll definitely pass that along.'

'Very well. Battleax out.'

The transmission did not break off immediately, and for a moment Phule thought he saw a grin flash across the colonel's face as her image vanished.

Perhaps the most puzzling thing to me has always been that successful people invariably seem surprised by their own success. As a case in point, my employer had taken over the Omega Company with the express idea of building it into an effective unit. He planned to do this by raising the Legionnaires' self-esteem, and worked ceaselessly toward that goal. When his labor finally began to bear fruit, however, it seemed to take him totally unawares.

Of course, the speed of the company's development was a bit unnerving. In hindsight, I guess it's apparent that there is nothing quite as fanatically loyal as a stray that's found a home. At the time, however, the Legionnaires' sudden enthusiasm was more than a little unsettling.

. . . and finally, I am pleased to report that the holdings in the company portfolio have increased substantially since my last report. I'll have a detailed report available for those interested, but cutting through to the bottom line, we're currently up by eight, which is to say every dollar invested in our fund at the last report is now worth eight.'

A low murmur rippled through the assemblage at this announcement, with some Legionnaires whispering excitedly at what they could do with their increased wealth while others groaned and grumbled over the profits they had lost by pulling all or part of their money out after the last reported increases.

The entire company was gathered for one of Phule's periodic informal debriefings. Whether it was items too minor to warrant announcement by wrist communicators, but too important to trust to a general notice posted on the bulletin board, or issues he wished to discuss with the Legionnaires face-to-face, the commander felt it was important to keep this line of exchange open, and the company had responded with diligent attendance whenever word was passed of an assembly.

After waiting several moments for the reactions to run their course, he held up a hand for silence.

'All right,' he said. 'That pretty much wraps up the old business for now. Are there any questions or comments before I move on to new business?'

'*Yes, sir!*'

Lieutenant Armstrong was on his feet, face rigid, in the classic position of attention. The captain noticed that several of the Legionnaires were grinning and nudging each other, but dismissed it as their normal amusement at Armstrong's Regular Army practices.

'Yes, Lieutenant? What is it?'

Instead of replying, the lieutenant literally marched to the front of the room, squaring his corners with parade-ground precision. Coming to a halt directly in front of the commander, he drew himself up with a crisp salute, which he held until Phule, puzzled by his antics, returned.

'Sir! The company has asked me to speak for them in voicing a complaint . . . sir!'

As he spoke, all the Legionnaires in attendance rose silently to their feet and assumed stances approximating Armstrong's textbook pose.

The commander avoided looking at them directly, but was both aware of and taken aback by their actions. Whatever was coming, it seemed to be unanimous. What the hell could it be?

'At ease, Lieutenant . . . and the rest of you, too. These are supposed to be informal meetings. Now then, what seems to be the problem?'

'Well, sir . . . the company is unhappy with the uniforms you've provided them with.'

'I see. Which uniform specifically?'

'All of them, sir. We feel they lack color.'

'Color?'

Phule couldn't keep himself from glancing at the assemblage. To a man, they were grinning at him.

'I don't think I understand. Black is the designated color of all Space Legion uniforms. While it may be unimaginative, I don't see any reason to change that, even if we could get approval from Headquarters . . . which I doubt.'

'We don't want to change the color of the uniforms, sir . . . just request permission to add something for accent. Specifically . . . '

The Lieutenant removed something from his pocket and held it out to Phule.

'. . . we request the captain's permission to adopt and wear this flash patch as a designation for our unit . . . sir!'

The patch was a bright red, diamond-shaped piece of cloth. Embroidered on it, in black, was a skull wearing a belled jester's cap at a jaunty angle.

Phule studied it for a full minute as silence hung thick in the room. Then, still not trusting his voice, he removed the paper from the patch's adhesive backing and pressed it onto the sleeve of his uniform with his palm. With slow precision, he assumed the position of attention himself and raised his hand to salute the company.

As one, the Legionnaires returned his salute . . . then the room exploded in cheers and celebration.

'How do you like it, Captain?'

'Lieutenant Rembrandt did the art! Isn't it a beaut?'

'We all chipped in . . . '

As they crowded around him, the Legionnaires took time from babbling and slapping each other on the back to assist each other in installing the new patches on their sleeves. From the speed with which the decorations materialized, it was clear to the commander that the patches had been distributed in advance, with everyone carefully keeping them out of sight until they could spring the surprise on him together.

Phule was sitting alone in his room, staring at the patch on his just removed uniform, when his butler let himself in.

'Have you seen this, Beeker?'

'Yes, sir. If you'll look at your closet, you'll find that it has been added to all your uniforms.'

'So you were in on it, too, eh?'

'I was asked to keep it confidential, sir. They wanted it to be a surprise.'

The commander shook his head in amazement.

'It certainly was. I never dreamed they were cooking up anything like this.'

'I think you should take it as a compliment. It's my impression that they wish to show their appreciation for your efforts on their behalf, as well as pledging their support.'

'I know. It's just . . . I didn't know what to say, Beek. Still don't, for that matter. I had to sneak out of the party early before I made a fool of myself trying to find a way to say thanks.'

'I believe your own acceptance of the patch is sufficient, sir. Rather like a father showing appreciation for his children by hanging their artistic efforts on the wall of his office.'

Phule shook his head again, more emphatically this time.

'It goes way beyond that. Even my best-case scenario didn't cover how fast the crew is coming together. I'll tell you, Beeker, I couldn't be more proud of them if they *were* my own kids.'

'Well, sir, as they say, the proof is in the pudding. How did they take the announcement that the Regular Army is arriving tomorrow?'

'I never made it.' The commander sighed, sagging slightly in his chair. 'They sprang this on me before I got around to it, and I couldn't bring myself to change the mood once they got rolling. I decided to let them celebrate tonight . . . tomorrow will come soon enough.'

It might be of interesting historical note to some that use of the expression 'hookers' as a designation for prostitutes originated during the Old Earth American Civil War. At that time, General Hooker maintained an entourage of 'soiled doves' who accompanied him on his campaigns. If anyone visiting his encampment happened to ask one of the soldiers who these 'ladies' were, they were simply informed, 'They're Hooker's,' and the phrase took root.

Realizing this, it should come as no surprise that when the Legionnaires under my employer's command roamed the streets of the settlement, they were explained by the locals by the simple expression 'They're Phule's' – a nickname that was to follow them for some time.

13

Journal #122

While I have noted that my employer is not immune to surprises, it should be mentioned that upon occasions, he has also been known to outsmart himself. Though normally he excels at dealing with the media, it is his particular love of coverage that more often than not leaves him vulnerable.

A marked air of nervousness hung over the Legionnaires as they waited in full company formation for the arrival of the shuttlecraft. Though they were officially 'at ease,' meaning they could move one foot and talk with their neighbor, there was no conversation at all. Rather, they stood fidgeting anxiously in silence, each individual lost in his or her own thoughts.

'Are you sure this is such a good idea, Captain?'

The officers of the company were able to wander freely, though Phule forced himself to remain in front of the formation, trying to set a good example for the company by projecting calm rather than yielding to his natural desire to pace. He welcomed Lieutenant Rembrandt's soft question, however, as it gave him something to focus his attention on.

'Don't you think it's polite to be on hand to welcome our opposite number on their arrival, Lieutenant?' he said with mock severity.

'I suppose so, sir,' Rembrandt returned, taking his statement seriously. 'To be honest with you, though, I've never seen any politeness on the part of the Regular Army toward the Legion.'

'Neither have I,' Phule admitted grimly. 'For your

information, Lieutenant, the *real* reason we're out here has nothing to do with courtesy.'

'Sir?'

'Think about it. Everyone's nervous because they're afraid the Army's going to kick our butts in the upcoming competition. That's not surprising, considering how they've been conditioned into believing the Regular Army is manned by supermen, while the Space Legion scrapes the bottom of the barrel for their manpower. Well, if we're going to give a decent accounting of ourselves, we're going to have to shake that belief, and our presence here is the first step. I want everyone to see the competition as soon as possible, so they can realize that Army troops are human and put their pants on one leg at a time like everyone else. See my point?'

'I . . . I guess so, sir.'

Though obviously still unconvinced, the lieutenant was spared a further lecture by the cry that went up from the formation.

'*Incoming!*'

'Here they come!'

'Send my body to my first wife . . . she could use a decent meal!'

The shuttlecraft had dropped through the cloud cover and was maneuvering toward the end of the runway.

'All right, everybody. Stand ready!'

Though still 'at ease,' this was the signal to get ready to be called to attention. Those Legionnaires who had been sitting in place rose hurriedly and dusted off the seats of their uniforms, squaring away their position in the formation.

All eyes were on the shuttlecraft as it touched down and taxied slowly up to the terminal, coming to a halt a scant fifty meters from where the company stood waiting. After what seemed like an eternity, the hatch opened and a ramp lowered. Seconds later, the first passengers stepped into view.

There was a heartbeat before recognition sank in, and then a buzz began to ripple through the formation.

'Sir!' came Lieutenant Armstrong's urgent whisper. 'Do you know who they are?'

'I know, Lieutenant.'

'Those are the Red Eagles!'

'I said *I know*, Lieutenant!'

'But, sir . . . '

'Company . . . *atten-hut!*'

Phule bellowed out the command as much to stop the conversation as to present a proper military picture. Mostly, however, he wanted time to try to collect his own thoughts.

Resplendent in their dress uniforms and crowned with the red berets that were their trademark, there was no mistaking the identity of the soldiers filing down the ramp. The Red Eagles! For some reason, the Army had decided to send their elite combat unit on this assignment!

Unusual for the Regular Army, the Red Eagles were in some ways more like the Space Legion in that they represented a cross section of planetary cultures rather than being a single-planet unit. There, however, the similarities ended. Highly decorated and publicized, the Eagles were considered the *crème de la crème* of the Regular Army. Competition was fierce for inclusion in their ranks, as literally hundreds of soldiers vied for the honor each time there was an opening in their roster. More than one effort to 'introduce a more equitable mix' in the unit was repelled when it was pointed out, and defended, that the Red Eagles only had one bias: They required the best!

All this and more swirled through Phule's mind as he watched the soldiers mill aimlessly about at the foot of the ramp. The Eagles, in turn, ignored the formation of Legionnaires completely, not even sparing them a curious glance as they chatted back and forth.

Finally an imposing figure strode down the ramp.

Looking neither left nor right, it stalked across the runway with the easy, rolling gait of a trained athlete, setting an unswerving course for Phule.

'Captain Jester, I assume? I'm Major Matthew O'Donnel.'

Startled at being greeted by name, Phule nonetheless managed a snappy salute.

'Welcome to Haskin's Planet, Major.'

'O'Donnel neither returned the salute nor offered to shake hands.

'Yeah. I'm sure,' he said with a tight humorless smile. 'Look, Captain, I imagine you're about as happy to see us as we are to be here. Now, is there somewhere we can talk? Somewhere air-conditioned, if possible. I'd like to get this foolishness settled as fast as possible.'

Numbly Phule gestured toward the terminal, and the major brushed past him with his now familiar stride.

'Lieutenant Armstrong, Rembrandt,' the commander called, beckoning to his junior officers.

'Sir?'

'Yes, sir?'

'Get the company back to the compound and wait for me there. I'll be along as soon as I find out what the hell is going on.'

'But, sir.'

'Just do it! But be sure to leave me a driver. I have a hunch I'm not going to feel like walking back once this is over.'

Entering the terminal, Phule found that his disturbing surprises were not over yet. The first thing to greet his eyes was the sight of Major O'Donnel stiffly shaking hands with . . . Governor Wingas!

'Ah! Captain!' the governor beamed. 'Come join us, won't you? I understand you've already met Major O'Donnel.'

'Yes, I have,' the commander said. 'I'll admit I'm

surprised, though. I didn't expect the Army to send the Red Eagles on a simple honor guard assignment.'

'If it will make you feel any better, Captain,' O'Donnel growled, 'it surprised us, too. It seems the upper brass has been reading the media coverage you've been getting about this hot-shit crew you're putting together and decided they had to put their best foot forward to protect the Army's reputation. Next thing you know, we get pulled out of a firefight and shipped off to here, with *orders* to take you seriously.'

From his tone, it was clear the major didn't think much of those orders.

'Now, if you don't mind, let's get down to it. I want to get the terms of this so-called competition squared away so I can get my troops settled in.'

'I . . . take it you're already aware of the competition?' Phule said carefully.

'That's right. The governor here was good enough to send us word prior to our arrival.'

The Legion commander shot a glance at the governor, who smiled and shrugged benignly.

'It seemed the least I could do, since I contracted the Army in the first place.'

Phule decided to deny Wingas the pleasure of an explosion, though inwardly he was seething at the betrayal.

'Yes. I can see where that's fair,' he managed.

'As I understand it, Captain,' O'Donnel continued briskly, 'we're supposed to settle who gets the honor guard contract with a series of three contests with independent judges. The Army picks one event, you pick one, and the third we're supposed to mutually agree on. Is that right?'

Phule nodded stiffly, not liking the way the major was taking control of the meeting.

'All right. For our event, we choose close order drill, since that's most of what you do on an honor guard post. What's yours?'

The captain's heart sank slightly. Of all the skills normally associated with the military, close order drill was, perhaps, his company's worst.

'The confidence course.'

For the first time, the major showed surprise, his eyebrows nearly disappearing into the sweatband of his beret.

'The confidence course?' he repeated. 'All right, Captain. It's your funeral. Now for the third event, assuming we get it . . . ' He gestured at Wingas. 'The governor here tells me you and your crew fancy yourself to be fencers. How does a three-weapon match sound to you . . . foil, saber, and épée . . . best two out of three?'

A warning bell went off in Phule's mind. This seemed a little too pat.

'It sounds like the governor has told you quite a bit,' he said, stalling for time.

'Is that a yes or a no? Come on, Captain. Let's not take all day on this.'

'Tell me, Major. Do you fence yourself?'

'Me? I've played a little bit with épée.'

'Then let me add a little rider to your proposal. The same three-weapon match, but we fence épée last . . . between the unit commanders. That way, if it should come right down to the wire, we can settle this between the two of us.'

Major O'Donnel's face split in a wide grin.

'Nothing would give me greater pleasure, Captain. Agreed . . . though I doubt things will get that far.'

'You might be surprised, Major,' Phule returned with a tight smile. 'My troops have surprised a lot of people, including me.'

'So surprise me,' O'Donnel shot back. 'Forgive me, though, if I don't hold my breath.'

'Well, now that that's settled, gentlemen,' the governor said, rising hastily.

'Just one more question . . . if you don't mind,

Major,' the Legionnaire commander pressed. 'Assuming for the moment that the Red Eagles *do* win, is the Army really going to tie up their crack fighting unit on honor guard duty?'

O'Donnel's eyes slid sideways at the governor in a reptilian glance.

'Now that you mention it, Captain, I do believe there's a clause in our standard contract that states that while a unit of the Regular Army can be contracted for specific duty, the Army reserves the right to select which unit will be so assigned . . . *and* that they may replace said unit at their discretion depending upon the demands placed upon their manpower at any given time.'

'So they're sending in the Red Eagles to nail down the contract, then plan to swap them with a completely different unit once the deal is closed. Is that it?'

Phule turned to Governor Wingas, who shrugged his shoulders helplessly.

'That's show business, Captain . . . or, should I say, that's politics!'

I have been very open in the chronicling of my employer's fallibility. Lest the wrong impression be given, however, I would hasten to add that, without a doubt, he is the best fighter I have ever had the privilege to observe, much less serve, when pushed into a corner.

'Of all the double-crossing, ballot-stuffing, two-faced –'

'That's enough, Armstrong!' the company commander's voice cracked like a whip. 'We don't have time to discuss the moral or genetic shortcomings of the governor. Not if we're going to put together a plan of action before the competition tomorrow!'

'The company's still waiting in the dining hall, Captain,' Brandy announced, sticking her head in the door of the commander's office. 'What do you want me to tell them?'

'Tell them I'll be down to talk to them in about half

an hour. Oh, and Brandy . . . in the meantime start talking it up that we've already won.'

'We have?'

'Certainly. We won the minute the Army decided it would take the Red Eagles to compete with us. Even if we get out brains beat out tomorrow, there always will be the question in people's minds as to whether or not we could have beaten any *normal* Army unit.'

'If you say so, sir.' The top sergeant's voice was doubtful. 'Oh . . . almost forgot. Do-Wop said you wanted this.'

'What is it, Captain?' Rembrandt said, craning her neck to try to read the sheet of paper Phule was studying.

'Hmm? Oh. It's a copy of the personnel roster for the Red Eagles. I guess they left it lying around the terminal somewhere.'

'Shall I ask Beeker to run it through his computer?'

'Never mind, Armstrong I've already found it. Damn! I should have known!'

'What did you find?'

Both lieutenants were crowding in next to Phule now, staring at the paper as if the names listed were some kind of coded message.

'I *thought* O'Donnel was awfully eager to agree to a fencing match!' the commander muttered, almost to himself. 'See this name? Third from the top? Isaac Corbin! He was Tri-Planetary saber champion for five years running! What in the hell is *he* doing in the Army?'

'Getting ready to cancel our checks, I'd say.' Armstrong grimaced. 'At least it's just one bout out of three.'

'Maybe, maybe not,' Phule murmured thoughtfully. 'I think we'll – '

The shriek of his wrist communicator cut him short.

'Colonel Battleax wishes to view your classic features . . . sir!'

'Oh great . . . just great. On the way, Mother.'

'I see you're getting your usual amount of press coverage, Captain. Certainly taking on the Regular Army in a public challenge is an ambitious effort.'

'Look, Colonel. I didn't know they were going to run the Red Eagles in on us. I'll even admit it's my fault for letting the media wave a targeting flag over us, but . . . '

'Whoa. Relax, Captain,' Battleax insisted. 'I'm not trying to hassle you. I just called in to wish you luck in tomorrow's competition. If you don't mind my saying so, I think you're going to need it.'

'You can say that again,' Phule said with a snort. 'Sorry, ma'am. Didn't mean to snap at you, there. I'm just a bit pressured trying to get ready for tomorrow.'

'Well, I won't keep you, then. Just between you and me, though, Jester, do you think there's any chance at all you can pull it off?'

'There's *always* a chance, ma'am,' he replied automatically. 'But seriously . . . I'd just go ahead and concede the close order drill except for the fact that I don't think we should ever give up without a fight. I would have bet we could hold our own against a normal Army unit on the confidence course, but now . . . I don't know. About the only thing that's definitely in our favor is that, even though it's supposed to be impartial judging, my crew has gotten in pretty good with the locals here on Haskin's. It just might give us the home court advantage.'

'I'm surprised at you, Captain.' Battleax laughed. 'And with your business background, too. You may have inadvertently set yourself a rougher road to hoe. I don't mean to rain on your parade, but we both know that an expert is someone from off-planet with a briefcase. I just hope your success with the locals hasn't made your troops too familiar figures, so that they only make the Red Eagles seem that much more exotic . . . or expert!'

14

Journal #129

I was fortunate enough to witness the events which made up the Legion vs. Army competition firsthand . . . though as a spectator, not as a judge. Though I normally try to stay emotionally detached from the antics of the company beyond what has immediate effect on my employer, I will admit to having formed a certain affection for the Legionnaires as individuals and as a group, and felt they might need whatever moral support they could get in the conflict. As it turned out, I was right.

The competition itself took place at the Legion facilities, which seemed to impress the Red Eagles even if the Legionnaires did not. Governor Wingas was on hand, along with the entire Settlement Council and assorted other local dignitaries who were to serve as judges . . . and, as might be expected, the media.

The less said about the close order drill event, the better, save to note that it took place. The Legionnaires managed to stagger through their portion without too many mistakes which would be noticeable to a civilian eye, and thus managed to avoid any actual embarrassment. There was no question, however, as to which group had the greater expertise.

Rather than restricting themselves to the normal Manual of Arms – right-face, left-face, about-face, that sort of rubbish – the Red Eagles dipped into their knowledge of the Exhibition Manual of Arms. Again, for the enlightenment of my fellow nonmilitary creatures, this consists of a series of rifle spins, ripple movements, and toss-exchanging of rifles, more often than not carried out while the participants are marching in a bewildering variety of directions. Needless to say, this impressed the judges and spectators in the reviewing stand, who rewarded the Eagles with frequent and loud bursts of applause. I somehow managed to restrain myself, but noticed I seemed to be the only one of the spectators who exercised such control.

As a finale, it was announced that the Eagles would repeat one of their more intricate maneuvers, only blindfolded and without the benefit of anyone counting cadence or calling orders . . . which they proceeded to do with chilling precision.

It might be expected that this display would move the already nervous Legionnaires to the depths of despair. Strangely enough, it seemed to have the exact opposite effect. From where I sat, I was able to overhear some of the comments the company whispered back and forth within their formation while the Eagles were performing. The general thrust of the comments was that they felt that the Eagles could have won the event without resorting to 'the snazzy stuff,' but that the soldiers had chosen their specific routines to 'show off' and otherwise make the Legionnaires 'look worse than we really are'! By the end of the Red Eagles' exhibition, a new, dark resolve had settled over the Legionnaires. What had been a contest for a soft contract had suddenly escalated in their eyes to a full-blown vendetta.

I felt this boded ill for the upcoming confidence course event.

Standing at his post by the barbed-wire and machine-gun portion of the confidence course, Master Sergeant Spengler shook his head again in wonderment.

Of all the crazy things he had seen and done during his years in the Army, today had to be in a category all its own. These Legionnaires had guts . . . he'd give them that. More guts than brains, though. After the shellacking the Eagles had given them at close order drill, he wouldn't have been surprised if they had simply conceded the rest of the events rather than suffer additional humiliation. Instead, they had not only been willing to continue the competition, they had insisted on some of the roughest rules for running the confidence course that Spengler had ever heard of!

The sergeant momentarily slipped off his cherished red beret and ran a sleeve across his brow before replacing it. He was still sweating from the Eagles' run at the course, and though they might look jaunty, the berets tended to seal the heat in.

If he hadn't been standing within earshot to hear it all for himself, he never would have believed that the Legionnaire commander had posed these rules himself.

First of all, they were supposed to run the course in what he called 'full combat conditions,' which mostly meant they had to do it under arms and carrying a full field pack. There had been some discussion as to whether some of the Legionnaires could use their glide boards and hover cycles, but the major had stood firm and those particular pieces of equipment had been barred from the course.

The real surprise, though, came when the black-uniformed officer had insisted that the groups run the course and be timed *as a unit* rather than as individuals, with time penalties for any 'skipped' obstacles. The major had protested, pointing out that as there were only twenty Red Eagles and nearly two hundred Legionnaires, his rival could lose most of his 'dead weight' while paring his force down to an equal size, sending only his twenty best through the course against the Eagles. Sergeant Spengler had thought that even yielding this advantage to the Legionnaires would have little effect on the outcome, though at the time he held his silence rather than intervene in an argument between officers. Incredibly, however, the Legionnaire commander declared that he had no intention of paring down or otherwise reducing the number of his company, that he wished to match the timed run of his entire command against that of the twenty Red Eagles! The major had been so dumbfounded at this revelation that he agreed to the terms without further attempts at modification.

Even now, thinking back on it, the master sergeant found himself shaking his head with disbelief. Though he occasionally felt momentary flashes of admiration for a commander who had that much faith in his troops, the overwhelming evidence said that the man was crazy. Even if the forces were evenly matched in ability, which they weren't, trying to run that many bodies through a confidence course in one wave, much less while being timed, was logistically suicidal!

The Red Eagles' performance on the course had suffered a bit from the 'full combat conditions.' Not that they were particularly hampered by their packs and weapons, mind you. They had lived and slept with those implements often enough in actual combat that the extra bulk and required maneuvering space were almost second nature to them. Trying to perform the Mickey Mouse, basic training maneuvers of a confidence course whilst so encumbered, on the other hand, was a real pain in the butt. While the obstacles in the course were specifically designed to test and exercise the participants, such challenges were rarely encountered once one cleared training. As an example, in the master sergeant's entire combat experience, he had never been called on to swing across a ditch on a rope while holding a rifle . . . until this afternoon, that is. Then, too, there was the problem, and the sergeant had felt it himself, of taking the competition seriously. Every one of the Red Eagles *knew* that the Space Legion was a bunch of clowns, and nothing they had seen since arriving on Haskin's Planet had served to convince them otherwise. As such, it was difficult, if not impossible, to generate that hard drive and push necessary to really excel at an exercise. Rather, there was a tendency to loaf or coast whenever possible. The Eagles had run the course in a presentable time, and, of course, had not skipped any of the obstacles, but it was far from their top performance.

Shading his eyes against the sun, Spengler peered toward the starting line where the company of Legionnaires was massing.

It wouldn't be long now. Another half hour at the most and this whole harebrained competition would be over. He assumed it wouldn't take the Legionnaires longer than that to run the course . . . or give up. The Army would have its contract – and publicity – and the Eagles would have their promised night on the town.

With the conscientiousness that earned him his stripes, the sergeant began checking over his position. When the Legionnaires reached this point in the course, it would be his job to fire a steady stream of machine-gun bullets above their heads as they crawled under the strands of barbed wire, which were conveniently stapled to posts, something else one never saw in real combat. The obstacle was designed to demonstrate to the participants that they could move and perform minimal functions while under fire. It was also, invariably, the biggest bottleneck on the course and the one that ate up the most minutes during a timed run. There was simply no way to crawl under barbed wire fast, especially since the maneuver called for lying on your back and pushing through with your feet, all the while using your hands to guide the lower strands of wire up and over the rifle lying on your chest.

Stepping onto the raised platform that housed the machine gun, set back some twenty meters from the wire itself, Spengler immediately noticed something amiss. Specifically the small frame that normally held the weapon's muzzle at a pre-set height was missing! What that meant was that all that was keeping the weapon from raking the course participants with live ammo was the steady hand of whoever was firing it!

The sergeant cursed softly under his breath.

He had *thought* the tracer fire looked awfully low while he was going under the wire. Well, two could play that game. When this was all over, he'd have a word or two with the Legionnaire sergeant who had manned the weapon during the Red Eagles' run. What was her name again . . . Brandy? Yes, that was it.

Spengler allowed himself the ghost of a smile as he recalled the magazine spread that had been passed around when they got this assignment.

He had to admit, they didn't have anything that looked like *that* in his unit. While there were women in the ranks of the Red Eagles, their build and manner was from flat-faced, big-boned, muscular genes that would look more at home behind the wheel of a truck or a bulldozer than on a dance floor or in a centerfold. Maybe he wouldn't lean on this Brandy girl *too* hard. Perhaps a sociable drink or five . . .

The sharp report of a starting gun drew the sergeant's attention. The Legionnaires had started their run. There were many obstacles to clear before they reached his position, and since there was no sense in spraying bullets over the barbed wire when there was no one there, the sergeant had time to watch for a while before settling in behind the machine gun.

At first, he thought the Legionnaires had gotten their signals crossed and were following the normal procedure of running the course in 'flights,' as half a dozen figures darted out from the starting line. Then he realized that the entire company was, indeed, moving, but in a steady, ground-eating jog rather than a headlong sprint.

Interesting. The force was better organized and disciplined than he would have expected. Sending scouts on ahead, since that was the obvious role of the lead runners, was an innovative idea. Almost as if –

well, yes – like real combat conditions. Who would have thought to find such conscientious role-playing in the Space Legion?

Spengler was amused to note that the two weird-looking nonhumans – what were they again? Sinthians? – were literally being carried by some of their team-mates. The sergeant had both performed and super-vised similar exercises as a drill for carrying wounded comrades, but had never seen anyone attempt the prac-tice through an entire confidence course. And wasn't that . . . Yes! The unit's commanding officer he had seen earlier was running the course along with his troops! For that matter, so were the other officers and what looked like the entire cadre!

The master sergeant's normal disdain for the Space Legion was slipping away and being replaced by a growing, though grudging, admiration for this scrappy crew. They weren't the Red Eagles, to be sure . . . not even close. Still, if one couldn't make the grade in a *real* outfit, this wouldn't be a bad outfit to belong to.

A flicker of motion on the course ahead of the main force caught the sergeant's eye.

What the . . . ? One of the 'scouts' had apparently climbed up the wooden framework of the first obstacle and was cutting down the 'swinging ropes,' tossing them to his teammates on the ground who, in turn, scampered off down the course bearing their prizes.

They couldn't do that! What were they trying to pull, anyway? More to the point, how were the rest of the Legionnaires supposed to cross the ditch with the ropes gone?

As if in answer to his mental question, the first run-ners of the main body reached the edge of the ditch. Ignoring the remaining ropes, they simply stepped off the bank into the chest-deep slime . . . and just stood there! The Legionnaires behind them stepped on their shoulders, then dropped into the ditch taking similar positions farther on, until . . .

Stepping-stones! Even as Spengler realized what they were doing, the chains were completed, and the main body was moving across the ditch with next to no loss of speed, stepping from shoulder to shoulder of their teammates standing in the slime. The maneuver had obviously been painstakingly practiced from the smoothness of its execution. There were even a couple chains where the 'stones' were standing closer together to accommodate the smaller members of the company.

A short story he had read in high school, one of the few he remembered, flashed through Spengler's mind. 'Lennington vs. the Ants,' it was called, and told the tale of a plantation owner's fight against the advance of a force of army ants. Watching the Legionnaires advance steadily on his position, the sergeant experienced a chilling moment as his mind's eye superimposed the image of that merciless, unstoppable swarm over the black-uniformed figures jogging toward him. This Space Legion troop no longer seemed quite as comical as they had this morning. If they were . . .

The dull *whump* of a nearby explosion made the master sergeant duck reflexively. At first he thought there had been some sort of catastrophic accident on the course, but then the truth dawned on him.

They were blowing up the obstacles!

Horror and outrage warred within the sergeant as he witnessed another barrier, the three-meter wall this time, disappear in a flash-*boom*, followed by a shower of splinters and debris. Before the echoes of the explosions had fully died away, the advancing black company appeared, maintaining their dogged advance through the clouds of dust, unnervingly close now.

With the iron discipline of a combat veteran, the master sergeant turned his back on the spectacle and began loading the first belt of ammunition into the machine gun.

Let the major fight it out over whether or not the Legionnaires' tactics were acceptable. *His* job was to see to it that they kept their heads down while they went under the wire. *Nobody* passed *this* position rapidly. Not with tracers whining around their . . .

The world suddenly went topsy-turvy around him, as the sergeant was violently upended and slammed down on the platform. Shaken and confused, he tried to struggle upright, only to be pushed flat again, this time with teeth-rattling force.

'Mmmm . . . You . . . *stay down.* Okay?'

A berry brown face with obsidian-dark eyes swam into focus. One of the black-uniformed Legionnaires was squatting over the sergeant's fallen form, and Spengler could feel the light prick of a knife point under his chin.

'W-what do you think you're doing?' he gasped, trying hard to speak without moving his chin. 'You can't . . . '

He broke off speaking as the pressure under his chin increased sharply.

'The captain tell me, he say "Escrima, I want you to help remove the obstacles." Here, *you* are the obstacle . . . yes? I remove you by capturing. You want, I *kill* you instead.'

Reviewing his options quickly, for the sergeant was unwilling to bet his life that the Legionnaire was joking – or bluffing – Spengler opted to lie quietly where he was. This did not, of course, keep him from seething inwardly as he watched wire cutters clear the barbed wire from his position, and, scant seconds later, the entire company sweep by this supposedly challenging obstacle without breaking stride.

'You can't mean you're going to let them get away with it . . . sir.'

Sprawled in one of the 'guest rooms' of the Space Legion's incredible facilities which had been assigned to them for use during the competition, Major O'Donnel favored his master sergeant with a scowl.

'I didn't say we were going to let them get away with it,' he said tightly. 'I said I wasn't going to lodge a protest.'

'But they didn't run the confidence course . . . they totaled it!'

'And we could have, too . . . if we thought of it,' the major snapped back. 'We had the equipment in our packs, and it *was* declared as combat conditions. It's what we would have done in combat. We just got trapped into conventional thinking, is all.'

'Well, what they did sure wasn't regulation,' the sergeant growled.

'Neither is the Exhibition Manual of Arms we used this morning. All right, we had our chance to show off without them whimpering about it, and now they've had theirs. At the moment, we're even.'

'So we're going to let it stand as a win for the Space Legion?' Spengler said, trying to sting the officer's pride.

'Face it, Sergeant. We lost. They beat our time without passing up any obstacles . . . *and* they did it with ten times as many troops. Of course, we helped them. That was a pretty lackluster performance our boys put on today. Frankly I don't think we *deserved* to win this event. We goofed off while they busted ass. That's no way to come out on top.'

The master sergeant had the grace to look embarrassed.

'We didn't think they could come on that strong, sir,' he muttered, avoiding the officer's gaze.

'Uh-huh. We got cocky and overconfident to a point where we badly underestimated an opponent,' O'Donnel clarified. 'If anything, Sergeant, we owe these Legionnaires a vote of thanks for teaching us a valuable lesson. I think we were damn lucky not to have learned it in *real* combat. At least this way, we're still alive . . . *and* we get another chance.'

'You know, sir,' Spengler said carefully, as if surprised by his own words, 'I never thought I'd say it, but I don't think I'd relish taking that crew on in a real brawl.'

The major grimaced. 'Don't feel bad. I've been thinking much the same thing. Wouldn't mind having them covering my flank, though . . . as long as we were were *sure* they wouldn't confuse us with the enemy.'

He grinned mirthlessly at his own joke, then shook his head.

'Enough of that, though. I've got to start concentrating on the fencing match tonight. It's going to be our last chance to pull the Army's chestnuts, not to mention our own reputation, out of the fire.'

'Do you think there might be a problem, sir?' The master sergeant frowned. 'I mean, we *do* have Corbin on our side.'

'Yes, we do.' O'Donnel nodded. 'But that's only one bout out of three. After this afternoon, I wouldn't bet the rent money that those clowns are going to hand us the other two on a platter.'

15

Journal #130

It is doubtful that you have ever attended a fencing tournament unless you are directly involved in the sport, either as a participant or through some emotional or professional relationship with a fencer. This is due to the simple fact that fencing is not a spectator sport, the action being far too fast and subtle for the uneducated eye. (It might be of interest to note that fencing is one of the few sports where the competitors pay a fee, but the spectators get in for free.)

Usually such an event is held in a large gymnasium or field house, with anywhere from six to several dozen 'strips' laid out. The competitors are divided into groups or 'pools' and fence each person within their pool. The top two or three advance to the next round, where they are reassigned to new pools and the process begins again. The bulk of those attending are in the competition area, consisting almost entirely of competitors and coaches, while a smattering of spectators made up of friends and parents of the competitors loll about in the bleachers getting bored. Only the final bouts generate much interest, but even then there are few spectators, most competitors packing their equipment and leaving as soon as they are eliminated.

Needless to say, this was not *the situation for the final event between the Red Eagles and my employer's company.*

Major O'Donnel paused in his limbering-up exercises to glance at the growing crowd of spectators. Despite his resolve to ignore any distractions while mentally preparing for the competition, he found his mindset giving way to amazement.

Crazy!

The Legionnaires' tactics on the confidence course had been unorthodox, but this . . . This was unheard-of! It looked like the entire company of the Space Legion was in attendance, filling the bleachers at one end of the floor, while his own Red Eagles, unhappy at not having a direct hand in the deciding event, were fidgeting impatiently in the rows of chairs provided for them at the opposite end. What really surprised him was the audience.

He had, of course, known there were going to be spectators but had never imagined the crowds jamming the bleachers on both sides of the gymnasium floor . . . for a *fencing match*, for God's sake! Even the media had their holo cameras set up to record the event! This looked more like a gathering for a basketball or volleyball game . . . or a coliseum waiting for the gladiators to start!

The major quickly put that disquieting thought out of his mind, along with the nagging suspicion that he had somehow walked into a trap. He had been surprised by the confidence course, to be sure, but there was only so much you could do on a fencing strip. Here, at least, there were standardized rules!

Apparently this Phule, or Captain Jester, as he was called, was not surprised by the turnout. In fact, a few minutes ago he had announced a demonstration of stick forms by one of his men to hold the crowd's attention while waiting for the formal competition to begin.

The costumed figure who took the floor at that point created a small ripple of interest among the Red Eagles, as he was quickly recognized as the Legionnaire who had held their own Sergeant Spengler at knife point during the afternoon exercise. After watching the small brown figure twirl his sticks in a blurred, bewildering net of interweaving circles and strikes, however, whatever concerns O'Donnel might have had about an unofficial 'meeting of retribution' between his force and that notable quickly vanished. The Red Eagles were all hand-to-hand experts, and that expertise included the wisdom *not* to pick a fight with someone who used a martial arts form you were not familiar with.

Ignoring the flashing display being performed on the floor, the major took a moment to study the diminutive figure warming up quietly against the back wall.

He had been surprised (again) when the lists of competitors were exchanged and he realized the Legion was fielding a woman for the foil bout. Recovering quickly, he had offered to substitute one of his own women for the competitor listed in that event, but the rival commander refused to take him up on it. 'You've chosen *your* best, and we've chosen ours,' was his only comment.

Strangely enough, though it was the most commonly fenced weapon, foil was the Eagles' weakest event. Normally O'Donnel would have fenced that weapon, being the second best fencer in the unit behind Corbin, who would, of course, fence saber. That would have possibly brought the competition to a close after only two bouts, without having to field their weakest fencer. As it was, Jester had boxed him into fencing épée, and there was a chance it would all come down to the third and final bout. The problem there was that épée was an 'iffy' weapon. If your point control was not clicking or your timing was a hair off . . .

Again the major fought his concentration back onto his own preparations. There was no point in getting oneself wound up over speculations. Shortly the matter would be decided once and for all in the real thing.

The demonstration was over now, and the director – the coach from the university fencing club – was taking over the microphone to address the crowd. O'Donnel had met him earlier, a spry little man who was obviously nervous about directing for this confrontation in front of an audience, not to mention the holo cameras, yet his voice was firm and confident as he launched into his explanation of the sport for the benefit of the spectators.

This, at least, the major had no difficulty ignoring as he resumed his stretching exercises. He had heard it all before, even knew it by heart. He also knew that it was extremely difficult to explain some of the subtler points of fencing, like 'right-of-way', to those impatient to see 'people swinging from ropes while hacking at each other with swords,' the common misconception of the sport generated by countless swashbuckler movies and holos.

Simply put, 'right-of-way' was a set of rules designed to preserve the true spirit of dueling, from which fencing descended. By those rules, once fencer A had 'declared an attack' by extending his weapon to an arm's length, threatening a valid target area, fencer B had to parry or otherwise remove that threat before retaliating with an attack of his own. The logic was that if the competitors were using 'real' weapons capable of inflicting injury or death, it would be foolhardy, if not suicidal, to ignore an attack in favor of launching one of your own. Though the concept itself might be simple, a goodly portion of any fencing bout was spent with the competitors standing by impatiently after a blinding flurry of action while the director sorted out exactly who had the right-of-way at each moment during the exchange so that the touch, or point, could be awarded. This was, of course, a little *less* exciting than watching grass grow. The only thing duller than sorting out right-of-way was listening to it being explained.

Finally the director concluded his explanation – or gave up – and raised his voice, announcing the first bout.

'Our first event this evening will be saber,' the speakers boomed. 'With this weapon, either the point *or edge* can be used on the attack. The target area is from the hipline up, *including* the arms, head, and back.'

The man paused to consult his notes.

'Representing the Red Eagles of the Regular Army will be Isaac Corbin, who held the Tri-Planetary Saber Championship for five years in a row!'

O'Donnel swore lightly under his breath as a surprised murmur swept through the audience. He had hoped Corbin's record would go unnoticed or at least escape comment. As it was, before the bout had even started, the Legion's representative would be seen as an underdog. If he lost, it would be expected, and if he won, it would be an upset!

'And representing the Space Legion, Sergeant Escrima, who has never fenced saber before this evening!'

This time, the major ignored the crowd's surprised reaction as he snatched the lineup list from his pocket and studied it quickly.

There it was: Sergeant Escrima . . . Saber! He had been so wrapped up thinking about his own bout and the woman foilist that he had completely overlooked the posting for saber!

Sure enough, the demonstrator had surrendered his sticks and was being helped into a fencing jacket and mask by two Legionnaires.

Not a bad idea, O'Donnel thought with a tight smile, running a totally unpredictable opponent at the champion by bringing in a nonfencer. Still, he doubted it would make much difference. Corbin was simply far too seasoned a veteran to be rattled by the antics of a beginner.

As it turned out, the major was correct in his assessment. Corbin scored an easy win over his inexperienced opponent, though the victory was not as decisive as O'Donnel would have liked.

At first, Escrima scored a few hits, lashing out with lightning speed to 'slash' the wrist of his opponent as Corbin began his attack. As the major predicted, however, the champion soon learned to ignore these 'stop hits,' carrying through with his simple attack and scoring the hit on right-of-way. In short, he knew the rules of the weapon better and rode that knowledge to victory.

Time and again, Escrima would electrify the crowd with his speed, either closing with his tormentor or dropping low to slash at his legs, only to have his hits disqualified as being 'off target.' Twice he was warned by the director for bodily contact, a strict no-no in tournament fencing.

The crowd, not fully understanding the rules, cheered and applauded Escrima's moves, only to lapse into stunned silence spiked with a few low hisses and boos when the action was nullified or the touch awarded against him.

As a final indication of his ignorance of the sport, Escrima clearly missed when the bout was over. With the awarding of the final touch, Corbin whipped off his mask and stepped forward to shake hands, only to be confronted by an opponent who was still clearly ready to fight. For a moment it looked like a disaster, but then Escrima realized his opponent was no longer competing. Sticking his saber under one arm, he pumped Corbin's hand once, then removed his own mask and stood looking around in bewilderment as the weak applause rose and sank.

'Sergeant Escrima!'

The voice cracked like a whip, and Escrima turned toward the bleacher of Legionnaires.

The company commander, who had been sitting, suited and ready for his own bout, stood pointedly in a position of attention. With careful deliberation, he raised his weapon to Escrima and held it in a salute. In a slow wave behind him, the entire company of Legionnaires rose and joined their commander, saluting their sergeant in his defeat.

The Eagles' commander was puzzled for a moment. It had been his understanding that the Legion didn't go in much for saluting. Of course, proper military form would have been for the salute to be given only by whoever was in charge of the formation, which was to say Jester, rather than by every individual simultaneously. Still, it was a nice touch.

Escrima stared at the company for a moment, then acknowledged their salute with a curt nod of his head. Holding himself stiffly erect, he turned and marched off the floor, ignoring the new burst of spontaneous applause that rippled down from the spectators.

'Our next event will be foil. This is a point weapon only, and the target area is the main torso, including the groin and back, but *excluding* the head and arms. Representing the Space Legion will be Private . . . Super Gnat, and for the Red Eagles, Corporal Roy Davidson.'

Without being conscious that he was ignoring the announcement and the beginning of the next bout, O'Donnel found his attention arrested by a small drama being played out outside the spectators' line of vision.

From his vantage point, the major could see the wall behind the bleachers which held the Space Legion company. What caught his eye was the figure of Escrima, who had just challenged the Red Eagles champion saber man. The stick-fighting sergeant was squatting by the back wall facing away from his company, his head bowed and shoulders hunched forward, a picture of abject misery.

To O'Donnel, the reason was immediately clear. Everyone else might have expected Corbin to win, and his rival commander might have fielded Escrima as a long-shot chance, but either the strategy hadn't been snared with Escrima or the message had failed to sink in. The proud, scrappy little warrior had apparently expected to emerge from the bout triumphant, and was now suffering the crushing aftermath of not only having lost but of having let down those who had counted on him as their champion.

As the major watched, Captain Jester appeared, first standing behind the sergeant, then kneeling to talk with intimate, earnest intensity. Though they were too far away for him to hear the exact words, O'Donnel had no difficulty constructing the conversation in his mind.

The commander would be explaining again the impossibility of the fight Escrima had just undertaken, possibly even apologizing for sending the sergeant into a hopeless situation instead of undertaking the job himself. It would be pointed out that the sergeant had scored several hits against a seasoned champion, which was more than many practiced fencers could do, and that he had, indeed, more than upheld the honor of the company.

Eventually the sergeant's head came up, and a few moments later he was nodding at what his commander was saying. The two men rose to their feet, and the captain clapped Escrima fondly on the shoulder, leaning close to share a few last words before leading him back to the bleachers.

O'Donnel found himself nodding as well.

Good. The little sergeant was much too good a man to be abandoned by his own during such a trauma. The major's appreciation of his rival went up yet another notch as he turned his attention to the bout in progress.

' . . . the initial attack misses . . . *passé* . . . *then* the counterattack lands *before* the final replacement of the point. The touch is right . . . Score, three to one! . . . *Gardez!* . . . '

Three to one?

O'Donnel focused his attention on the action.

What was going on here? How could his man be down 3–1 so fast?

'*Allez! Fence!*'

In the quick flurry of swords that followed the director's signal, it became clear what was happening.

The little fencer representing the Legionnaires – what was her name? Oh yes, Super Gnat – had found a way to compensate for her shorter reach. She would hang back at the edge of Davidson's lunge range, obviously too far back to launch an attack of her own, and bait the Eagles' fencer into initiating the action. Sometimes she would simply step back out of the reach of the attack, but then . . .

The major scowled as Super Gnat dodged the oncoming point and stepped in close to her taller opponent. Davidson tried to reverse his advance to bring his point to bear again, but she followed him back down the strip and . . .

'*Halt!* The initial attack falls. On the recovery, the counter-attack lands! Touch is right! Score, four to one!'

The bitch was so small, her target area was almost nonexistent! Hell, she could inhale and disappear behind her foil! And that footwork she was using . . .

O'Donnel watched closely as Super Gnat skipped and danced backward down the strip, leading Davidson like a terrier teasing a bull. He had seen that floating, pivoting footwork before. He couldn't quite put his finger on where, but it wasn't on a fencing strip! The Legionnaires had run another off-style martial artist in on him, but *this* one had managed to translate her moves into fencing! What was more, Davidson lacked Corbin's experience and was clearly thrown off his normal form by his opponent's unorthodox movements.

The Eagles' fencer managed to rally and score two touches in a row, but to the major the outcome was already a given. The scrambling little fencer was simply too resourceful to let a three-point advantage slip away, and . . .

As if in response to his thoughts, Super Gnat launched a running, diving *flèche* attack, taking the offensive for the first time and catching Davidson napping as he planned his own attack.

'*Halt!* The attack carries! Touch is right! Five to three! Bout to the Space Legion! The meet is tied at one bout each!'

The spectators exploded with cheers and applause as Super Gnat saluted her opponent and pulled off her mask, revealing a beaming face that shone like the sun. She pumped the hands of her adversary and the director, nodding her thanks at their murmured compliments, then turned toward the Legion bleachers.

No cue had been necessary from their commander this time. The entire company was on its feet saluting its victorious champion. Still holding the jubilant smile that seemed to pass her ears, Super Gnat returned the salute with a flourish of her weapon that ended in an exaggerated mock curtsey. At that, the Legionnaires broke their stiff poses and swarmed out of the stands to surround their teammate.

'All *right*, Gnat!'

'Way to go!'

The first to reach her was the tall, misshapen nonhuman Legionnaire whose mere presence made the Red Eagles uneasy. In a move that could only be genuine affection, he snatched her into the air in a huge bear hug that was at once enthusiastic and gentle, then, without setting her down, shifted his grip and held her aloft to the cheers of the rest of the company.

'Sorry about that, sir.'

The terse apology pulled O'Donnel's attention back from the other end of the gym.

'Don't worry about it, Davidson,' he said firmly, lightly punching that notable on the arm. 'Nobody wins all the time. Looks like it's up to me to try to settle up.'

'Yes, sir,' the corporal said, shooting a glance down the floor to where the Legionnaires were still celebrating. 'Do you think you can do it? They may be goof-balls, but they're tricky as hell.'

The major nodded his agreement of the corporal's assessment.

'To tell you the truth, Corporal, I don't know. Ask me again in about ten minutes.'

Davidson flashed him a quick smile.

'Right. Good luck, sir.'

'Our next and final bout . . . ' The director's mike boomed through the loudspeakers, and he paused to wait for the Legionnaires to quiet down and take their seats again before continuing.

'Thank you. Our next and final bout will be épée. For those of you who have been confused by my explanation of the right-of-way rules, you'll be glad to know *there is no right-of-way in épée! Whoever hits first, gets the touch!'*

A brief ripple of applause and laughter greeted this announcement, which the director acknowledged with a grin.

'This is because the encounter épée is re-creating a duel from the period *after* the Code Duello was changed to accept "first blood" rather than death to settle an affair of honor. First blood can be drawn from anywhere on the body, including the hands and feet, and accordingly the entire body is fair target when fencing épée.'

O'Donnel gathered up his mask and his weapon, plugging his body cord into the socket hidden inside the weapon's bell guard. The movements were automatic and ritualistic as he began to mentally set himself for the upcoming bout.

'By watching the lights on the scoring machine,' the director was continuing, 'it is easy to see who has scored the touch. The machine, which both fencers will be attached to by means of feed reels and body cords, determines within a twentieth of a second who hit whom first. If both fencers score a hit within that time frame, which happens more often than you might think, both lights will come on and it will be scored as a double touch. That is, a hit will be awarded to *each* fencer for that particular exchange.'

The major wished the bout would get under way. He was starting to feel the tension of the deciding bout creeping into his shoulders. Nervously he shook his sword arm to keep it loose. Tension meant stiffness, and stiffness meant slowed reflexes, a potentially fatal error in a sport where the winner and loser were often divided by split seconds.

'The final bout will be between the commanding officers of the competing groups. For the Red Eagles of the Regular Army, Major Matthew O'Donnel . . . and for the Space Legion, Captain Jester!'

'*Go get him, Cap'n!*'

'*LEGION!*'

The cheering section at the other end of the gym was obviously wound tight as a drum, bellowing out encouragement in their excitement that would be more appropriate at the opening of a boxing match than in a fencing meet. O'Donnel noted, however, that his opponent seemed oblivious to the racket as they moved onto the strip and hooked their body cords into the spring retrieval reels at either end. Saluting each other and the director, they donned their masks and stepped up to their respective on-guard lines.

'Fencers ready?'

'Ready, sir.'

'Ready!'

'*Allez! Fence!*'

Judging from what he had seen before, both this evening *and* this afternoon, the major had expected Jester to be an off-the-wall, unorthodox fencer, relying on weird, unexpected moves to score his points. Instead, he was pleasantly surprised to see his opponent take a conventional, textbook guard stance as they began to jockey for position.

Fine by me, mister. By the book it is. Let's see how good you really are.

Unlike foil and saber, where the hits are usually scored 'deep' to the body in flashy, driving attacks, épée is more of a sniper's weapon where the touches are made with sudden quick jabs to the arm and hand – and, rarely, the leading foot – of one's opponent.

Silence slowly descended on the crowd as the two men edged back and forth on the strip, watching each other for the slightest opening.

O'Donnel was now oblivious to the audience as he studied Jester's guard stance.

. . . weapon arm ramrod straight at shoulder level, hiding the entire arm and hand behind the oversized bell guard . . . never a waiver in the coverage as he advanced and retreated in small, coiled spring steps . . . Classic! . . . No cheap, easy touches here! . . . Maybe if he invited an attack to . . .

In a flicker of movement, the Legionnaire attacked . . . not with an explosive burst of energy, but seeming to almost collapse as his sword dropped and . . .

BZZZ!

'*Halt!* One light! Touch is right! Score, one to zero! Fencers ready?'

The major barely heard the director's call, much less the applause from the stands as he mentally raged at himself.

The foot! He had been hit on his leading foot! Of all the . . .

While foot hits were, of course, permitted, they were rarely tried in actual bouts. If the defender simply withdrew his lead foot, the attacker would be left with no target, and his entire arm exposed for the counter hit! Still, occasionally a low attack would catch the defender flat-footed, but your opponent had to be . . .

O'Donnell pushed his self-criticism from his mind,

focusing instead on the next touch as the director placed them on guard again.

Okay, wise guy. You know I'm ticked at having gotten caught that easy. If you've got any smarts at all, you'll fake your next attack to that same foot, counting on me to overreact in defense. When I do, you'll be back on the high attack before I can cover. Well, I'm waiting for you, buster, so just . . .

'*Allez! Fence!*'

BZZZ!

'*Halt!* Again, there is one light . . . '

Jester had attacked as soon as the director dropped his hand to signal the start of the action. No feint . . . no tricky fake . . . just a quick darting jab . . . *to the foot again!*

Two-zero!

The major tried desperately to get his annoyance under control as they came on guard again.

The sonofabitch caught him twice with the same sucker move!

'*Allez! Fence!*'

The progress of the bout was relentless, giving O'Donnel little or no time to regroup mentally.

Jester stamped his foot noisily, and the major had to fight to keep from twitching defensively at the sound.

Don't fall for a sound feint! It's just the kind of thing this joker will use to . . .

The Legionnaire surged forward, catching and controlling O'Donnel's sword with his own weapon, moving the deadly defending point to one side with a flick of his wrist while slamming his own point squarely into his opponent's mask.

BZZZ!

'*Halt!*'

The major turned his back on the proceedings, shaking his arms and rotating his shoulders as the touch was awarded.

He had tightened up! Fighting the reflex to move at

the sound of the foot stomp, he had tensed his arm, and Jester seized the opportunity before he could regain enough flexibility to evade the attack on his blade!

Three to zero! No! Put it out of your mind! Think of it as coming on guard for the first touch . . . except now Jester would be going for double touches! Two double touches and the bout would be over!

'Fencers ready?'

'Ready!'

'Just a moment, sir!'

O'Donnel took a deep breath and blew it out slowly. His opponent might protest the delay, but even that would buy him some time to get himself under control . . . and break Jester's momentum.

As it was, nothing was said by either the director or the Legionnaire until the major stepped up to his on-guard line and raised his sword.

'Ready, sir!'

'*Allez! Fence!*'

To O'Donnel's surprise, Jester did not immediately press the attack. Instead, he stood waiting in his guard . . . just a second! The classic picture wasn't there! Instead, the point of Jester's épée was *above* his bell guard . . . not much, barely an inch, but . . .

The major was attacking even before he finished the thought.

BZZZ!

'*Halt!* One light! Touch is left! Score is three to one!'

That was more like it! In an épée guard, holding the sword at an angle to the arm, however slight, was a dead giveaway that there was target exposed, even if you couldn't see it. Slipping his point past Jester's bell guard, O'Donnel had caught a piece of the underside of his opponent's arm . . . not much, but enough for a touch. Now to see if the bastard had figured out his mistake!

'*Allez! Fence!*'

BZZZ!

'*Halt!*'

Got him again! Three to two now!

The major was waiting at the on-guard line as the touch was awarded, eager for the bout to resume before his opponent had a chance to analyze the hole in his defense.

'Fencers ready?'

'Ready.'

'Ready, Sir!'

'*Allez! Fence!*'

BZZZ-UZZ!

'*Halt!* Both lights are on! Double touch! Score is four to three!'

Four to three! He had to be careful now. One more touch and . . . No! Jester had been lucky to catch a piece of his arm as he came in on the attack. He had to keep the offensive. Still, his opponent was expecting the shot to the underside of the arm now. Maybe a feint to draw his reaction . . .

'*Allez! Fence!*'

The major deliberately gave the point of his weapon a small twitch, and was rewarded by a quick flash of light reflected from his opponent's bell guard as it moved.

BZZZ!

'*Halt!* There is one light! Touch is left! Score is four all. Bout and match point, gentlemen. Fencers ready?'

Got him! Now, just one more. C'mon . . . think! One more touch!

'*Allez! Fence!*'

For a moment, it was as if neither fencer had heard the director's signal. Motionless, they stared at each other, watching for an opening yet unwilling to make a move which might create a vulnerability. Then, with slow deliberation, Jester raised his sword arm six inches, exposing the target his opponent had been scoring on, daring him to try again. That frozen tableau was held for a few heartbeats, then O'Donnel went forward in a gliding rush, accepting the invitation. Jester's point darted down, racing to intercept the attack, and . . .

BZZZ-UZZ!

'*Halt!*'

The major whipped his head around, looking to the electronic box to see who had scored the touch first.

Both lights were lit! *Double touch!*

Jester jerked his mask off and stuffed it under his arm as he saluted the director and his opponent, then strode forward with his hand outstretched for the traditional handshake that signaled the end of hostilities.

'Excellent bout, Major. Thank you.'

Startled, O'Donnel found himself shaking his rival's hand reflexively.

'But . . . the bout . . . ' he managed at last.

'Tournament rules, as agreed,' the Legionnaire said firmly. 'Isn't that right, sir?'

That last was addressed to the director, who shook his head and shrugged. 'Well . . . in a double elimination tournament, it would be scored as a double loss . . . '

'There! You see?'

' . . . but I suppose we could have a fence-off to decide a winner. Perhaps a one-touch sudden-death bout,' the director rallied gamely. 'It's really up to you gentlemen.'

'Well . . . ' O'Donnel hedged, removing his mask as he tried to organize his thoughts.

'Major.'

The word was said so softly that it took O'Donnel a moment to realize Jester had spoken it rather than it being a random thought flitting through his mind. Their eyes met.

'Take the tie.'

'What?'

His rival looked away, smiling at the audience as he spoke, like a ventriloquist, without moving his lips.

'Take the tie. We'll split the competition . . . *and* the contract. I wouldn't want to see *either* of our forces lose at this point . . . would you?'

Good combat commanders do not survive by agonizing over decisions, and O'Donnel was no exception.

'Tournament rules were agreed upon.' He shrugged dramatically, turning to the director. 'The Red Eagles *and* the Space Legion stand by their word. Announce the double loss, sir.'

Turning on his heel, he marched unswervingly back to his men, barely remembering to unhook his body cord, as the director's announcement echoed in the silent gym. Weak applause greeted the explanation, though the confused babble in the audience nearly drowned it out.

From the look on the faces of the Red Eagles, the audience wasn't alone in its puzzlement.

'What the hell happened . . . sir?' Master Sergeant Spengler said, rising to meet his commander.

'Well, Sergeant, what we have is – '

'*Company! Atten-hut!*'

O'Donnel turned to look down the floor.

The Space Legionnaires were on their feet, Captain Jester centered in front of them. With a picture-book precision they had not shown during the close order drill competition, they were saluting the Red Eagles.

The major stared at them for a few moments, but their pose didn't waiver. Correct military procedure called for holding a salute until it was returned or the person or unit you were saluting was out of range.

This time, O'Donnel's decision was easier.

'*Red Eagles . . . Atten-hut!*'

And for the first time since their arrival – in fact, in the history of the Red Eagles – the crack unit of the Regular Army saluted the Space Legion, and meant it.

Soaking in a hot tub can be of mental, as well as

physical, therapeutic value, and Phule was enjoying it to the fullest as he felt his muscles slowly begin to relax.

'Sir?'

Slowly, reluctantly, he raised his head and opened his eyes.

'Yes, Beeker?'

'Will that be all, sir?'

'Have you asked Mother to hold all calls until this morning?'

'Yes, sir. Actually it seems she was already doing that without instruction. There are several messages of congratulation, and it seems that young reporter has been trying to reach you.'

'Again?' Phule closed his eyes and sank a few inches deeper into the tub. 'How many interviews does she need in one day?'

'I don't believe she's calling about an interview . . . sir.'

'Oh?'

'That's the impression I got from Mother, though she didn't relay the messages word for word.'

'Oh!'

'Will there be anything else?'

'No. Go ahead and call it a night, Beek. It's been quite a day . . . for all of us.'

'Indeed it has, sir.'

'Good night, Beeker.'

There was no response.

Strange. Usually his butler was quite fastidious about such social pleasantries.

Mildly puzzled, Phule opened his eyes to discover Beeker still in attendance, but looking uncharacteristically uncomfortable.

'Something bothering you, Beek?'

'Well, sir . . . you know I rarely pry or question your actions, but . . . '

The butler hesitated, as if at a loss for words.

'Yes, what is it?'

'In your bout this evening . . . I mean, I've watched you fence in competitions before, sir, and flatter myself to think I know something of your abilities and style . . .'

Beeker's voice trailed off again.

'And?' Phule urged.

'And . . . for my own curiosity, you understand, and in strictest confidence . . . I was wondering . . . Well, sir . . . did you throw your bout? Deliberately fence for the tie, I mean?'

Phule exhaled a long breath, closing his eyes and sinking deeper into the tub before answering.

'No, I didn't, Beek. I thought about it . . . that's why I let him pull up even instead of finishing him off when I got the lead . . . but I chickened out at the end. If I could have been *sure* of the tie, I would have gone for it, but it would have been chancy at best. In the final analysis, I decided I didn't have the right to risk the company's success on a gamble, so on the final touch I was genuinely going for the win. The way it turned out – getting the tie I really wanted – was pure luck, nothing else.'

'I . . . I'm afraid I don't understand, sir. Why would you prefer a tie to a win?'

Phule opened his eyes and raised his head again, his face splitting in a wolfish grin.

'You weren't watching close enough, Beeker. We *did* win.'

'Sir?'

'Think about it. Our little Space Legion Omega Company, the dregs of the dregs, just held its own with the Red Eagles – the best the Regular Army has to offer. What's more, as far as the spectators were concerned, Escrima *won* his bout. The points favored Corbin because he knew the technicalities of the rules better, but it was obvious that in a *real* fight with no rules, Escrima would have made mincement out of him. On that basis alone, we were the winners *before* I even stepped onto the strip. In fact, the only event the Eagles won clearly was the drill competition – parade-ground flash that doesn't impress anyone with their fighting ability.'

'I see.'

'Do you?' Phule's voice was suddenly very earnest. 'We had them beat, so there was no point in kicking them, too. The Red Eagles are a top outfit that deserve the reputation they've built. If preserving that reputation, helping them save face, means sharing the idiotic honor guard contract, then it's a price I'm willing to pay. There's no point in making enemies when you don't have to.'

'Of course, your *own* force is disappointed. I may be doing them a disservice, but I doubt they would understand the subtleties of your logic.'

'Yes. Isn't it incredible?' The Legionnaire was grinning again. 'Do you realize how much they've changed their mind-set in just one day? This morning they didn't believe we had a chance against the Red Eagles; but tonight they're disappointed that we *only* tied them! They're really starting to believe that we can do anything!'

'That *is* how you've trained them, sir. Of course, it would have been nice if they could have celebrated a victory tonight.'

'True, but instead, they're in town drinking with the Red Eagles, as equals. Unless I miss my guess, there's more than one argument going as to whose commanding officer would have won if we had gone to a fence-off . . . as if that were any indication of the caliber of men we are or the forces we lead.'

'Quite so, sir. As long as *you're* aware of it.'

This was, of course, my true *concern. It was one thing for the Legionnaires to draw confidence from their success in a controlled contest with set rules, as long as my employer maintained his awareness that it was no indication of how they would fair in real combat. Unfortunately, despite his assurances to the contrary, I continued to be plagued by the nagging fear that he, too, was sliding into the belief that his force could do and accomplish anything.*

History has shown that, while soldiers can draw confidence and esprit de corps *from such conviction, the same attitude in a commander can breed disaster.*

16

Journal #152

[Note: The more numerically aware readers will have observed there are more entries than normal missing between this portion of my chronicle and the last. While there were numerous interesting incidents and observations made during this period, they are not particularly pertinent to this account, and I have therefore withheld them to focus on the more crucial occurrences which followed. Perhaps, if time allows, I will publish some of those episodes at a later date, probably thinly disguised as fiction. For now, however, I will simply insert a brief summary of the two or three weeks following the competition.]

The Regular Army was apparently less than pleased with the Red Eagles' inability to achieve better than a tie against the Space Legion force under my employer's command. Then again, there is also the possibility that their new orders simply got lost in the shuffle of paper that is the bane of any organization of a size worthy of mention. For whatever reason, whether punishment or bureaucratic incompetence, the Red Eagles were not reassigned after the contracts were signed, but left to cool their heels for a while with us on Haskin's Planet. It is my hope that this was due to an oversight, for if punishment was the Army's intent, they failed dismally.

Despite the stormy nature of their initial introduction, the Eagles and the Legionnaires got on like a house afire. Between intra-unit dating and the inevitable bar crawling, the two groups drew even closer together and friendships grew and blossomed. (No reference need be made here of the methods of frequency of cross-pollination.)

The Red Eagles were particularly enamored of The Club which the Legionnaires called home, and soon were spending as much or more time there as they were at their own quarters. Of course, there is no doubt in my mind that the Legionnaires benefited greatly from this association, as the Eagles were more than happy to show off by sharing tips and pointers on the firing range and confidence course. There was also, as might be expected, a notable increase in interest among both groups in the fencing lessons which had been available all along.

Perhaps the most notable development during this period was that my employer finally felt satisfied that he had at least a passing knowledge of those under his command, and turned his attention to the job he should have been doing all along, which is to say administration. More and more he was willing to rely on his lieutenants to oversee the company's field operations while he filled his time managing things on a grander, more long-term basis.

Unfortunately this meant that he was not standing swamp duty with the company when, as they say, it hit the fan.

'Are you sure this guy can deliver the goods, C.H.?' Phule said impatiently, glancing at the door of the cocktail lounge for the twentieth time. 'If this turns out to be a waste of my time . . . '

'Don't fret yourself none, Cap'n,' his supply sergeant said, desperately signaling the bartender for another round for his commander. 'If my man says he's got 'em . . . he's got 'em. I just thought it would be best if the two of you met face-to-face *before* any money changed hands, is all.'

The subject of this oblique discussion was knives. Harry claimed to have found a source who could supply them with a large quantity of the latest design in 'action' knives, which was to say spring-loaded. These beauties were unusual in that not only did the blade emerge straight out of the handle at the touch of a button, as opposed to the more traditional switch-blades which opened from the side like a jackknife, but if one held down the locking lever while triggering the blade, it would keep going, launched like a dart by the forty-pound spring that powered the mechanism. All in all, they were deadly little beasts. They were also illegal . . . hence the cloak-and-dagger approach to closing the deal.

Harry's connection had refused to come out to The Club to discuss the matter, but had agreed to meet them at their old watering hole, the Hotel Plaza lounge. Not surprisingly, the Legionnaires were well remembered at that establishment, and part of Phule's nervousness was that he was afraid their supplier would be scared off if Bombest or any of the rest of the hotel staff were talking to them when he arrived.

'How are things going with the inventory?' he inquired, more to make conversation than anything else. 'Are you going to be ready by next week?'

'Ready anytime you are, Cap'n.' The sergeant grinned. 'Just be sure to wear one of your old uniforms. Physical inventories can get kinda dusty.'

'Oh, I'm not going to be doing the audit.'

'Yer not?' Harry scowled. 'You mean my boys have been doin' all that prep work for nothin'?'

'Not exactly,' the commander said. 'I've asked Sushi to handle the first couple rounds with you.'

'Sushi? Aw, c'mon, Cap'n. That's not exactly fair.'

Sushi's partner, Do-Wop, had proved to be less than discreet when it came to bragging about his crony's criminal achievements. As a result, that notable's history as an embezzler was already legend throughout the company.

'Think of it as setting a poacher to catch a poacher,

C.H.' Phule smiled. 'I figure he knows more about what to watch for than I do. Of course, I'll be spot-checking *his* work as well.'

'But don't you think . . . Uh-oh. Here comes trouble.'

Phule followed his sergeant's gaze. Chief Goetz had just entered the lounge and was making a beeline for their table.

'Just relax, Harry,' he murmured. 'Let's not be too eager to post bail until we're charged.'

'Haw! Hey, that's a good one, Cap'n.'

'Good afternoon, Willard . . . Sergeant.' Goetz was standing over their table now. 'Mind if I join you for a drink, or am I interrupting something?'

'As a matter of fact, Chief' Phule said, glancing pointedly at his watch, 'we *are* waiting to meet someone.'

Ignoring the hint, the policeman pulled up a chair and parked himself on it as if he had been invited.

'You know, it's funny you should mention that.' He smiled, waving for the bartender. 'We've got a guy down at the station, name of Weasel Honeycutt. Picked him up for questioning on a couple break-ins last night, and you know what? Instead of pushing for a lawyer like he usually does, what he wanted was for someone to come down here and tell you he wouldn't be able to meet with you today . . . and here I am, being a conscientious public servant. Would that, by any chance, be the appointment you were waiting for?'

'Uh . . . '

'Good. Then you've got time to have that drink with me, and maybe answer a few questions yourselves . . . like *what's up between you and the Weasel?*'

The last came out as a snarl, as Goetz abandoned his pleasant manner and glared at the two Legionnaires.

'He wanted to talk to the cap'n here about enlistin',' Harry answered quickly.

Phule barely managed to avoid choking on an ice cube.

'Enlisting?' The chief's eyebrows collided with his hairline. 'I knew the Legion wasn't picky about whom they recruited, but don't you think that the Weasel is stooping a bit . . . even for you? I mean, you've already got one fence and black marketeer working for you.'

He stared pointedly at Chocolate Harry, who shifted uneasily in his chair.

'Regulations require me to speak with anyone who expresses an interest in enlisting,' Phule interceded smoothly. 'One's pre-Legion history is unimportant to us. As you've so tactfully noted, we take anyone . . . we've even been known to accept ex-cops.'

That earned a guffaw from the policeman, though the best Harry could manage was a weak smile.

'You got me there, Captain,' Goetz acknowledged with a mock salute. 'I don't think you'll get the Weasel, though. It would mean too much of a pay cut for him . . . unless you're supplementing his enlistment bonus personally, that is.'

'It was just talk,' Harry mumbled, playing with his empty glass. 'You know . . . nothin' definite.'

The chief pursed his lips for a moment, then nodded.

'All right,' he said. 'We'll let it drop for now and keep it social. I'll tell you, though, if there's a chance it might get the Weasel off-planet and out of my jurisdiction, I'll help with the paperwork myself.'

He paused as the bartender delivered his drink. By unspoken agreement, he paid for his own, lest there be any question as to whether he was accepting bribes from the Legionnaires.

'Mebbe I should get on back to The Club, Cap'n,' Harry muttered, starting to rise, but Phule waved him back into his seat.

'Relax, C.H.,' he said. 'The chief here says it's just a social visit, and besides, it's about time you two got to know each other a little better.'

'Where are the rest of your bandits, if you don't

mind my asking?' Goetz said, taking a sip of his drink. 'Haven't seen any of them around town today.'

'It's a duty day,' Phule explained. 'The fearless forces of the Space Legion are hip-deep in muck, protecting the miners from the local ecology, and vice versa. The fact that C.H. and I happened to schedule our . . . meeting the same day as we would be normally joining our comrades in their discomfort is mere coincidence.'

'Amen to that,' Harry acknowledged with his first genuine grin since Goetz entered the lounge.

'Say' – the chief frowned, peering at one of the other groups in the lounge – 'isn't that the Eagles' commander sitting over there with that little reporter . . . whatzername?'

'Jennie,' the Legion commander said without looking. 'I believe it is. Why do you ask?'

'I thought you had her staked out as private property. Or is she part of the settlement between you and the Army?'

'She's her own woman,' Phule said. 'Always has been, from all I can tell. Just because we had dinner together a couple of times doesn't mean – '

The shrill screech of his wrist communicator interrupted him in midsentence.

Annoyed, since he had left word he was not to be interrupted, the commander debated for a moment as to whether or not to acknowledge the call. Then it occurred to him that it would have to be important to override his orders, and he reached for the controls.

'Excuse me a moment, Chief . . . Phule here, Mother. What's the problem?'

'We've got trouble, Captain,' came the communication specialist's voice without any of her normal banter.

'What . . . '

'I'll let you hear it direct. Stand by for a patch from field operations . . . Go ahead, Lieutenant.'

'Captain Jester? Rembrandt here.'

'Go ahead, Lieutenant.'

'We have a situation here. I thought I should alert you as soon as possible.'

Phule felt a sinking sensation in his stomach, but kept his voice calm.

'Very well. What's happened? Start at the beginning.'

'Well, Do-Wop took a shot at a lizard . . . '

'A lizard?'

'It sort of looked like a lizard . . . only bigger. Currently unidentified. Anyway, it shot back at him, and –'

'*It what?*'

'It shot back at him, sir. Hit him with some kind of a stun ray. He's alive but unconscious. We've got a force of previously unknown aliens in the swamp. Intelligent and armed.'

17

Journal #153

I had the privilege of being the only civilian present at the confrontation with the 'alien invasion force.' This is not to say that I had any actual role in the proceedings or had any real business being there, but when those Legionnaires not on active duty for the initial contact scrambled to join their comrades in the field (leaving only Mother at The Club to serve as a communications link with the settlement), simple curiosity got the better of me and I decided to tag along. Normally I believe my employer would have sent me back, but he either decided he couldn't spare anyone to provide transportation or simply didn't register my presence at all. He was rather preoccupied at the time.

The bulk of the company was scattered along a one-hundred-meter line, crouching or flattened behind what little cover the swamp provided, as Phule huddled with Brandy and Rembrandt for his briefing. As they spoke, they kept their voices lowered to a conspiratorial whisper, occasionally raising their heads or leaning to one side to peer around the hummock they were kneeling behind.

The object of their attention, and the focal point of nearly two hundred primed weapons, was a scant thousand meters in front of them: a bulky ungainly-looking spacecraft which floated on pontoons at the end of a tether in one of the swamp's countless small pools of open, shallow water. There had been no signs of movement in or around the craft since the commander joined his force, but its proximity was enough to hone their caution to a fine edge.

'. . . they're small . . . well, big for lizards, but small compared to us,' Rembrandt was explaining. 'I'd put them at roughly half our height, judging from the few we've seen.'

'Weapons make them taller,' the commander commented grimly. 'You're sure Do-Wop is all right?'

'As sure as we can be without having him checked over by a doctor.' Brandy said. 'It was like he got hit with an electrical jolt. It knocked him out, but doesn't seem to have done any permanent damage. Mostly he's hollering to rejoin the company.'

'Let's keep him out of it for the moment. We don't know for sure if there are any hidden aftereffects yet, and there's no point in risking him unless he's really needed.'

'Right.'

'Any word from Armstrong?'

'He's still with the team escorting the miners back to the settlement,' Rembrandt reported. 'He wanted to break off and rejoin once they were a kilometer out of the area, but the way I understood your orders you wanted the miners under our protection all the way back to the settlement.'

'That's correct, Lieutenant,' Phule said. 'Until we know for sure how many of them there are and where they are in the swamp, we have to keep the miners covered.'

Though it had been proposed that Armstrong supervise the holding action while Rembrandt commanded the miners' escort, Phule had decided to reverse those assignments. Armstrong was clearly the better combat commander of the two, which to Phule's thinking made him the logical choice for escort duty in the event that another group of aliens was encountered during the miners' withdrawal. Rembrandt, on the other hand, had a better feel for the normal swamp terrain thanks to her earlier sketching expeditions, which made her a valuable asset to the scouting and information-gathering efforts.

'Has the settlement been alerted yet?' Brandy said, sneaking another look at the dormant craft.

'Goetz was with me when the call came in,' the commander supplied. 'He's standing by for further information from us as to what we're up against. In the meantime, he's pulling in all off-duty officers so that they'll have manpower ready to mobilize if things get rough.'

'How rough is rough, sir?' Rembrandt pressed. 'We've already had one person shot.'

'*After* he opened fire first,' Phule pointed out. 'What's more, from what you tell me, he's unharmed. There hasn't been any more shooting, has there?'

'No, sir . . . as per your orders,' the first sergeant said hastily. 'There was a bit of activity around the ship a while back, but no firing from either side. I think they saw us, but I can't be sure.'

'What kind of activity?'

'Spartacus reported it. Hang on, you can ask him direct.'

Before Phule could comment, Brandy gave a low, attention-getting whistle, then beckoned to the Sinthian to join their huddle. The Legionnaire came skimming across the open ground, his body compressed low so he looked a bit like a bean bag draped over the glide board.

The nonhuman would not have been the commander's choice for a scout, since the swift motion of his glide board would tend to catch and hold the eye more than would the slow, stealthy movements of his human teammates. Still, it was more maneuverable over water, and apparently he had completed his mission without drawing attention, or at least without drawing fire.

'Tell the captain what you saw, Spartacus,' Brandy

ordered. 'He wants to know what the aliens were doing around their ship.'

'Well, Captain,' the Sinthian began, 'they opened a panel on the side of their vessel and tinkered around inside for a while . . . I couldn't see exactly what they were doing. Then they sealed it up again and retreated back inside.'

The nonhuman's voice, as supplied by the translator he had hung diagonally across his body, was high and musical, almost like the tinkling of a bell. Try as he might, Phule could not escape the impression that he was receiving a military briefing from a Munchkin.

'Did it look like they were arming a weapon?'

'I . . . I don't think so, sir. There was no opening or fixture on the outside of the panel to suggest a firing capacity.'

'Did they see you?'

'A few of them looked my way from time to time, but they were looking all around, not just at me. I don't think . . . '

A flicker of motion to the rear of their position caught Phule's attention, and he held up a restraining hand which silenced the Legionnaire in midsentence. There was a tense moment, then a small group of figures appeared, moving carefully from cover to cover.

'What are *they* doing here?'

It was Brandy who voiced the muttered question, though it echoed the thoughts of everyone in the huddle, as well as those Legionnaires positioned near enough to note the group's approach. The answer was forthcoming, as one figure detached itself from the group and crept forward to join them.

'Sorry to take so long getting here, Captain,' Major O'Donnel said, nodding a curt acknowledgement to the others in the huddle. 'We hadn't expected to need our full combat gear for a simple honor guard assignment, and it took us a while to get it all unpacked and issued.'

He paused to survey the Legionnaires within his line

of vision, then shot a glance back at his own Red Eagles.

'If you just fill me in on what you've got so far, I'll get my troops disbursed. Then you can pull your force out a few at a time while we cover you.'

'Excuse me Major.' Phule said coldly, 'but what exactly do you think you're trying to pull here?'

'Pull?' O'Donnel was genuinely puzzled. 'I'm not trying to "pull" anything. We're simply taking command of the situation.'

'By what authority?'

'Oh, come now, Captain. Isn't it obvious? Dealing with a new alien race, particularly one which is potentially hostile, is much more in the Army's line than the Legion's.'

'I don't think it's all that obvious.'

'Do you mean to say you think . . . '

'In fact,' the Legion commander continued, raising his voice slightly to cut off the major's protests, 'what's obvious to me is that the *Legion* has been contracted to protect Haskin's citizens from whatever dwells in or comes out of these swamps, and that you and your force, Major, are interfering with our operation. Now, while I appreciate your offer of help, and would love nothing better than discussing military protocol with you, we're rather busy at the moment. Would you kindly take your force and retire?'

'You want authority?' O'Donnel said tightly, fighting to control his temper. 'All right. I'll play your game. Pass me one of your communicators and I'll get authorization for you.'

'I'm sorry, Major. Our communication network is for Legion personnel only. I'm afraid you'll have to hike back to the settlement to find and open – '

'Damn it, Willard!' the major exploded. 'By what right do you have the gall to try to give orders to a unit of the Regular Army?'

'Well, Matthew,' Phule said softly, 'how about

because at the moment we have you outnumbered by roughly ten to one?'

O'Donnel was suddenly aware that most of the nearby Legionnaires were listening to their conversation and that an uncomfortable number of weapons were now pointed in the general direction of the Red Eagles rather than at the alien ship.

'Are you threatening us?' he hissed, still watching the Legionnaires' weapons. 'Would you actually order your troops to open fire on friendly forces from the Regular Army?'

'In a minute,' Brandy said levelly.

'That's enough, Sergeant,' Phule snapped. 'As to your question, Major . . . Lieutenant Rembrandt?'

'Yes, Captain?'

'Do we have any hard evidence that the aliens are *not* capable of shape changing or low-level illusionary mind control?'

'No, sir.'

'So for all we know, they may have the ability to disguise themselves as humans, even a people we already know, to infiltrate our positions?'

'Well . . . I guess so . . . sir.'

'There you have it, Major. If necessary, I would feel more than justified in allowing my troops to defend themselves from any intruders, even if those intruders happened to *look* like a Regular Army unit.'

'But . . . '

'And especially,' Phule continued, dropping his voice, 'if they were conducting themselves in a manner inconsistent with known behavior patterns. You're losing it, Matthew. Cool down and we'll try it again . . . from the top.'

O'Donnel wisely followed the advice, taking and releasing several long breaths before resuming the conversation.

'Am I to understand,' he said at last, 'that you are

refusing to relinquish the situation to the Regular Army?'

'That is correct, Major O'Donnel,' the Legion commander confirmed. 'In my opinion, it still falls within our contracted services and is therefore our responsibility and ours alone. Simply put, it's our fight, so back off.'

The major glanced at the waiting Eagles again.

'Seriously, Captain, are you sure you wouldn't like to have my boys around – at least as a backup?

Phule wavered. There was no denying the benefits of having a team like the Red Eagles around.

'Would you be willing to serve as a reserve unit under my command?'

O'Donnel straightened slightly and saluted.

'If that's the only way we can be included in this waltz, then yes, sir! Reporting for duty, sir.'

It was far from an unconditional surrender, and everyone present knew there would be a reckoning later on. Still, if O'Donnel said he would take orders from the legion, then his word would be good . . . at least until the engagement was over.

'Very well, Major,' Phule said, returning the salute with equal formality, 'then I want you to take your force and pull back about two hundred meters. I'll let you know when and if we need you . . . and thanks.'

'How will we know if we're needed?' the major pressed, ignoring the offered thanks.

The Legion commander looked around, then raised his voice slightly.

'Tusk-anini!'

'Yes, sir?'

The large Legionnaire came crawling on his elbows at his commander's summons.

'I want you to go with Major O'Donnel and the Red Eagles while they take up a reserve position. We'll use your wrist communicator to send instructions if we need backup.'

'*No, sir!*'

'What?'

Phule was momentarily stunned by the refusal.

'No send away. I work hard . . . train hard. Have much right anybody be here for fight. Send someone else . . . *Please*, Captain.'

At a loss as to how to deal with the Voltron's obvious sincerity, the commander glanced about, seeking someone else to take the assignment. None of the other Legionnaires would meet his eyes, however, everyone suddenly developing intense interest in the alien spacecraft.

'All right, Tusk. Then give me your communicator.'

'Sir?'

'Give it to me, then get back to your position.'

After a moment's fumbling with the straps, Tuskanini handed over his precious wrist communicator, then went squirming across the ground to resume his post.

'I thought he was supposed to be a pacifist,' O'Donnel said, watching the Voltron go.

'So did I,' Phule acknowledged absently as he worked the communicator's settings. 'All right, Major. I've keyed this thing for a beeper cue so it won't give your position away when it goes off. Three beeps means we need you, then press this side lever here to go into talk/receive mode for specific instructions. Except for that, don't touch any of the controls. If you're not familiar with the unit, you might end up making noise at someone's else's position by mistake. Clear?'

'Got it.' The major nodded, accepting the communicator. 'We'll be waiting if you need us.'

'All right, get moving. And Major . . . thanks.'

O'Donnell threw him a wry salute and scuttled off to join the Eagles.

'Do you really trust him, Captain?' Brandy said skeptically.

'Just a moment . . . ' Phule was busy working his own communicator. 'Mother?'

'Com Central here, Captain.'

'Major O'Donnel and the Red Eagles are now on the network using Tusk-anini's communicator. Do not – repeat, do *not* – allow him to make any calls outside this area. Also monitor his position and inform me immediately if he starts moving. Copy?'

'Got it.'

'Jester out.' Phule shut down his communicator and turned to Brandy. 'In answer to your question, Sergeant, of course I trust him. Trust is the cornerstone on which intra-service respect and cooperation are built.'

'Right, sir. Sorry I asked.'

'Now then, returning to the original reason for this party' – the commander flashed a quick smile – 'I think we've learned about as much as we can about our visitors from watching them. Spartacus, I'm going to have to borrow your translator.'

'My translator?' the Sinthian chimed.

'That's right. Then switch your position to where you're close enough to Louie for him to translate for you if necessary.'

'Excuse me, Captain,' Lieutenant Rembrandt said, scowling, 'but what do you need a translator for?'

'I'm going to try to open communications with the beings in that ship, and I don't think it's safe to assume we speak each other's language.'

'But that's . . . I mean . . . do you think that's wise, sir?'

'I figure it's wiser than opening fire on them if there's a chance they're friendly . . . *or* cooling our heels out here while they get ready to attack if they're not,' the commander said. 'One way or the other, we've got to find out what their intentions are.'

'By setting yourself up to be a duck in a shooting gallery?' Brandy frowned. 'Don't you think it would be better to send someone out who's a little more expendable than you are, Captain? We really don't need our chain of command blown apart on the first salvo.'

'Lieutenant Rembrandt will be in command in my absence, however temporary or permanent that may be. Besides' – Phule flashed his smile again – 'I don't intend to be *completely* vulnerable out there. How far did you say Do-Wop was from the alien when he squeezed off his shot?'

'About fifty meters. Why?'

'That means they can't be sure of the maximum range of our weapons. It's my intention to try to set up this little powwow well *within* small-arms range. Believe me, I won't mind having a little extra cover while I'm out there. Now pass the word . . . I'm going out in five minutes.'

'Yes, sir.'

'And Sergeant? If you don't mind doing me a favor, double-check to be sure everyone has his safety on. I'm not *that* wild about being downrange of this trigger-happy bunch.'

Obviously I am not privy to the personalities or procedures present in the alien force we were facing, so this next portion is pure speculation as to the goings-on in the alien craft. Two things, however, lead me to believe my reconstruction is not totally inaccurate.

First, of course, is the eventual outcome of the confrontation.

Second is the logical observation that, since the humans and their allies had never encountered this race of aliens before, the alien force were as far or farther away from their home base as we were. That is to say, it is doubtful that those chosen for such an assignment were viewed as elite or exemplary by their own hierarchy.

Flight Leftenant Qual of the Zenobian Exploratory Forces was far from pleased with the situation. If anything, his frame of mind was closer to blind panic as he felt any chance of personal redemption slipping away from his grasp with each new report.

It had been his hope that the success of his mission, if not the length of its duration, would mollify the annoyance of the part of Second Supremo Harrah which had led to this assignment. Zenobians were not supposed to be a grudge-holding race to begin with, so how long could Harrah remain upset with one little lapse of judgment . . . really? Besides, could a lowly leftenant reasonably be expected to be able to distinguish between a 2,000-cycle-old antique urn and a fancy receptacle for the disposal of bodily wastes? Especially after an entire evening's drinking at a mating reception? That particular social blunder, however, was rapidly being eclipsed by the current disaster.

'How could you be so stupid as to shoot an intelligent alien, Ori?' he hissed at the crewman before him. 'Didn't it even *occur* to you that it was a flagrant violation of our standing orders to avoid direct contact with any alien cultures we might encounter?'

'But Leftenant, they shot at me *first*!'

'That in itself is an indication of intelligence on their part.'

'Excuse me, Leftenant,' his second-in-command said, joining the conversation, 'are you saying that the aliens' possession of weapons and uniforms is a sign of intelligence . . . or their specific choice of Ori as a target?'

'Both,' the leftenant retorted heatedly. 'But don't note that, Masem. In fact, none of this conversation should be entered in the log.'

'But sir, the completeness of the mission log is one of my specific duties, and I would be negligent if I – '

'Scanning for signs of intelligent life before we landed was one of your duties, too!' Qual interrupted. 'What happened to your sense of duty *there*?'

'If I might remind the leftenant,' Masem said,

unruffled, 'the scanners were inoperative at the time. In fact, they were partially dismantled in an effort to comply with the leftenant's order to repair our communications gear at any cost.'

Qual found himself wondering, not for the first time, if the crew he had been assigned was, in fact, part of his punishment.

'Well, are they operative now?'

'Almost, Flight Leftenant. Of course, to effect *those* repairs, we had to – '

'I don't care what it takes! Just get those scanners working! We've got to find out – '

'*Leftenant! The scanners are working!*'

The conversation as well as the niceties of rank were forgotten as the two officers joined the rush to the viewscreens, treading on more than one tail in the process.

'What's out there?'

'How many . . . ?'

'Great Gazma! Look at that!'

'There must be thousands of them!'

Actually there were barely hundreds of the glowing blips on the screen, but substantially more than the scant half dozen Zenobians crewing their own vessel.

'That's interesting,' Masem said thoughtfully. 'Look at these two – no, there's a third! Flight Leftenant, these readings indicate there's more than one intelligent life-form out there. It would seem that we're being faced by a combined force of alien races, though one race is clearly in the majority.'

'I don't care if they're talking mushrooms!' Qual snapped. 'There are more of them than there are of us – lots more – and probably armed, to boot. Stand by to lift off! We're getting out of here while we can!'

'I'm afraid that won't be possible, Leftenant.'

'Now what, Masem?'

'Well, we used parts from the lift-off relays to repair the scanners . . . as you ordered, sir.'

Qual wondered briefly if the craft's self-destruct mechanism was functioning, then remembered there wasn't one.

'You mean we're stranded here while an unknown hostile force is surrounding – '

'Leftenant! You'd better look at this!'

One of the blips had detached itself from the bulk of the force arrayed before them and was approaching their position.

'Quick! Put it on visual!'

The screen display changed to show the actual scene outside the ship. Whatever or whoever the blips had shown before were now visible behind brush and fallen trees, except for the one black-garbed figure standing out in the open.

'What a revolting creature.'

'Big, though, isn't he?'

'What does that have to do with anything?'

Qual was studying the figure in silence as the crewmen chattered nervously.

'I wonder if there's any significance to the white cloth he's waving?' he said finally.

'You know, sir,' Ori piped up, 'I remember back in basic training, we used little pieces of cloth like that to sight in our weapons.'

The flight leftenant favored him with a withering glare.

'I seriously doubt, Ori, that he's inviting us to shoot at him.'

'Well, they shot at *me*!'

'True, but indications are that *they're* intelligent.'

'Look, Leftenant,' Masem broke in, interrupting the exchange.

The figure on the viewscreen was making a big show of holding up its weapon, then carefully setting it on the ground at his feet.

'Well, *that's* pretty clear.'

'Unless it's some kind of ritual challenge to fight.'

'For the moment we'll assume that it means they want to parley,' Qual said, reaching his decision. 'I'm going out there.'

'Do you think that's wise, Leftenant?' his second-in-command queried.

'No . . . but I don't see where we have much choice at the moment. See if you can get the lift-off units repaired while I try to buy us some time.'

'Do you want us to cover you with the ship's guns, sir?'

'That would be great if we *had* any ship's guns. This is an exploration vessel, not a battleship, remember?'

'Oh. Right. Sorry, sir.'

'Leftenant,' Masem said softly, drawing him to one side, 'it might be prudent to be guarded in your conversation with the aliens. We wouldn't want to betray how strong the Zenobian Empire really is.'

'Believe me, Masem,' Qual hissed, giving one last glance around the control room, 'I *certainly* don't want them to find out our true strength.'

'Now that we've established communications, Leftenant,' Phule said, 'I'd like to begin by apologizing for the unprovoked attack on one of your crew. It was a fear reaction to the unexpected, made before we realized yours was an intelligent species. Further, I'd like to thank you for the merciful nature of your force's counterattack. It is impressive that my underling was only stunned and not killed outright.'

Qual was impressed with the translator, though he did his best to act as if it were commonplace. It had taken some time for him to realize he was to hang it around his neck, but once it was in place and in contact with his hide, the various grunts and clickings this strange alien used for speech were readily transformed into images and contacts in his mind. The translation of his own foremost thoughts into those same weird noises was a bit disquieting, but it was worth it to be able to establish that neither force was particularly eager to fight.

'Thank you for the apology, Captain Clown, but – '

'Excuse me, but that's Captain *Clown.*'

'I . . . see.'

The image provided by the translator was identical to the one Qual had formed in his mind when addressing the alien commander. Apparently the mechanism was not as effective as it first appeared.

'Anyway, as I was saying, Captain . . . Captain, I'm afraid there has been a minor misunderstanding. You see, my crewman was hunting for food when he was attacked, so the weapon he was carrying was designed specifically for that purpose.'

'I . . . I'm afraid I don't understand, Leftenant.'

'Well, we Zenobians prefer to eat our food while it's still alive, so hunting weapons are made to stun instead of kill like our war weapons.'

'Oh. I see. Well, no harm done,' Phule flashed his smile again.

'Pardon me, Captain, but is that supposed to be a friendly gesture?'

'What?'

'The baring of your fangs. You've done it several times now, but your manner does not indicate a matching hostility.'

'Oh. That's a smile . . . and yes, it's a sign of friendship. I'll try to stop doing it if it offends you.'

'No need. I just wanted to be sure I was interpreting it correctly.'

There was an awkward moment of silence, as each representative mentally dealt with this new awareness of the differences between their species.

'Tell me. Leftenant,' Phule said at last, 'now that we've established that your purposes here are not hostile, might I ask what your actual assignment *is*? Perhaps we could be of assistance.'

Qual considered the question carefully, but could see no danger in answering truthfully.

'We are an exploratory expedition,' he explained, 'assigned to search for new planets suitable for colonization or research stations. We landed here because swamps such as this are ideal habitats for our needs.'

'I see.' Legion commander nodded thoughtfully. 'Unfortunately this particular swamp has been designated as a preserve by my people. In fact, the presence of my force is to specifically serve as guardians.'

'Oh, I understand, Captain,' the Zenobian replied quickly. 'Believe me, we have no intent to contest your possession of this territory. Space is large, and there are sufficient habitats that we see no need to fight for those already inhabited. Now that we have discovered that these areas are already occupied, we will simply explore in another direction. In fact, we'll be on our way as soon as . . . soon.'

'Now, let's not be hasty,' Phule said. 'Perhaps we can work something out – something mutually beneficial to both our peoples.'

'How? Excuse me, I don't wish to challenge your veracity, but I thought you said the swamp was unavailable for use.'

'*This* swamp is, but there are others within our system which might serve your needs equally well. Information on their locations could ease or eliminate your need for exploration, and if permissions were obtained in advance, there would be no conflict involved in their settlement.'

Qual was suddenly very attentive. Such an arrangement would make him a hero within the Exploratory Forces as well as nullify any lingering disfavor he might be suffering under. Still, he had learned from past experience that offers that sounded too good to be true were usually just that.

'I don't understand, Captain,' he said cagily. 'Our races may be different, but I've always assumed that intelligence implies a certain degree of self-interest. Why should your people simply *give* us something which is theirs without asking for anything in return?'

'Oh, we'd want something in return, all right.' Phule smiled. 'Remember I said an arrangement which would be *mutually* beneficial. I think you'd find, however, that our demands for return on the use of our swamps would be minimal.'

'How minimal?'

'Well . . . before we get down to specifics, would you mind telling me what the maximum accurate range is for those sporting stun weapons of yours?'

'What happened, Captain?'

'Is there going to be a fight?'

'What do they want?'

Discipline fell by the wayside as the Legionnaires swarmed out to meet their returning commander. Ignoring their questions, Phule waved them to silence as he activated his wrist communicator.

'Com Central.'

'Yes, Mother. Patch me through to an off-planet line. I need to get a call through to my father . . . '

He gave the code number, then glanced up at the impatient Legionnaires who were circling him.

'If you'll listen in on my end of the conversation, you'll hear the answers to most of your questions. For the moment, however, you can all stand down. The alien force is not – repeat, *not* – hostile. There will be no fight, unless someone – '

'Willie? Is that you?'

Phule turned his attention to his wrist communicator.

'Yes, Dad. I'm here.'

'What's the problem? Don't tell me you're tired of playing soldier boy already.'

'Dad, I don't say this to you often, but *shut up and listen!* I have a situation here that potentially involves

you, and I don't have time to trade jibes and insult
this time. Okay?'

There was a few moments' pause, then the repl
came through, in notably more serious tones.

'All right, Willard. What have you got?'

'Does Uncle Frank still own that development com
pany? The one that buys up cheap swamps, then trie
to convert them to usable land?'

'I think so. Last thing I heard, he was using it as
tax write-off. It's always been a marginal operation
and – '

'Get on the horn to him as fast as you can and bu
it up . . . along with any other swampland you can ge
your hands on.'

'Just a second . . . '

There was another pause, this one broken by muffle
comments through the speaker.

'Okay,' came the elder Phule's voice again. 'Th
wheels are in motion. I suppose there's a reason I'n
doing this?'

'You bet there is. I've got a deal on the line: a whol
new alien race looking for swampland. No developmen
necessary. Just let them know where it is.'

'New aliens? What have they got to offer i
exchange?'

'I figure there's a wealth of new technology to b
bartered for, but for this particular deal how doe
exclusive production and distribution rights on a nev
weapon sound to you?'

'How new?'

'We're talking a stun gun . . . easily portable powe
pack . . . effective range approximately three hundre
meters. Law enforcement is the most obvious market
but I'm sure you can think of others.'

'Sounds good so far. Who's their agent?'

The Legionnaires smiled along with their com
mander.

'That's the bad news, Dad. I am. Don't worry, though . . . I'm sure we can work something out.'

'Yeah . . . sure. Just like last time. Well, give me a call when you're ready to squat down on the horse blankets and hammer out the details. Just do me a favor and don't ever tell me what your commission is. Okay?'

'It's a deal. Over and out.'

Phule shut down his communicator, drawing his first deep breath since the initial call on the aliens had come in.

His commission. He hadn't even thought about that. Wonder if the Zenobians had any need for the mineral rights to their swamps . . . here *or* within the territory they already controlled?

18

Journal #162

While it is difficult to clearly define where one segment of my employer's career ends and another begins, the first phase of his time with the Space Legion came to its climax, not with his encounter with the Zenobians, but with a 'visit' from certain high-ranking members of the Legion Headquarters staff.

It seems that, with the single-mindedness so typical of bureaucracies everywhere, they were less concerned with the results of my employer's actions than with the methods and procedures he utilized to achieve them.

The general public was usually apathetic regarding the movements of the Space Legion – even its high-ranking officers. As such, the party from Legion Headquarters was more than a little surprised at the crowd of civilians waiting for them when they disembarked from the shuttlecraft at the Haskin's Planet spaceport. Most were curiosity seekers, to be sure, but there was at least a token attendance from the fifth estate, as the party was quick to discover.

'Jennie Higgens, Interstellar News Service,' the reporter announced, blocking the path of the first Legionnaire in the party with her body, microphone, and camera crew. 'Is it true that you're here to punish Captain Jester, the commander of the Space Legion company stationed here on Haskin's Planet, for his recent confrontation with the Zenobians?'

'No comment,' Colonel Battleax mumbled, trying to edge around the obstacle. Despite her criticisms of

Phule's activity with the media, the truth was she herself only had limited experience in dealing with reporters, and those encounters had left her wary and guarded in their presence.

'But if Captain Jester is not going to be punished, why was he relieved of command and placed under house arrest right after that incident?' the reporter persisted.

'The Space Legion felt it was its obligation to the citizens of the civilized planets we serve to suspend Captain Jester's authority until an investitgation could be conducted to determine the propriety, not to mention the legality, of his actions.'

General Blitzkrieg was one of the three ranking officers who made up the board which governed the Legion. Though he was as startled as Battleax at their reception, he was also nearing retirement and quickly reached the decision that a little media exposure wouldn't hurt his efforts to obtain postretirement employment. If nothing else, it might increase his chances of finding a publisher for his memoirs.

'So your actual purpose here is to perform that investigation rather than to court-martial Captain Jester as rumored?' Jennie said, shifting her attention easily to the talker of the group.

'That is correct,' the general said, 'though we are prepared to convene a court-martial if the investigation warrants it.'

Blitzkrieg had only meant to cover himself for when the anticipated court-martial took place, but the reporter pounced on his implication.

'Could you tell our viewers why Captain Jester, who recently averted a potentially hostile alien invasion of the settlement here on Haskin's Planet, might be subject to court-martial and discipline by the Space Legion?'

The general leveled his best steely gaze at the reporter.

'Young lady,' he said, 'you are employed by the Interstellar News Service as a reporter . . . is that correct?'

'Yes, I am,' Jennie answered firmly, though she was unsure where the question was leading.

'Do you feel that position authorizes you to negotiate a peace treaty with an alien race, such as the Zenobians?'

'Of course not.'

'Excuse me, Ms. Higgens,' Colonel Battleax said, breaking her self-imposed silence, 'but if, as a reporter – or in any other capacity – you were the first to make contact with a force of potentially hostile aliens, would you feel justified to do or say whatever was necessary to remove the immediate threat to yourself and others, regardless of your actual authority?'

'That will be enough, Colonel,' Blitzkrieg snapped before the reporter could answer. 'I believe this interview is over, Ms. Higgens. We will release a formal statement of the Legion's position upon the completion of our investigation.'

Turning on his heel, he strode off toward the spaceport terminal, with Battleax trailing along behind.

Bringing up the back of the party, Major Joshua made no effort to hide his grimace of distaste. He had been the silent witness to this argument between the colonel and the general for the entire trip here, and they seemed no closer to an agreement than when the voyage started. At least it would all be over soon, except that indications were that he would be placed in command of the Omega Company to oversee its dismantling and reassignment after the court-martial . . . for the general was determined that there would be one. The major viewed both these occurrences with equal lack of enthusiasm, yet both seemed inevitable.

' "Saved the planet from an invasion by hostile

aliens," ' Blitzkrieg fumed, mimicking the reporter's voice. 'Do you *believe* this bullshit?'

'You must admit though, General, it's a pleasant change to have the Legion getting hero treatment by the media, isn't it?' Colonel Battleax said, unable to keep herself from twisting the knife a little.

'It would be nicer if it were justified,' the General snarled irritably. 'From the reports that were filed, the Zenobians were scared to death and just wanted to get back off-planet with their hides intact. To my thinking, that's a far cry from an invasion.'

Both the colonel and the major refrained from pointing out that the general himself had passed up numerous opportunities to correct the mistaken impression created and maintained by the media. By unspoken agreement, the Headquarters delegation was united in its desire to keep the favorable publicity generated for the Legion by the stories of the Zenobian 'invasion.' What divided them was the question of whether or not they retain that impression while punishing the man who was at the focus of the incident. Battleax didn't think it could be done . . . not that she had any real desire to punish Phule in the first place.

The party was ensconced in one of the spaceport's courtesy meeting rooms, the general having repeatedly rejected suggestions that they hold their proceedings at the facilities currently enjoyed by the Legion's company.

'Captain Jester *does* seem to have achieved a certain popularity locally,' the colonel tried again. 'Justified or not, he and his crew of cutthroats are currently the toast of the settlement.'

'All the more reason to get this over with and get him out of here as soon as possible,' Blitzkrieg muttered, deliberately missing the point Battleax was trying to make. 'What's the delay, anyway? Where is this Captain Jester?'

'He's waiting in the next room,' Major Joshua supplied. 'Has been since before we disembarked.'

'Then what are we waiting for?'

'We're trying to locate the court recorder, sir. She seems to have wandered off.'

'Shall we get started, anyway?' Battleax suggested casually. 'At least with the inquiry?'

'Oh no,' the general said. 'I want everything legal and by the book when I nail this guy's hide to the wall . . . no "procedural mistrial" loopholes for him to wiggle out of. Major, go out and see if you can find . . . What the hell is that?'

There was a loud rumble of powerful engines outside. The sound had begun softly as they spoke but had slowly risen in volume until now it could no longer be ignored.

Joshua had moved to the window overlooking the shuttle pads and was staring at something outside the line of vision of the other officers.

'General,' he said without turning away from his post, 'I think you should look at this.'

The sound was from a full dozen hover cycles, whose Legionnaire riders kept revving the engines noisily despite their slow pace. What was even more attention-getting, however, was the procession they were escorting.

The entire company of Legionnaires was marching into the area between the shuttle pads and the spaceport. There were no flashy maneuvers such as the Red Eagles had performed during the intra-service competition, yet something in the grim determination of their approach made them nonetheless impressive, if not intimidating, as they drew up in full formation. Of course, this image was enhanced by the fact that they were garbed in full combat uniform and gear, including what appeared to be loaded weapons.

At a barked command echoed by the sergeants, the formation halted and stood at attention. At the same ime, the hover cycle riders shut down the engines of heir vehicles, and for several moments the resulting ilence seemed even louder than had the earlier noise.

'What are they doing out there?' the general said as he three officers stared at the display outside their vindow.

'If I had to guess, sir,' Battleax murmured, not aking her eyes from the formation, 'I'd say it was a lemonstration of support for their commander.'

'A demonstration? It looks like they're getting ready o assault the spaceport.'

'I didn't say it looked like a *peaceful* demonstration.' The colonel smiled humorlessly.

'They've got clips of ammo in those weapons,' Blitzrieg noted. 'Who authorized that? Whom did you put n temporary command when you relieved Jester?'

'Lieutenant Rembrandt had the most seniority,' Batleax said. 'That's her at the head of the formation. I elieve that's the other lieutenant, Armstrong, standing eside her. Ummm . . . is it necessary for me to point ut to you gentlemen that they're between us and the huttle?'

'Do you want me to call the local police?' Joshua sked nervously.

'Those are supposed to be *our* troops out there, Major,' the general retorted tersely. 'We'd look pretty lamn silly asking the police to protect us from them, now, wouldn't we?'

'Yes, sir. Sorry, sir.'

'I want you to go out there and take command of hat formation, Major Joshua. Break it up and tell hem to return to their barracks and await further rders.'

'Me, sir?'

Fortunately rescue appeared that moment in the orm of the missing court recorder, who slipped into he room and took her position by her equipment, lissfully unaware of what was going on outside the spaceport. She was one of those drab, horse-face women who gave lie to the holo-movie stereotype c the sexy secretary.

'Sorry I'm late, General,' she said.

'Where the hell have you been?' Blitzkrie demanded, finding a focal point for his anger and ner vousness.

'Begging the general's pardon,' Battleax interceded 'but isn't it more important that we begin th proceedings . . . without further delay?'

'Oh! Yes . . . quite right. Thank you, Colonel. Some one tell Jester we're ready for him.'

The trio of officers barely had time to settle into thei seats before the captain entered. With careful precision he strode to the center of the room and saluted crisply

'Captain Jester . . . reporting as ordered, sir!'

General Blitzkrieg returned the salute with a sketch wave of his hand as he looked over at the cour recorder.

'Let the record show that a court of inquiry is con vened to review the actions of Captain Jester. Genera Blitzkrieg presiding, Colonel Battleax and Majc Joshua in attendance.'

He turned his attention to the figure in front of hin

'Well, Captain,' he said conversationally, 'I assum you know why we're here.'

'No, sir, I don't. I was told my actions were to b reviewed, but I am unaware of any activity on my par which might warrant such scrutiny.'

Even Battleax was startled by this statement. Sh had been prepared to favorably review whateve defense Jester might have to offer, but it had neve occurred to her that he would attempt to defend himse by arguing his innocence.

This was potentially disastrous. The captain *migh* have been able to obtain special consideration b claiming that extenuating circumstances forced him t overstep his authority, but not acknowledging he wa in error at all indicated a permanent, not a temporary, lapse in judgment.

The general sensed an easy victory, and his smile took on shark proportions as he pressed on.

'Captain Jester, do you feel that you, or anyone else in the Space Legion, has the authority to negotiate a peace treaty with a culture or society of aliens previously unknown to us?'

'No, sir. That power rests solely with the Alliance Council.'

'Well, then . . . '

'But I fail to see where the question has anything to do with me or anyone in my command . . . sir.'

'You don't?' Blitzkrieg frowned.

'General . . . if I may?' Battleax broke in quickly. 'Captain Jester, how would you describe your recent interaction with members of the Zenobian Empire?'

'Well, sir, I was informed that there had been an altercation between a member of my company and what seemed to be a previously unknown alien race. After first taking measures to ensure the immediate safety of the miners we were contracted to protect, I established contact with the commander of that alien force to determine whether or not they constituted a threat to the settlement or the Alliance as a whole. In that conversation, it was discovered that the alien presence was due to equipment failure on their part rather than any premeditated plan or attack, and that the altercation had been caused by nervousness and ignorance on both sides. Apologies were extended and accepted.'

'And . . . ' the general prompted after several moments' silence had passed.

'That was the total extent of my official exchange with the Zenobians, sir, which I believe is well within the guidelines set down for a Legion officer.'

'What about the agreement to trade swampland for weapons, Captain?'

Phule's expression was guileless.

'I *did* serve as a combination middleman and agent in such an agreement, sir. But that was at a later time while I was off duty. What is more, that agreement was a business deal between two individuals . . . specifically, Flight Leftenant Qual of the Zenobian Exploratory Forces and my father. To the best of my knowledge, and I was involved in all exchanges surrounding that agreement, at no time was it stated or implied that the deal committed or involved either the Alliance as a whole or the Zenobian Empire. As I said, it was simply a trade arrangement between two individuals, and my own part in the matter was permissible under Article – '

'We *know* the article in question, Captain,' Battleax interrupted, fighting a smile. 'It's referenced frequently in your file.'

General Blitzkrieg was shaking his head in amazement and confusion.

'Is it legal? Doing business with an alien race outside the Alliance, I mean.'

'To the best of my knowledge,' the captain answered smoothly, 'there is no law specifically *forbidding* such an arrangement. If we were at war with the Zenobians, it might be a different matter, but I don't believe there are any provisos for dealings with intelligent aliens that are not either in the Alliance or actively at war with us.'

He paused to smile at the reviewing officers.

'I imagine the tax boys might try to find some basis to challenge the deal, but I suggest we leave that to the battery of lawyers Phule-Proof Munitions employs for just such disputes. Repeating my initial assertion, I see no reason why such a question of legality, if it arises at all, should involve the Space Legion . . . or, specifically, me or my command.'

After the brief media conference where it was

announced that Captain Jester of the Space Legion had not only been cleared of any charges of misconduct but decorated for his handling of the Zenobian episode, that notable retired to the nearest bar, which happened to be in the spaceport, for a quiet drink.

'I'll tell you, Beeker, that's a load off my mind. For a while I thought they were going to shoot me just out of general principles.'

'It's good to see you vindicated, sir . . . if I may say so,' the butler agreed, raising his own glass in a small toast.

'The company showing up like that didn't hurt at all,' the commander mused. 'How did they react when the company portfolio profits were announced?'

'I don't believe the announcement has been made yet, sir. The lieutenants seemed a bit preoccupied with the preparations for today's demonstration when I passed the information to them.'

'Good,' Phule said. 'I'll tell them myself. I wonder how they'll take to being suddenly wealthy?'

'I've been meaning to ask for some time, sir. Is what you're doing with the portfolio aboveboard . . . legally *and* ethically?'

'What do you mean, Beek?'

'Well, it seems to me that buying stocks in corporations where you are a majority stockholder, particularly just before mergers or new product developments are announced, might be viewed by some as "insider information." '

'Nonsense.' Phule smiled easily. 'Coincidences *will* happen . . . and besides, if I don't have enough faith in my own ventures to invest in them, how can I expect anyone else to?'

'If you say so, sir.'

'How about dinner tonight, Beeker? Truth to tell, I'm a little tired of looking at Legionnaire uniforms today.'

'I'm sorry, sir. I already have a dinner date.'

'Oh?' The commander raised an inquiring eyebrow
'The court recorder,' his butler said in explanation.
'Really? I wouldn't have guessed she was your type.
Beeker sighed. 'Normally she wouldn't be. The con-versation did, however, keep her occupied until *afte* the company arrived for its demonstration.'
'I guess it did at that,' Phule said. 'Tell you what Beek. Go ahead and put the dinner on my account.'
'Very good, sir.'

Aboard the shuttlecraft, Colonel Battleax was em-broiled in a conversation of an entirely different nature
'I tell you, General, he's completely turned the Omega Company around. You saw how they rallied when they thought he was in trouble. What's more, the media loves him. As far as they're concerned, the orig-inal reports were correct: He's heading up the Space Legion's crack outfit. Now, you and I may know differ-ent, but I think we should capitalize on that publicity They're wasted on this swamp guard contract.'
'Oh, I fully intend to reassign them, Colonel,' the general said. 'There are a few situations on my desk I'd like to try them out on. We'll find out once and for all exactly how good these "elite troubleshooters" really are . . . or aren't.'
His smile was devoid of any warmth.